SPINNING
STARLIGHT

Spinning Starlight

R.C. LEWIS

HYPERION

LOS ANGELES   NEW YORK

Also by R.C. Lewis

Stitching Snow

Copyright © 2015 by R.C. Lewis

First Edition, October 2015
10 9 8 7 6 5 4 3 2 1
FAC-020093-15196

Printed in the United States of America

Library of Congress Cataloging-in-Publication Data
Lewis, R. C. (Rachel Christine), 1979–
Spinning starlight / R.C. Lewis.—First edition.
pages cm
Summary: "Sixteen-year-old heiress and paparazzi darling Liddi
Jantzen must save her brothers in this outer-space retelling of Hans
Christian Andersen's The Wild Swans"—Provided by publisher.
ISBN 978-1-4231-8515-4 (hardback)—ISBN 1-4231-8515-3
[1. Science fiction.   2. Rescues—Fiction.
3. Brothers and sisters—Fiction.]   I. Title.
PZ7.L587687Sp 2015
[Fic]—dc23   2015010731

Reinforced binding

Visit www.hyperionteens.com

SUSTAINABLE FORESTRY INITIATIVE   Certified Sourcing
www.sfiprogram.org
SFI-00993

THIS LABEL APPLIES TO TEXT STOCK

TO MY MOM FOR STARGAZING,
AND MY DAD FOR MAKING ME
LOOK UP MY OWN ANSWERS

✹ – – – ✹

1

AFTER SIXTEEN YEARS, you'd think I'd be used to the incessant buzz of vid-cams swarming to chronicle every breath I take. I'm not. Good thing, too, or I might not have noticed when one of the tiny airborne devices slips into the hovercar with me like an errant bumblebee. I shoo it like the pest it is. The lights and hustle of Pinnacle blur by until the city thins, then disappears as I enter the country—or the closest thing to "country" you can find on Sampati. A small river winds through fields and woods extending for several miles, with no sign of any neighbors. The house greets me with a few warm lights along the front path.

As nice as it is to be away from the noise of the city, the two seconds of silence as I open the door press in on me, twist in my ears. I hate the sound of an empty house. It isn't natural.

"Welcome home, Liddi." The disembodied voice breaks silence's hold, the same voice that's greeted me most of my life. Sometimes I wish it weren't the *only* voice greeting me now. "You've returned earlier than scheduled."

"It was like every other party, Dom. Loud music, too much lip gloss, and Reb Vester's existence. I got bored." Bored, and tired of the weight of myriad eyes watching me, manifesting as an ache in my lower back. Or maybe that's just from these shoes. I kick them off and pull the pins from my hair before tapping a touchscreen to activate the wallscreen in the main room. "Pull up those news-vids I was watching earlier. Resume playback."

The first vid loads with a familiar face, sienna-skinned and dark-haired like all us Jantzen kids, and I settle on the couch to watch. I'm not sure why I bother. I could recite these start to finish.

"Among technologists more than twice his age, eleven-year-old Durant Jantzen presented his biometric exercise unit at the Tech Reveal today. Athletes from Pramadam gave the system high praise...."

"Jantzen twins Luko and Vic followed in their big brother's foot-steps at this year's Tech Reveal, debuting a customizable pesticide. Ecologists on Erkir have already placed orders for ten thousand units...."

"This year's Tech Reveal brought young Fabin Jantzen and his Domestic Engineer and Itinerary Keeper...." I wonder if Domenik ever feels all meta hearing about his program's debut.

On and on they go. The first year Anton presented at the Reveal, then the triplets. Marek, Ciro, and Emil were only ten, so tiny next to the other technologists and already dubbing themselves the Jantzen Triad. That was the first year after Mom and Dad's accident. The year everything changed.

I watch more years, more Tech Reveals with all my brothers presenting inventions and innovations and upgrades. The narrative changes, though, becoming less about the technology, more about my brothers themselves.

More about me.

"Durant Jantzen attended the opening of a new art exhibit on Yishu before returning for the Tech Reveal...."

"Vic Jantzen presented two different technologies before rushing off to the luserball title match...."

"No sign of the Jantzen girl at this year's Tech Reveal...."

"Luko, will your sister be presenting this year?"

"Emil, when will your sister stop partying and take her place in the family business?"

"Fabin, do you think your father made a mistake, leaving the majority of the company to the youngest of you?"

My brothers answer the same way every time, staunchly supporting me. I don't go to that many parties—it just seems like I do because the media-grubs follow my every move. I'm taking extra time *because* of the responsibility I bear. Our father knew exactly what he was doing, seeing how competitive my brothers were with each other, but how they all doted on me. When I turn eighteen and take control of Jantzen Technology Innovations, the boys will support me. It won't tear the family apart the way it would've if Dad had picked one of them to take his place. They say I'm the best of the Jantzens, that everyone else will realize it soon.

That's been the story since I was six years old. I only believe some of it. Only the parts about my brothers. Somehow I have to make the rest come true.

"Turn it off, Dom."

I get up and go into the adjoining room, the workshop that takes nearly half of the house's first floor. Plenty of space, but I stick to the bench in the corner that's always been mine. This room used to be so noisy and busy, with computers beeping and tools whirring, Dom interrupting to tell us we forgot lunch and that if we didn't eat, he'd cut power to the whole shop.

Used to be, right up until last year when "the Triad" turned eighteen and moved to the city, becoming full-time technologists for JTI like everyone else.

The silence makes me itch.

"Dom, music."

"Genre?"

"Whatever they're saying is the new thing on Yishu. Surprise me."

A syncopated beat fills the room, followed by a point-counterpoint melody on electronic instruments engineered to sound like they're not electronic.

Durant designed some of those. I wonder if this is one of the recordings he's done under a false name. Maybe I'll ask next time I talk to him.

I fiddle with a few of the half-finished projects on my workbench for more than an hour, but it's no use. None of them are any good. Either they won't work, or they're inferior knock-offs of things my brothers came up with when they were half my age.

I can't do it. Not when everyone's watching. Not when my picking the wrong skirt is cause for its own media-cast.

"No Tech Reveal for me this year," I mutter. *"Again."*

The volume of the music cuts in half. "Please repeat, Liddi."

"I wasn't talking to you, Dom. Check my message queue. What have I got?"

He rattles off media-casts of my appearance at tonight's party, requests for interviews, invitations to parties and concerts and fashion shows. I cut him off in the middle of relaying that some senator's daughter from Neta wants me to go shopping with her.

"Nothing from the boys?"

"No."

It's been weeks since I've seen any of them, enough to deepen the ache when everything is quiet. As much as I tell them they don't need to worry about me being on my own, they don't usually believe me for this long at a stretch. Not that it's a big deal. They're busy with the work I'll be part of, if I can ever get my defective neurons to cooperate. Still...

"Dom, send a message to Emil. I'd like to see him." Emil's the youngest other than me. Not only will he drop everything—all my brothers would—but he'll tease me less for asking.

"Message sent. It's getting late. Time for bed?"

"Not yet. Discontinue music."

The house goes silent again as I tidy up my workbench, but I'm not sticking around long enough for it to bother me. I walk out the back door, the grass of the yard cold on my bare feet. Luna Minor is straight overhead, giving plenty of light, and there'll be even more when Luna Major rises in the next half hour. The night phlox is blooming pink and maroon, and the scent of the flowers brings back memories of playing hide-and-seek when we should've been in bed. A time when wondering what we'd have for breakfast tomorrow was my biggest worry about the future. When the scarier future and potential failures were still far enough away to forget sometimes.

I cross the yard into the stand of trees, letting the sound of the river draw me; the grass gives way to smooth pebbles, warming my feet a little with the heat they've retained from the day. It's never silent out here, not even at night. The water rushes along, and nocturnal insects chirp and chitter, the noise wrapping around me. Calming me. A little, anyway.

The Tech Reveal is just fifty-one days away. Hardly enough time to create something groundbreaking when I don't even have an idea yet. My brothers would never say so—they'd never pressure me—but I know everyone worries that I haven't come up with anything to present. Ever. At this rate, I'll be as old as an average technologist at debut. The idea of someone saying the word *average* in the same breath as *Jantzen* and it being my fault makes me shudder. I walk along the river's edge, hoping something will click.

Maybe the ecologists on Erkir could use a less disruptive way to irrigate their agricultural zones.

Maybe there's a way to help data flow more smoothly in the computer networks.

Maybe the tiny moths fluttering by could serve as a model for better vid-cams, with less buzzing.

Bad idea. The annoying buzz lets me know the cams are watching me, which they always are. Everywhere but here, because Luko set up an interference field like a bubble over the property so they can't get through.

Maybe I'll go to some of those events tomorrow so everyone can keep thinking my "busy social schedule" is the real reason I haven't lived up to the Jantzen name.

Domenik was right. It's late, and as nice as it is to walk down the river, it's not helping. I should get some sleep. That means getting back to the house. I've gone farther than I meant to, but at least the return trip means I'll be tired enough to fall right to sleep. Always a bright side.

Except comfortable thoughts of my bed leach away in the

not silence of the trees and river. Some noises are missing; others don't belong, but I can't place them. A little closer to home, I figure it out.

Voices.

I didn't intend for Emil to drop everything *this* quickly, and he should know better. My feet slip on the bank's wet pebbles as I hurry to tell him off. Really, though, I'm hurrying to see him, so the telling-off will have to be brief. A few steps later, I curl my toes into the rocks.

That's not my brother's voice. None of my brothers sound like that, gruff and sharp-edged, and the voices are too near me, too far from the house.

If the media-grubs have trespassed on the property, my brothers will kill them for crossing that final line, especially in the middle of the night. It's breaking the law. Instinct pulls me into a crouch, then I'm sidling up to the closest tree and straining my ears.

"Team Two, are you in position?"

Not a media-grub. Then another voice, maybe over a live-comm. My pounding heart obscures the words.

"Team Four, hold the perimeter."

I don't like the sound of that. Another tree, a larger one, is nearby and closer to the voice. I creep over to it and peer around its trunk.

Five men all in black stand several yards away. Without the light from Luna Major, I might not see them in the darkness of the woods. They're carrying some kind of equipment and facing the house.

Three options present themselves. I can confront them, I can run, or I can wait and see what happens. Options One and Two are no good. If I heard the voice right, at least three other teams lurk out here. I don't know enough.

Option Three it is.

"All teams, on my mark . . . go!"

The men race toward the house, dodging the remaining trees before cutting through the yard. It's hard to see but it gets loud quick. A *boom* as they force the door open, maybe breaking it, then gunshots.

Guns.

Charge-bullets flying in my home. Where I should've fallen asleep more than an hour ago.

I brace myself against the trunk and force my legs to straighten out of my crouch. The bark scrapes my palms. Everything shakes.

Boys, what do I do? Why aren't you here? Why couldn't even one of you be here?

A few more shots, then an unmissable shout from somewhere inside the house.

"Find her!"

I'm running before the words fade from my ears.

The other teams could be anywhere—I don't know where their "perimeter" is, the edge of the property or closer in—but I run anyway. I run back along the river, back to where the trees beyond the banks are thicker. Faint sounds follow, then not-so-faint shouts of "This way!" and "Move it!" and "Box her in downriver!"

Boxed in. I picked the wrong direction. The river bends up ahead. If they're positioned right, they'll have me cornered.

The trees to my right block my view of anything useful, but across the river to my left is one of the clearings where the boys and I used to play. Something there catches my eye, and I slow enough to look through the darkness. A lone, shadowy figure stands in the middle of the clearing, waving to me. He's familiar. One of the twins, either Luko or Vic—I can't tell from this distance.

I don't dare call out, and he must not, either, because he just beckons me to him. Across the river. It's small enough, as rivers go, but my brothers always forbade me from setting foot in this part—during the hottest summer days, we swam in a slower stretch upstream.

The gunmen are getting closer, either in my imagination or in reality—doesn't much matter which. I wade in, cold water shocking my feet, the silty bottom squishing under my toes. The force of the current on my ankles, then calves, then knees threatens to push me over and sweep me along, but I fight. As I step toward the middle, the ground drops from beneath me and water rushes up past my chest.

I cry out briefly before clamping my mouth shut. Luko-or-Vic might hear and know I need help, but so might the gunmen. I have no purchase, no traction, and I'm carried several yards downstream. I stop fighting it and just try to make progress toward the opposite bank. A quick glance along the path of the river reveals just what I need—the dark shadow of an old log stretching halfway across. I brace myself and grab hold, the bark cutting into my hands and arms, but I don't lose my grip. It's enough that I can pull myself along the length of it until my feet are under me again.

My soaked skirt and top cling to me as I climb out of the river, the light breeze chilling every inch of my skin. It doesn't matter. I doubt the river is enough to stop the men after me,

whoever they are, and I'll warm up soon enough. I force myself up the bank into the clearing and look for my brother.

He's not there.

I blink three times and rub the river water from my eyes. The light of both moons must be combining to play shadow games. But he's still not there.

You imagined him, Liddi. You're scared and wanted one of your big brothers to protect you, so your subconscious pointed the way out of the river-bend trap. And guess what—you're still scared.

The men across the river shout to each other, maybe asking if anyone sees me, if anyone's caught me yet.

I'm alone, and right now I'd give anything for some silence.

The woods continue past the clearing. No roads that way, but I don't need a road to find my way to Pinnacle's edge. The ground is rougher, not smooth pebbles and soft grass like it is on the house side of the river, and I curse my bare feet, but that doesn't matter, either.

I need to get to my brothers, so I run again.

✳ – – – ✳

I'm pretty sure my feet are bleeding but I can't look. I keep moving. The sight of blood isn't my favorite, and seeing it won't help the pain any. It's been ages since I heard any sign of the gunmen. I keep moving. Between the sweat and the dirt, everything itches, and my body aches. I can't remember which designer sent my latest party outfit. He'll die when he sees what I've done to it, filthy and ragged with a hem torn where it snagged on a branch. Still, I keep moving.

The trees thin, revealing the edge of Pinnacle in the dim

predawn light, and I finally stop. The city means civilization, protection. It means getting to my brothers, making sure we're all safe, and figuring out what in the Abyss is going on. I take a moment to orient myself. Anton's place is closest.

About a million people stand between me and the boys, and at least as many vid-cams. That keeps me frozen at the last tree. I'd had no reason to bring a com-tablet for my walk along the river, but now I would cut off my bleeding feet for one. I could live-comm one of my brothers, they could come get me, and I wouldn't have to walk alone into the city full of watching eyes.

Then again, maybe those eyes are a good thing. The gun-men came out to the house, the one place the vid-cams can't go, and in the middle of the night. Whatever they were planning to do, they wanted to be invisible. Maybe ransom. It would make sense as much as anything.

For once, having every sneeze caught on a vid might be exactly what I want. It might keep me safe long enough to get to my brothers.

Or I might have to run for it again.

If only my feet didn't hurt so much.

It takes ten minutes for the first vid-cam to find me. I'm still on the outskirts of the city, where there wouldn't be much hov-ercar traffic even if it weren't so early. The cams usually stick to downtown or the trendy entertainment districts, but a few wander the edge of the city, looking for something interesting.

Liddi Jantzen, dirty and bleeding, definitely qualifies as interesting.

One vid-cam turns into two or three, then a swarm buzzing around me. I'm too tired to care, too tired to do anything but force one throbbing foot in front of the other. But not too tired to

notice when the buzz turns into voices and the swarm becomes a crowd of people. As the media-casts go out, people backtrace my position and realize I'm in their neighborhood. People who are up early to get ready for work, or insomniacs who haven't been to bed yet—I can tell them apart by whether their clothes are pressed or rumpled—all kinds gather around me. Talking, shouting, jostling . . . It's too much to process when the white-hot fire of my feet demands all my attention. The only other things I feel are the eyes. My rules kick in: never make eye contact. Just keep going.

"Look, I told you it's her—it's Liddi Jantzen!"

"Liddi, what happened? You're hurt."

"Get her off her feet."

"You need to see a doctor."

"More like she needs the police. Someone did this to her."

"She needs both. Get out of the way. Liddi, look at me. Do you remember me?"

I turn, afraid the voice belongs to someone from one of dozens and dozens of parties and clubs I've been to in the past couple of years. Most of those faces disappear from my mind as soon as I leave, so the chance I'll remember isn't good.

But I do recognize this one, and I find myself nodding. A man in his forties, his features slightly rounded and his hair graying. He's familiar, but the name won't come to me.

He must read the question in my eyes. "It's Garrin Walker. I was your father's assistant before . . . well, before. Come on, let's get you some help."

Of course. Walker-Man. That's what I called him when I was little. He was younger, thinner, but his eyes were the same back when he'd let me play by his desk outside Dad's office. Back when I was the boss's daughter rather than the boss-to-be. Those eyes were sharp and intelligent, but also gentle. They still are. All I have to do is nod again, and he takes charge, guiding me through the crowd and into a waiting hovercar. The chatter and questions are sealed off outside the doors, and Garrin enters a destination in the hovercar's computer before turning to me.

"What did you do, Liddi? Walk all the way from the country estate?"

"Ran, mostly."

"Why? What happened?"

As much as Garrin was kind to me when I was five years old, I can't make the answer form in my mouth. The men breaking into my house. The shouts. The guns. Images flood my eyes, making Garrin less real than the memory.

"I need my brothers," I murmur. I need to know they're safe.

He might restrain a sigh—hard to tell—and nods. "Of course, I'll contact them. First, a doctor for you."

My head's getting too heavy for my neck, and my gaze falls to the floor. "I'm bleeding on your car."

"Don't worry about that."

I don't. Worrying takes too much strength, and I'm using it all thinking about the boys. How Marek would make me laugh, taking my mind off the pain, and how Luko would give me a hug. I need one. I need *them*.

My vision blurs with a combination of tears and exhaustion. I end up in a hospital room, quiet except for the light rush of air sanitizers and the meticulous efforts of the doctor taking care of my feet. His ministrations sting, then cool, then numb, and that final effect seems to spread through most of my body. I break out of the fog when raised voices erupt in the hallway.

Loud enough to know it's an argument, but not loud enough to hear what it's about.

"Doctor, have any of my brothers arrived?" I ask.

"I'm not sure, Miss Jantzen. If they haven't, I'm sure they will shortly." He finishes with my feet and raises a scanner to the scrapes on my hands and arms. "You say you got these injuries running to the city from the wilderness preserve?"

It's not a preserve, it's my home, but there's no point in arguing with him. Like everyone else on Sampati, he's strictly a city-dweller, so I nod. "Well, and crossing a river."

His brows knit as he studies my expression. "A river. Why did you do that?"

"To get to the other side."

The doctor doesn't get to press further—thank the Sentinel—because the door to the hospital room bursts open. Two women stride in with Garrin trailing behind them. He's saying something about talking to me alone, but the women ignore him. The younger one wears the dark green uniform of the Sampati Police Force, but with black sleeves. So she's not just any cop—she's here on assignment from the military divisions on Banak. Her tall, muscular build and sleek haircut reinforce that fact, but even her formidable presence can't distract me from the other woman who entered with her.

"Ms. Blake," I greet, habit forcing me to sit up straighter. I may have played by Garrin's desk as a child, but there's no silliness with Ms. Blake, ever. The woman has been managing JTI for most of my life, running day-to-day operations for my brothers. Coordinating the various departments, evaluating which projects have the most promise . . . doing a lot of the things I'll have to know how to do someday.

"Liddi, are you well? Garrin says you were hurt. I assure you, Doctor, if she's not receiving the absolute best possible care, you'll—"

"I'm fine," I cut in. "Or, fine enough."

Ms. Blake stands right in front of me, her gaze cutting through. "Tell me exactly what happened."

I've been resisting all morning, resisting the words that make it real. My brothers should be the first ones I tell, but with Ms. Blake here, there's no choice. She needs to know.

"Men with guns came to the house. I was outside, walking... thinking. When they realized I wasn't in bed, they came looking, and I ran."

The women are frozen, but Garrin takes a half step forward. "Did they hurt you? Did you get a good look at any of them?"

I shake my head, answering both questions at once. His concern reminds me of my father, which only strengthens my need to see the boys. "Ms. Blake, please, has anyone told my brothers? They should be here. They might be in trouble, too."

Garrin inhales sharply. "That's just the thing," Ms. Blake says. "Liddi, no one's heard from your brothers in at least nine days. We can't find them."

Some of the boys were roughhousing while the others vied for their father's attention, showing him the little devices they'd tinkered together that day. Mrs. Jantzen took Liddi's hand and they slipped away, up to the roof of the townhouse.

The city surrounded them, the lights of each building reflecting off the next, the streets a distant memory below. A breeze cut through, lifting Liddi's hair and blowing it across her eyes. Her mother sat her down on one of the benches and twisted her hair into a braid to hold it in place.

"Those boys are so noisy sometimes," she said. "It's nice to get away once in a while."

"Yeah, it's nice," Liddi agreed. She craned her neck up toward the sky. "Where are the stars, Mommy?"

"Right where they always are. We just can't see them because there's too much light in the city."

"They should turn off the lights. I want the stars back like at the other house. They shouldn't be gone."

Mrs. Jantzen wrapped her arms around Liddi's shoulders and pulled her close. "Sweetheart, they aren't gone. Just because you can't see something doesn't mean it isn't there. The stars are always there."

2

NINE DAYS AND NOT A BLIP from my brothers, to anyone. "How is that possible?" I demand. "How do eight of the most famous men in the Seven Points go comm-silent without anyone noticing? Without *you* noticing?"

"It's possible it's nothing," says Ms. Blake. "They've all been traveling off-Point recently, and you know how they are when they're away."

True, I know how my brothers are. They keep busy, and when they go to other worlds—which, thanks to the interstellar conduits, they can do almost instantaneously—they like to stay focused on their business. Sometimes that makes them a little fixated on a project, though, and they tune other things out. That's why they have Ms. Blake in the first place, so they can spend more time on their own work. They're technologists to the core, and a lot like our father was in that way. At least, that's what I'm told. It's possible they're all busy and not paying attention to their messages. Possible.

But it doesn't feel right. It's normal enough for me to be out of the loop. Upper management at JTI, though? Not so much. The scowl tightening Garrin's mouth says he agrees with me.

I don't want to ask the question out loud, but someone has to. "Could the same gunmen— Could my brothers be..."

Garrin shakes his head. "All eight of them, so quietly? Highly unlikely. I don't care who these gunmen are. They're not that good."

"I agree," Ms. Blake says. "Far more plausible that the two are unrelated, or that these men noted your brothers' absence and seized the opportunity."

The police officer finally speaks up. "Besides that, inter-Point communication can be awful spotty. I remember when I was in training, a bunch of us went cliff diving on Pramadam. Had a wretch of a time contacting our commander when Freitag broke his leg."

My estimation of the woman nudges down. Communication between the seven worlds may have been "spotty" in her youth, but Anton redesigned the interlocks himself just to make sure he could reliably contact his then-girlfriend on Yishu. They're so solid, you could whisper across the light-years. My brothers wouldn't have any such trouble.

Ms. Blake cuts off my retort. "Liddi, this is Officer Svarta. I imagine she'll need your report."

She nods, tapping away on a com-tablet. "Indeed. And a patrol is heading out to your estate right now. We'll get this sorted out quick enough."

"Meanwhile, once the doctor and officer are finished, we should get you settled somewhere safe."

"I can see to that, Ms. Blake," Garrin says.

The upturn in the manager's lips barely qualifies as a smile. "A kind offer, but under the circumstances, I prefer to see to those arrangements myself. You understand."

I'm not sure how I feel about either of them making arrangements for me. But I do what I'm told. What's expected. I tell Officer Svarta every detail I remember of the attack, and she makes me repeat nearly everything. There were four teams? At least. None of them followed me across the river? Not that I know of. Did I see anyone else?

I hesitate at that last question. I was so sure I saw Vic, but if it were really him, he wouldn't have run off again without seeing me to safety. The late hour, the shadows, the adrenaline... it adds up to a trick of the light and my imagination. Maybe. I tell Svarta I saw no one, and the officer leaves to supervise the investigation.

The doctor finishes just as Ms. Blake's assistant arrives with clothes and shoes for me. I wonder where they came from, and a glance at the tag emblem answers that. They're from Beyond, a boutique that's always trying to get me to chat up their fashions in media-casts. I've never liked their pushiness, but it's clothes, and that's all I care about right now.

"That's much better," Ms. Blake says after I clean up and change. I have to agree. She tries to usher me from the room, but I hold back.

"Garrin, thank you," I say. "Thanks for finding me."

"Of course," he replies, his eyes steady on me despite Ms. Blake's impatience. "When I saw the media-casts, I couldn't leave you out there alone. If you need anything, contact me right away."

I nod, but Ms. Blake won't wait for further sentimentality,

nudging me into the hallway. "Come on, Liddi. Let's get you out of here."

Out of the hospital is fine, but it raises a question. "Where are we going?"

"Your parents' townhouse has been prepared. It's secure, and you'll be able to get some rest. You should be safe here in the city—plenty of eyes keeping watch, of course—but this security-cam will accompany you door-to-door if you need to go anywhere."

The townhouse. Thinking about it distracts me from the hum of the heftier cam following us. I haven't been there since Mom and Dad died. Someone held a reception there after the funeral, and then the boys and I were sent out to the country. Durant and the twins were already grown—just barely—but they stayed for a few years until Fabin was old enough to keep an eye on the rest of us. Eventually, Fabin left, and Anton, and finally the triplets, leaving just me. But no one went back to our home in the city. They got their own places, either here in Pinnacle or somewhere else on Sampati.

I could tell Ms. Blake I refuse, that she'll have to find another place for me to stay. But I don't. A place where we were all once happy together might be exactly what I need. For a little while.

"Ms. Blake?"

"Please, Liddi, you're not a child anymore. You can call me Minali—your brothers do."

I can, but it's weird. Like calling Dom the Domestic Engineer and Itinerary Keeper, but in reverse. One too formal, the other too casual. But it's true that my brothers have called her by her first name for years, so I can try.

"Okay. Minali. Will I be able to go back to the estate eventually?"

She considers during the two seconds it takes to program the hovercar. "I certainly hope so, but there's a lot we don't know right now. Let's wait and see what Officer Svarta and her team find out. I know this must be frightening, but we'll figure it out. I promise."

Her promise lends some reassurance, but the fear lingers. She must see it in my eyes, as she offers a small smile.

"Meanwhile, maybe some distraction is in order. Are you working on something for the Tech Reveal? I can have it brought into the city for now."

That thing again. Color heats my face, equal parts shame, frustration, and anger. "No, still in the idea stage."

"Well, if you can come up with something we can preview before the Reveal, it will likely help the situation. Media-casts are running rampant with recordings of you entering the city on foot. We could use a touch of spin."

Spinning for media-casts... something I can definitely do. Parties and pretending I like expensive shoes that are barely anatomically possible to wear, that was always spin. In this situation, though, it feels off. Men attacked my home and my brothers are missing. That's a lot to overlook.

"What difference will spin make now?"

She tilts her head uncertainly. "It's always important to show strength. You know how the worlds rely on this company, its technology. And, by extension, you."

I can't help but think if that's true, the Seven Points are in more trouble than they know.

— – – —

It turns out I remember more about the townhouse than I thought I did, because the moment I enter, I know nothing has changed. The wallscreens are set to the same artwork—landscapes of the Seven Points, from the senatorial complex on Neta to a mountain range on Erkir—the windows have the same blue curtains, and the main room is full of the same furniture to accommodate our large family. The edge of that chair in the corner cracked open my forehead when I tripped while chasing Ciro. He'd threatened to cut my hair.

One of Dad's spare toolkits is on a small table against the wall.

Everything's perfect, still in its place, and yet so wrong. Smaller, the walls closer together, but big with the emptiness that should be occupied by the rest of my family. The emptiness that aches alongside my worry.

I wander for a while, reacquainting myself with everything, climbing the stairs and testing my memory with which room was whose. When I get to mine, I realize I won't be able to sleep there. The bed is tiny.

Dad said at six years old I was getting big enough for a new one. Mom agreed and said she'd take care of it as soon as they finished trials on whatever they were working on. She never had the chance. One wrong move during a delicate experiment. One mistake. One accident.

One is such a deceptively small number.

I could sleep in the master bedroom, but after a peek in there, I close the door. That won't work. Durant and the twins, being

oldest, were full-grown when we left, so their shared room will be fine. Everything smells a little sterile. Fitting for a place that's been kept clean but unlived-in for ten years. Still, Durant's bed is soft and his blankets warm, and I don't care that it's midmorning and the sun's out. I curl up and try to keep the images of gunmen at bay when I close my eyes. To silence the questions of where my brothers could be. It doesn't work very well at first, setting me into a fitful doze, but eventually my exhaustion decides it's more powerful than my dread.

When I wake up, it's dark outside. Night again. And I'm not alone.

Durant stands at the window, moonlight illuminating him.

I grin and roll out of bed, ready to tackle him with a hug and demand to know where he's been. I've only crossed half the room when he disappears. It's impossible. He was right there, then faded, like an image being deleted.

Except maybe he wasn't right there. Something didn't look quite right, just like Vic—or Luko—hadn't looked quite right in the clearing. Less than solid. Ghostlike.

Spirits pass on to Ferri, some damned to serve the Wraith in the Abyss, others sent to live with the Sentinel.

A spike of pain jars me as my knees hit the floor and knocks sense back into my head. Everyone knows those ancient stories are superstitious nonsense. *I* know it. The names survive as meaningless words that make old ladies scold us for our lack of manners.

But I saw Durant. I did. No confusion about my mind playing tricks on me this time—he was right there. Unless I'm having a full psychotic break, but I can't let myself believe that. And if spirits aren't an option, what does that leave? Things that look

like ghosts, that people have mistaken for ghosts. Nothing to do with gunmen and their bullets.

I force myself to my feet and tap a touchscreen to activate the computer. "Link Domestic Engineer and Itinerary Keeper from country estate to current location. Dom, you there?"

"Yes, Liddi. I see you're at the townhouse. Is everything to your liking?"

"Well enough. I'm doing some research. Get me everything you can find on phenomena that make people look like ghosts."

"Could you please clarify what you mean by 'look like ghosts'?"

"Translucent. And transient. Like appearing and disappearing."

"Compiling ... done."

I'm already heading upstairs to the top floor. "Cue it up in the workshop."

Once there, I sit down at my old spot and narrate my observations into the computer—the time and place of each sighting, my brothers' behavior, everything I remember. Then I have Dom start playing his findings on the wallscreen.

I watch media-casts of people who claimed to have seen ghosts in "haunted" locations, like the site of an old concert hall collapse on Yishu. Maybe I was wrong about *no one* believing the old legends. The witnesses always sound either mentally disconnected or more interested in the attention than anything else, so I quickly dismiss them. Listening to treatises on life after death is a little more enlightening, but the philosophers on Tarix are still just theorizing without any thought to evidence or hard facts.

It takes hours to sift through everything, and nothing helps.

Finally, though, Dom cues up a technologist's working notes from centuries ago when the conduits were first being tested.

"The conduits are holding now that we've attuned the energies at each end. Several trips to each Point have been completed successfully. The dimensional shift from the origin Point and the shift back into phase at the target Point are separated by an average of eleven seconds. We'll continue to monitor stability, but it looks good. A side note: some of the conduits on Erkir have outdoor exit points for now, since the citizens prefer we not build facilities until success is confirmed. When making transit on moonlit nights, we've observed a strange visual phenomenon. The traveler appears before he's arrived, while he's in the neither-here-nor-there hyperdimensional state. 'Appear' may be too strong a word. More a ghost of an appearance. May be linked to the frequency variance we've observed. We'll try to tighten that up."

Both times I saw my brothers, it was at night. In the moonlight, even. And "neither-here-nor-there" sounds similar to what I witnessed. But not exactly. My brothers aren't in transit. I don't think. Or if they are, they're not completing the transition, getting back into phase with our reality's dimension.

Like they're stuck.

I go up the final flight of stairs and out onto the roof. Still the middle of the night, still dark. Luna Minor has set, but Luna Major is high above me. I sit on the bench where Mom and I used to look for the stars against the city lights, but now I watch everything else. Every corner of the roof, every flicker of movement. Nothing.

But just because I can't see them doesn't mean they aren't there.

"Boys, I have an idea where you might be . . . maybe." It feels weird, talking into the nothing, but I keep going. People hear voices on the other end before completing a conduit trip all the time. It might work here, too. "If I can see one of you again, here while I'm talking to you, I'll know it's not a coincidence. And I'll find a way to help you. Please, I need to know I'm right."

More silence, more nothing, but only for a moment. Then a patch of moonlight takes shape. It's Anton. Since I'm watching carefully this time, expecting it, I see the effort it takes from him. He smiles, but it's not one of the easy smiles I've known all my life. It's strained, its tightness echoing across my chest. He opens his mouth like he's going to say something, but he slips away again before he can.

It's the beginning of an answer that only creates a hundred more questions. I hate that Anton couldn't tell me anything, that I can't solve the problem *right now,* but this beginning is more than I had. "Okay, I'll figure it out. I'll get you home."

I race downstairs and change into some of the clean clothes Ms. Blake—Minali—had sent over from the estate yesterday. As much as I don't want to, I take an extra five minutes to brush and braid my hair. After everything Minali said about spin, she'll be more likely to listen to me if I'm not running around the city looking like a lunatic . . . again. I scarf down a protein bar, too. I'm starving.

The sun is barely teasing the horizon when I leave the townhouse, my security-cam humming along behind me. Much too early for anyone to be in at JTI, but I told Dom to send an urgent message for Minali to meet me right away. The alert will wake her up if necessary.

It isn't far, so I walk, even though that means picking up plenty of vid-cams on the way. Their presence is so common, it gives the illusion of everything being normal. Almost

comfortable when everything is so definitely *not* normal. Some aren't on autopilot, it turns out, because the voices of their media-grub owners come out of minuscule speakers.

"Any comment on yesterday's unusual events, Liddi?"

"Not yet." I keep my eyes on my destination. Just a few more blocks.

"Doesn't seem like you to head into the office so early in the morning. Or at all."

That's true in a way, but I bristle. I don't come in to JTI, but I'm in the workshop at all hours, usually trying not to smash my head against the bench. "Let's face it. How much do you guys think you *really* know about what is or isn't like me?"

"We know you prefer clubs on the east side of the entertainment district, and fashions from the aquatic zones of Yishu."

Several other cameras prattle off bits of minutiae gleaned from my attendance at parties and galas and whatever else qualifies as "not working for JTI." I don't say anything until I've reached the door.

"Exactly. You know what I've wanted you to know. And that's how it stays."

I wave to the guard at the security desk—he knows better than to slow me down—and go straight to the elevator bank. Minali's office is empty, but not for long. She arrives three minutes after I do. Every hair is in place, her pants are perfectly pressed, so only the weariness in her eyes betrays the early hour.

"What is it, Liddi?" she asks. "Did something happen?"

"I think I figured it out." I quickly summarize everything, from seeing Vic-or-Luko as I ran from the house to the technologist's notes I stumbled on. "Could that be it? Could they be in the conduits, stuck in transit without an exit point?"

My words spilled out so quickly, Minali's face didn't have much chance to react until the conclusion. Now her eyes widen and her hands flex.

"No. I mean yes. It makes sense. I should have thought of it."

She should have? I thought the way-out-there nature of the idea explained no one figuring it out. "Why?"

After another moment of thought, Minali taps and swipes a few commands on her desk, activating the wallscreen. Seven icons are arranged with a web of thin lines connecting all of them. Off to the side is some kind of fluctuating meter.

"Is that the conduit network?" I ask.

"It is. This is how it looked when the conduits were first established." She swipes the panel again. The lines connecting the Seven Points turn fainter, flickering. The meter fluctuates more wildly, and at a higher level. "This is how it is now. Has been for a while."

"What does it mean?"

"The conduits have never been very efficient. That over there?" She points to the meter. "It's the energy intake per trip, making the hyperdimensional shift and back again. It's quadrupled. Yet even with all that energy, the conduits are destabilizing."

I try to swallow against the dust that seems to coat my throat. Destabilizing does not sound good. "What does it have to do with my brothers? How did they get stuck?"

"I'm not sure exactly. But I do know they've been working on this destabilization problem for almost a year. It's obviously a top priority."

That feels right. Just after the triplets moved out, all of the boys got busier than ever, more distracted . . . and that was saying something.

But none of them told me anything. They kept me in silence, and I don't know why, but I refuse to stay in it now.

"Okay, fine. Maybe they were doing some experiments and got stuck. How do we get them out?"

"That's the question. And I don't know if there's an answer."

Nevi Jantzen was the most important man on Sampati—
and arguably on all the Seven Points—with near-constant
demands on his attention.

That didn't stop him from sneaking away from the office
during lunch to spend time in the park with his kids. Especially baby Liddi and the triplets. Ciro, Marek, and Emil had
been born after Nevi's father died, passing the reins of JTI
officially into Nevi's hands. They would have no memory of
life before their father was the head of the company, but he was
determined to ensure they would have memories of him being
their father.

One day brought such a lunch hour with Nevi in the park
with Liddi. The boys hadn't wanted to stop their work, and he
wasn't going to force them to. So Liddi had him all to herself,
squealing with exhilaration as he pushed her on the swings,
or going down the slide on her own as long as he caught her
at the bottom.

As she went to climb to the top of the slide again, her little
face screwed up and she waved a hand by her ear like she was
shooing a bug away.

Her father spotted it, though. Not a bug.

"Hey," he said sternly. "I've told you to stay away from
my kids."

The vid-cam persisted, barely moving out of range of
Liddi's hands.

"Have it your way."

Nevi reached in his pocket and pulled out a tiny device he'd been meaning to test. He touched the button to activate it, and the vid-cam fell to the ground, dead. The device in his hand likewise sparked and shorted out, though.

"Bad bzzz-bzzz, bad!" Liddi said.

"That's right, Liddi-Loo. And this thing has some promise. Daddy'll work on it this afternoon. But first, one more time down the slide!"

3

MINALI SENDS MESSAGES to the top technologists at JTI, anyone who's ever worked on anything related to the conduits, right down to the communication interlocks. Everyone's reassigned to the new project, but she asks me not to mention my brothers, just sticks to a general story that the conduits *may* have malfunctioned, someone *might* be stuck, so we need to collect and analyze all the data possible. She doesn't want news getting out and starting a panic, which makes sense. The whole building thrums with people murmuring into their earpieces, and images I'm not familiar with flash across wallscreens.

They work all that day. And the next, and the one after that. I go home just long enough to sleep each night, and only when Minali shuts everyone down because sleep-deprived brains don't do great work. Except, thinking of my brothers trapped in a hyperdimensional state just outside our reality makes sleep impossible.

I try to keep up with the technologists. I try to follow along and offer suggestions. I try to dig in and find the missing pieces, because these aren't just the top technologists in the Seven Points who need help. These are *my brothers*. Even if they never touch another piece of technology again, I need them. The eight of them are all I have.

Half of what I hear makes sense, but the other half is missing a connection. Someone states a fact about the conduits. I ask why it's so. Their explanation feels as useless as saying, "Because it is."

Just like when I try to come up with something for the Tech Reveal. I'm a step behind.

Worse. I'm in the way. That much is obvious when Minali finally pulls me aside.

"Liddi, you're exhausted. Maybe you should get some rest."

I get the message. "Tell me something first. Where do we stand?"

She smooths a hand over her hair. "Hard to say. The conduits are failing. We have time, but if we don't do something, they *will* collapse and each planet will be left isolated. As for getting your brothers out...I'm not sure we know enough about how the conduits really work. Designing them in the first place was guesswork with half-understood energies, and failing conduits aren't the right ones to study. We'll keep looking. But we still have you, and it's more important than ever that you take care of yourself, okay?"

I nod, because I don't want to hear any more. Definitely not anything that hints at me being the only Jantzen left. Minali ushers me toward the door, offering to arrange a hovercar home, but I decline.

I don't want to rest. So I wander. There's been no further sign of the gunmen, making the attackers look more and more like some opportunistic ransom-takers. With the security-cam keeping an eye on me, freeing my brothers is a much bigger concern.

Regular vid-cams notice me quickly enough, but I don't pay any attention to them. My feet carry me in random directions. Away from JTI, away from home, away from the entertainment district. If it were night, I'd try to see my brothers, hope that they could give me some clue. Knowing exactly how they got trapped would help so much in getting them back. But it sounds like sunlight is too bright for them to be seen, so that's not an option, and I keep walking.

The last Jantzen. The only one left. The one everyone has been counting on.

The world presses on me, crushing with its weight. Maybe all seven worlds. I find a bench on the side of the road and sit, hoping if things settle, a solution will pop out of the ground like it's been waiting for me to notice the obvious. The first ten minutes aren't promising—nothing obvious yet—and my still silence is so boring that the vid-cams following me back off and try to find something more interesting in the vicinity.

I don't know if it would count as "interesting" to the computer algorithms, but something is happening in a schoolyard across the street. Several little kids are playing with a skip rope, including the rhyme everyone learns around the time they begin to walk:

If you found a portal high, if you found a portal low,
Where in the Eight Points would you go?

Each child takes a turn calling out one of the Points and jumping as long as they can according to the matching rule. Sampati means jumping with a fast left-left, right-right pattern.

Yishu has to dance and spin. For Pramadam, the twirlers move onto a low wall or curb so the jumper has just a few inches of width to stand on. Erkir jumps gently, Tarix jumps backward while the twirlers move across the playground, and Neta does the opposite, with the jumper moving forward so the twirlers have to follow. Banak is the favorite for show-offs, with the rope swinging at knee-level off the ground. Most kids don't last long on that round.

The Eighth Point is Ferri—Death. Not a real Point, no planet to match, just the mythical afterlife ruled by the Sentinel and the Wraith. When a kid chooses Ferri, the twirlers have to drop the rope and everyone runs from them. Anyone who gets caught within a minute is dead and out of the game.

During the brief time I attended school, we got bored with the game pretty quickly. Not so with this group. Round after round they go, laughing at the silly dance moves of a boy who chooses Yishu, cheering on a girl who manages to complete fifty Banak-jumps.

> *If you found a portal high, if you found a portal low,*
> *Where in the Eight Points would you go?*

Portals. Not conduits. I remember Fabin telling me something about portals, the natural phenomena the conduits were based on, the original connection between the seven worlds. There's a reason the rhyme goes the way it does, about *finding* portals. They had to be found every time you wanted to use one, because they don't stay in place. Anyone who looked hard enough seemed to find one, but they're unreliable, unsafe, and unpleasant, from what Fabin said. That's why technologists developed the conduits—artificial, stable, and simple.

Except the conduits are failing. Emil says mimics are never

as good as originals, in anything. It seems especially true in this case. And my brothers got trapped trying to repair those mimics. The originals are better, somehow, but they're still similar. Maybe similar enough and better enough to help.

The portals must still be around, even if it's been centuries since anyone used them.

My thoughts are interrupted by the children screaming. Someone called out Ferri, so everyone's running from the two twirlers.

I have some running of my own to do, but that'll draw the attention of the vid-cams to me. Instead, I walk as quickly as I dare. I have to get back to JTI.

Minali's assistant rapidly becomes my least favorite person.

"Ms. Blake isn't in her office. She's busy," he says.

"And I need to make her even busier. She's here somewhere, so tell me where."

He says something about appointments and makes a show of having the computer list available times. With his attitude, I'm not going to get anywhere with the nice approach, and this is too important to let him brush me off. Time for the approach I never use.

"Computer, voiceprint override. Identify Liddi Jantzen."

"Liddi Jantzen, identified," says the electronic voice. "How may I help you, Miss Jantzen?"

I ignore the way the assistant glares. "Locate JTI manager Minali Blake."

"Minali Blake is in Lab One on the thirty-eighth floor."

In a last-ditch effort to assert his authority, the assistant physically blocks me from the door. "You have no right to interfere with daily operations here."

"I have every right. I may not have taken control yet, but this is still my family's company." I shove past before he comes up with another futile argument.

The lab is easy to find. It's also locked—standard for all the upper-level labs at JTI—but that's no problem with my voice-print logged in. Minali is inside, working a bank of equipment with several wallscreens running. She turns, startled to see me. Her assistant must not have commed ahead, but I'm too excited to apologize for the rudeness.

"Minali, I had an idea about the conduits."

Her startled expression fades, smoothing to a curious one. "What kind of idea?"

"The old portals are still out there, right? It's been ages since anyone studied them, centuries at least, and even then, we didn't have the technology to really understand them. Like you said, barely enough to model the conduits after them. But maybe now we do. And if we do, maybe we can figure out what's going wrong with the conduits, and how my brothers got trapped. Come at the problem from the side instead of head-on."

"That's good thinking. I'll get—"

"Simulation complete," the computer interrupts. "Summary: eighty-two percent chance of success under Variant A. Thirty-three percent chance—"

"Pause results," Minali says. "Tell me more, Liddi."

On the surface, it makes sense that she stopped the computer to be polite and hear out my idea. But a moment of clarity slices through the cloud of worry and helplessness that's been surrounding me. That clarity punches right to my gut and says no. Says there's something tiny in Minali's face that I don't like. Microexpressions . . . Ciro studied them so he'd have a better idea who to trust, with all the people wanting to use our family to their advantage, and particularly regarding some of the girls Anton dated.

"What are you working on?" I ask, forcing curiosity into my voice rather than accusation.

"Just a few theories, nothing solid."

No, that's a lie. I glance at the wallscreens, which she hasn't bothered to blank. Each shows a waveform I'm not familiar with, though they all look related. Something at the corners catches my eye. Identifier icons. I recognize all eight. They're my brothers'.

"Explain it to me," I insist. "You have something about my brothers."

"Just some readings on the conduits."

"But you've isolated waveforms for each of them. Do you think you can use those to locate them? And you ran a simulation—on what?"

"Random ideas, a bit complicated. I really *am* busy, Liddi."

She probably is, but I'm tired of being put off, tired of being told to wait, that I'll understand later. "Computer, resume results summary and disable pause."

Minali glares—there's a familiar impatience in it—but I just listen. The computer details the results of the simulation. She was right about the complexity. I don't understand all of it, but I get the idea.

And I don't like the idea I'm getting.

"Conclusion: hyperdimensional stabilizing using biological catalyst remains feasible with multi-stage implementation. Stage one complete. Time to stage four completion is forty-five days, with levels of success greatest for Variants A, F, and C."

A cold void forms inside me, numbing everything. The simulation has projected possible results of an experiment... an experiment that's already in progress. "My brothers are the 'biological catalyst,' aren't they? What have you done?"

Minali smacks a workstation with her palm, sending me back a step. No mere microexpressions now. Her eyes are bright with panic. "You don't understand. First your brothers, now you. The conduits are *failing*. The Seven Points won't survive if they do. Without resources from the other Points, Sampati will crumble, and without leadership from Neta, the others will fall to chaos. Not one of the planets can survive alone, not without being set back centuries, even a millennium."

Yes, the conduits' failing is a problem, but this is wrong. *Minali's* wrong, something's sick or broken in her mind if she thinks sealing *people* inside is the solution. "So you trap my brothers? Even if that made any kind of sense—which it does not—they're our best chance at fixing everything!"

"No, they're not. They refused to acknowledge what it'll take, refused to move forward and act. And you...nothing *ever* goes right with you, does it? Computer, execute primary contingency."

I have no idea what that means until a column of blue light shines on me, and then it's too late. The computer emits a signal calibrated precisely to my brain waves, and everything goes black.

Liddi's plastic robot man needed to climb to the top of Metal Mountain, but he was only one inch tall. He'd need help. So she took the blocks from the tub in the corner and started building a tower with steps. Robot-Man was good at climbing steps.

"Garrin, can you get me the schematics for the conduits?" Mr. Jantzen said. "I have a few thoughts."

"Certainly, sir."

Liddi's fingers slipped, knocking one of the blocks off-balance, and the noise drew her father to the other side of the desk. "Liddi, I said you could play in my office. You don't need to bother Garrin."

"But Walker-Man's desk is better, Daddy," she protested. "Yours is bumpy." She couldn't easily brace her tower against the wooden carvings on her father's desk.

"It's no bother, Mr. Jantzen," Garrin said. "And you're busy. I can keep an eye on her."

"All right. If she gets in the way, send her in. Durant will be by to pick her up this afternoon."

Once Jantzen disappeared back into his office, Garrin peered over the edge of the desk at Liddi. "Nice tower. Try adding a few more blocks to the bottom before you start building higher."

4

EVERY CELL IN MY BODY ACHES, and I'm not surprised. That's a side effect of the neural incapacitator. There's a sharper pain and tightness somewhere on my neck, and again where my shoulder blades and hips rest against a hard surface. I open my eyes, knowing I won't like what I see.

I'm laid out on a metallic table surrounded by computer displays and other equipment. It's a lab, but not the same one I was in before. The aches make it difficult to even think about moving, but it doesn't matter. All I have to do is tell the computer to contact the police. Or the media. Or everyone on the whole planet and beyond. I don't get further than opening my mouth.

"You'd better not do that." Minali, standing in the blind spot behind me, of course. I open my mouth again, but she keeps going. "No, really. I've implanted a device near your larynx, and I'm activating it right now. Programmed with internal voice-recognition and a hyperdimensional transmitter. A pulse will be sent through the conduit substrata, one specifically calibrated to disrupt the pattern cohesion of any living beings inside . . . not that you understand any of that. All you need to know is if you speak, your brothers die."

My hand goes to my throat. There's no mark—she healed the incision perfectly—but I can make out a tiny, hard lump under the surface that shouldn't be there. It explains the odd tight feeling. The cold void inside me hits new depths beyond freezing, the emptiness echoing in my ears. Her footsteps approach, and I reflexively force myself off the table onto shaky legs.

"I'd really rather *not* kill them," she says. "Conduit stabilization is a bit more certain if they remain alive. So please, mouth shut."

I look around at the equipment—next to useless without being able to use voice commands. Minali stands between me and the door. All I can do is glare, so I do it the very best I can.

"You have to understand, it wasn't supposed to be like this, Liddi," she says. "If those incompetent mercenaries had done their job and gotten you implanted days ago, we wouldn't have all this attention pointed here. They were supposed to hold you at least until the Tech Reveal. You wouldn't have been harmed; I just needed you out of the way until I'm finished. The mystery of your kidnapping and your brothers' coinciding disappearance would've been a perfect distraction. Then again, you gave me a reason to get more people collecting data on the conduits, letting me run the simulation sooner, so there's that. But I need time. Stabilizing the conduits, it's like constructing a fifty-story building from the ground up, knowing each girder is laced with explosives. I can't do it overnight."

The tightness near my voice box intensifies alongside my urge to speak, to rage until that perverse look of regret is burned from her face. She sent those men with guns into my house, then acted all concerned and helpful when I dragged myself into Pinnacle. The knowledge pulses through me, making it difficult not to scream.

Something else she said is more important, though. Minali needs me out of the way for a while, at least until the Tech Reveal. The only threat I've posed is in trying to rescue my brothers, so maybe that means doing so is still possible. Before the Reveal. Before "stage four completion." The computer said that's forty-five days away.

The kidnapping ruse might've worked, but she's lost all claim on sanity if she thinks she can get away with *this*. I try to figure out how to say so without saying anything and spot a computer display that's already running the right subroutine. Minali tries to cut me off when I step toward it, but I hold up my hand, rolling my eyes in an attempt to convey I'm not going to *do* anything. Then I scroll through icons on the touchscreen until I find the one for a popular media-cast. I tap it and get exactly what I expected—vids of me walking through the city barefoot, interwoven with studio commentators.

"We still have no idea exactly why the Jantzen girl arrived in such a state."

"No, reports out of JTI have been less than informative. An unspecified 'minor' emergency, nothing to worry about? Come on, JTI, it's not that 'minor' if she's shredding a new Igara skirt."

"The Jantzen boys are all off-Point and reportedly unavailable for comment. We contacted Reb Vester to see if he had news on his girlfriend, and even he doesn't know what's going on."

I hold back a growl at that last bit—Reb only wishes we were dating, because gorgeous or not, he's been hit in the head by too

many laserballs for my liking. I point at the display as it switches to vids of me at various parties and raise my eyebrows at Minali.

"Ah, you think your sudden silence will tip off the media? Liddi, after all these years, surely you know how easy it is to spin. With your brothers attending to pressing matters off-Point, you're finally taking a more serious, substantial role in the company. You're ignoring the media because they're a distraction."

This passes beyond madness. I want to explode, to scream, or at least to break Minali's neck, but I can't. Not without endangering my brothers further. Instead, I mime stabbing myself and shrug.

"Why not just kill you?"

I nod.

"Your brothers will serve their purpose alive or dead—the simulation results just look better if they're alive. Killing *you*, however, isn't an option. I can't have those useless thinkers on Tarix getting control of the company."

Oh, right, the implant I got when my parents died. I didn't understand until years later when the boys explained. A safety measure for an inheritor not yet of age, just a simple thing that does nothing but monitor my vital signs and send a signal to Tarix if they cease.

But I remember something else, too. My brothers have similar implants. Not with my priority level, but they have them. Maybe I can use that. Maybe I can find the monitoring codes for them. Maybe a lot of things, but none of it while I stand here listening to this null-skull who's attacked my family.

"Liddi, stop," she says warningly. "I see the plotting in your eyes. This *has* to be done to save the Seven Points. I know you don't understand what we're facing, and that's not your fault.

Your parents put a check on your genes to ensure you wouldn't be as smart as your brothers, so you would still need their help. If you ask me, it was cruel of them, but there's nothing for it now, is there?"

Checked genes. Not as smart. The words echo and ricochet in my head, leaving dents and gouges in their wake, trailing down into my lungs so I can't breathe. But my parents couldn't have done that. They wouldn't have.

Then again... All these years with no debut at the Tech Reveal, never meeting my family's standard, hitting a thousand walls with every attempt...

I miss Minali saying something, but it's not to me. One of the company drivers is at the door to take me home.

I look to Minali, but she spares me the barest glance before returning her attention to the console. Like I'm beneath her notice now that I have no way to threaten her. There's nothing I can do.

"Officer Svarta cleared the grounds and tightened security measures on the perimeter of the country estate, so you won't need that noisy security-cam anymore. You'll be safe there now."

I bet. I bet I'll be as safe as a caged dog. Those men weren't meant to kill me, after all. Just to hold me hostage until it was too late to save my brothers, until they were locked in as a permanent part of the conduit infrastructure. Maybe Minali even had elaborate plans for "rescuing" me, and I'd have been too grateful to question whatever tragic story she gave for my brothers' demise. Even the botched kidnapping didn't matter, though. I came running straight to her with my theories about my brothers, full of naive trust.

I'm an idiot. Checked genes is right.

The driver either knows I can't talk or isn't inclined to make conversation. Whatever the reason, the ride home is silent except for the faint hum of the car's hover-struts.

Tears don't make much noise.

Everything on the outside of the house looks completely normal. The door is on its hinges, no windows are broken, and even the flowers are tidy. I remember the noise of the attack. I expected more destruction, but Minali must've had it repaired.

"Welcome home, Liddi," Dom says as I walk in. "Has there been a change to your schedule? I could update it if you like."

The tears press harder, and the pressure to cry out becomes unbearable, but the tiny extra weight at my throat reminds me I can't. I can't use my voice, and I can't respond to Dom.

Dom figures out after three more tries that I'm not going to talk. Still achey and tired from the neural incapacitator, I curl up in bed, hoping the silence won't suffocate me in my sleep.

※ - - - ※

"Liddi, do I assume correctly that you don't wish to hear the usual messages in your queue?" Dom asks two days later.

I tap the icon for Yes and stare at the otherwise blank screen.

"Very well. One new message has just come in that doesn't fit the 'usual.' Would you like to hear that one?"

Yes again. Why not?

"Liddi, it's Garrin. I'm not buying Blake's story about you taking some 'quiet time.' Something's wrong. Holding back the truth about your brothers' disappearance is the wrong move—we need all the eyes possible looking for them. Get back to me. I can help."

A nice sentiment, but I can't record a message back to him, and I can't get into the city to see him without Minali knowing it. I can't just sit and do nothing either, though, so I don't. Unfortunately, doing anything using just the iconographic interface takes *forever*. All the computer networks have been voice-activated for ages now, with the touchscreens mostly for quick jumping between subroutines. Good thing Dom is such a smart system. He makes up a few new icons and tells me what they mean, hoping to help me get where I'm going. When that's too much, I draw pictures for him to decipher, and he uses the in-house cams to watch my gestures.

"Your refusal to speak does make things inefficient," he says after the fourth wrong try in a row. "And my flexibility regarding icons is limited. But I suspect the information you seek isn't relevant to the databases I have access to."

Relevant databases. There's something Marek told me. Something he joked about. *"Those archivists on Tarix are so afraid of losing everything obscure, they don't realize they lost their minds centuries ago."*

Archivists and historians and philosophers. "Useless thinkers," Minali called them. Useless to her, maybe. But they have the collected history and knowledge of the Seven Points, including everything ever dreamed up by the technologists on Sampati. If someone ever knew more about the portals and we forgot, the information would still be there somewhere. Maybe I could find the connection my gut tells me I'm missing between the old portals and the way the conduits work. And even if the people on Tarix don't have my brothers' monitoring codes, they might have details on the implants themselves. That would be a starting point.

If I can figure out a way to communicate and access their systems . . . but maybe they'll have something for that, too.

Even then, what makes me think I can figure it out? Checked genes, the only non-smart Jantzen in history. A waste of all the energy put into building me up. Hopeless and pointless . . .

I shake off the creeping doubts. It doesn't matter. Trying is what matters, because my brothers have always expected my best effort. It's *all* they've ever asked of me. Besides, if my parents set control of the company to pass to Tarix if something happened to me, they must have trusted some people there. If I can find those people, if I can make them understand, I'll get the help I need.

But there's no way I can go to a conduit terminal and ask them to send me to Tarix. Even if I could talk, Minali will have all the terminals monitored by more attendants than usual.

If you found a portal high, if you found a portal low . . .

So I guess I'll have to find one.

I pull up the blank screen to draw on and sketch out the icon of the Seven Points. Seven interlocking circles in a partial ring, lines joining their centers, with a web in the middle and flames through the gap at the top.

"The Seven Points," Dom says.

I nod and lock the drawing, then point to the web in the middle.

"The hyperdimensional conduits interconnecting the worlds of the Seven Points, used for near-instantaneous travel between—"

I shake my head. After a moment of thought, I delete pieces of the lines forming the web and lower their contrast, making them faded and broken.

It takes Dom a full five seconds to make a guess. "The ancient portals originally serving the purpose now fulfilled by the conduits." When I nod, he continues. "Would you like the complete compilation of data or a summary?"

Two fingers up— our signal for the second option.

He talks, and I listen.

※— — — ※

The summary isn't good enough, so I have Dom dig into the full compilation. That takes time, especially since I can't do much to help him filter it down to what I need. The records are sketchy and vague, and most of the best information comes from my family. Pieces creep together, so slowly, and I'm not sure whether it's the lack of material or my checked brain that's at fault.

Dom interrupts himself on our second day of digging. "Liddi, there's a news-vid you may want to see."

I nod. The break couldn't hurt. I just hope it's not about the laserball tournament standings.

A picture flashes onto the wallscreen. Police outside a residential building in the city.

"This is the home of Garrin Walker, who was formerly the assistant of Nevi Jantzen and has worked for Jantzen's sons in an advisory capacity in recent years. Police found Walker's body inside a few hours ago, an apparent suicide."

My stomach clenches and the tightness in my throat triples. I hit the No icon, which Dom correctly interprets, stopping the vid. But it means more than that to me.

No.

Impossible.

Garrin can't be dead.

The man who let me build block-towers by his desk, who helped my father every day, who got me away from the vid-cams and the mob when I ran to the city . . . he can't be gone, too. My hand shakes over the touchscreen but the icons have blurred. I can't see. I can't breathe. He sent me a message yesterday, wanting to help.

No one offers help one day and commits suicide the next, do they?

Not someone who suspects Minali is up to something and still has a voice. She hasn't killed my brothers yet, but if she's killed Garrin just for nosing in, getting in her way . . . She says she can't afford to kill *me*, but she can do worse. Saving the conduits is important, but she's obsessed. And I know from a lifetime in vids that obsessed people are the scariest kind.

Walker-Man. I remember. I didn't call Garrin that just because of his last name. It was because of something he often said to my father that made little-kid me think he was really interested in walking.

"Always take the next step before anyone catches the one before."

I get it now. I can't waste more time looking for information that probably doesn't exist. I have to make the next move before Minali realizes the path I'm on. The bits I have will have to be enough to get me to Tarix. I'll figure out the rest as I go. Hopefully.

She's watching the house—I'm sure of it. From the media-casts, I know people are getting more and more desperate to catch a glimpse of me. Dom knows better than to mention interview requests and event invitations at this point, but I'm sure they're clogging up my message queue. The new security

measures are holding, but if any media grubs break through, it'll be reason enough for Minali to bring me back into the city. Especially if Garrin's concern already has her worried about people going public or trying to help me, she'll want to keep a closer watch.

Can't have that—I need the woods. Fabin's research said portals were more prevalent in natural areas, and when all I have to go on is "look really hard," I need the best odds I can get.

Evening walks have been part of the routine since I was silenced. Even before that, it was common enough. Cams still don't work on the grounds—I checked—so if Minali is watching, it's with satellite imaging, and that doesn't provide much detail.

If she's watching, she won't notice I'm carrying a small pack with some clothes, food and water, and a com-tablet.

When I walk out the back door, the fragrance of the night phlox is almost too much, reminding me of the night of the attack. My first instinct is to hold my breath, but instead I inhale deeply, letting other memories flood and flow. Playing tag or stickball, Vic lifting me so I could climb trees whose lowest limbs were still too high, Durant nagging him about using two hands, making doubly sure I wouldn't fall.

I'll get them out. I will. Somehow.

Luna Major is already well above the horizon, so visibility isn't an issue. My only plan is to wander until I find a portal. It's not much of a plan, especially given the vastness of the property, but it's the best I've got.

Just as I'm wondering whether I should try up- or downriver, movement flashes in the corner of my eye. My first instinct is to duck and hide, but then I see what it was.

Fabin.

 51

Every night I've walked the grounds, hoping to see one of them. Now, the night I need them most, here he is! Still faint and ghostly, but I don't just see him. I hear him.

"Liddi, come on! This way."

His voice is strange, weak and muffled like there's a wall between us. But it's my brother's voice, and I've never heard anything so beautiful. I run toward him. He runs as well, making me follow.

He's in such a hurry. A pulse of panic surges through me, alongside my adrenaline. I missed a piece. There can't be vid-cams on the grounds, but there could be people. More merce-naries. More guns.

I run faster.

We head upriver to the old footbridge, but I lose Fabin in a tangle of trees on the other side. The panic hasn't left me, but before I can pick a random direction to keep running, I spot Ciro ahead, beckoning to me.

Two of my brothers in short order. It can't be a coincidence. They know something. I don't know how, but they know.

This is going to work.

I follow Ciro, and he leads me along an unfamiliar path for several minutes before I lose him. The pattern continues as each of my brothers finds me and leads me in turn.

Durant is the last, but when I lose him, I don't have to wonder where to go. A light filters through the trees ahead that definitely doesn't come from either of the moons. It crackles, like light making sound. I come to the edge of a large meadow—larger than any clearing I've found in the woods—and see the source.

It's an enormous knot of white-blue energy hovering in the middle of the meadow, twisting and snapping at itself. But

it's more than that. As I walk closer, I feel it. Not like the hair-raising tingle of an electric field. I felt that plenty of times in the workshop as my brothers fiddled with electricity. This is so much more, so much "other." It's like walking on a laser beam, like if this massive spark weren't twisted so tight, holding itself together, it'd tear the entire world apart. More than the world. Tear space and time and thought and everything until there was nothing left whole.

My cells writhe in its presence.

I don't understand how there haven't been reports of anybody seeing one more recently, or why the old reports were so sketchy and vague. There's nothing vague about something this terrifying. Every detail sears itself in my memory, whispering promises to haunt my nightmares forever.

The very real possibility of turning around and walking home presents itself. The part of me that doesn't want to stand here looking at this vortex of destruction, contemplating stepping *into* it willingly, seriously considers that possibility. It's not like it's going to take long for Minali to notice I left. It might take some time to figure out I went to Tarix, but there are only so many Points, and they know my face on all of them. So not *that* long. More than likely, not long enough for me to accomplish anything useful. I could go home and forget it. Play along.

Pretend I didn't even hear about Garrin's death.

No, I can't.

Every one of my brothers' innovations started out as a long shot they took a chance on, then worked at until they succeeded. It's my turn to take a chance. But at the same time, the portal evokes a bone-deep desire to run.

I drag my eyes away from the snapping, convulsing energy and see something else. My brothers are here. All of them, spaced along the edge of the clearing. I wish they'd come closer so I could hear their faint voices, so they could tell me what to do. But they don't. If they won't come to me, I'll go to them.

One step toward Emil stops that idea. Even from a distance, I see how they all tense. Shake their heads. Then I notice something else. They're not just standing on the perimeter; they're moving along it. Not by walking. More like gliding, adding to the ghostlike effect of their appearance.

I turn back to the portal. Beneath the complex lashes of energy, the whole thing revolves slowly, in time with my brothers. They're bound to it, under its control.

Or they're controlling it, holding it in place long enough for me to use it. If that's even possible. But something about the idea feels right.

If that's what they're doing, it can't be easy. It could be why only one at a time could guide me, and only for a little while, until he had to get back to wrangling his "corner" of the vortex. And even all eight can't do it forever.

I tighten the straps of my pack, fix my thoughts on Tarix, and run right at the whirling mass of energy.

The reports said travel by portal was uncomfortable.

The reports lied.

Fire freezes my skin. Air drowns my lungs. I'm torn apart by stitches piecing me together. Colors whirl in monochrome as the roar of silence fills my ears.

And pain. Pain is the one thing that makes sense.

I'm spinning and flying and sinking and dying and no matter how much I try to think about Tarix like I'm supposed to,

I'm just not getting there. I'm getting nowhere. Or nowhere is getting me.

Amid the whirling madness, something else breaks through that makes sense. A hand on my arm. Another on my shoulder. And another.

My brothers, real and solid, surround me. Emil tucks me into his arms, shielding me from the assault. The others push and pull and carry us through the storm, Durant leading the way, then Luko and Vic, each one taking his turn. Waves of chaos beat against us, but my brothers are strong, taking the brunt of it and continuing forward.

We go for hours, or maybe time moves backward. No way to mark the duration except by counting the number of times Emil murmurs reassurances in my ear. That I'll be okay, that I'll make it and be safe and that he's sorry-sorry-sorry, about Garrin, about being too late, about getting caught in Minali's trap, they all are.

The others murmur, too, but it's harder to understand. Vic saying it's not a game because games have rules, and he would know because he's played all the games and this isn't one of them. Fabin reciting properties of conduit substrata but no-no-no that isn't it, that's not the answer. Marek trying to tell a joke because it's his job to make me laugh, but it always turns out with me crying, only my tears are dry and cut into my skin. And the others, their words aren't even words, just sounds, and it's my fault, I'm not listening hard enough. If only I could listen, I would find the answer but I can't-can't-can't.

My awareness begins to fade a few times, but when it does, energy seeps into me, returning focus. I'm not sure where the energy comes from. When it happens, my brothers' grips loosen the tiniest bit. Like the energy comes from them.

A barrier stands in our way. I can't see it, but I feel it, the same way I felt the power of the portal from a distance. Emil tightens his hold, the others move in closer, and we launch forward—*what's forward?*—with a sudden burst of speed—*speed measured against what?*—to pound against it.

It's the other side of the portal, and the answer is simple. If I keep hold of my brothers, we'll come out the other side. *All* of us. They'll be free.

The barrier resists, trying to push us back, but we push harder. I hold on to Emil with everything I've got.

My skull splinters.

My limbs disintegrate.

My grip slips.

Blood blinds and chokes me.

Then the ground, hard and rough and scratchy, is beneath me with enough force to knock the air from my lungs. I'm not sure where I got the air in the first place, but its abrupt departure, along with the tightness at my throat, keep me from making a noise.

I can't move—it's like my body's forgotten how—except to turn my head and blink until my eyes regain focus.

Emil is still with me, but he's the only one, and he's back to ghostly not-quite-here form. He's on his knees, gasping for breath. I tell my hand to reach for his, and the signals sort themselves out. Our fingers touch. I feel it, but not like inside the portal. More like the faint touch of a soap bubble, light and fragile.

"Be strong, Liddi," he says. "We think you'll be safe here. We hope. We're trying to find some answers. Even when you can't see us, we'll keep an eye on you. Just . . . just be strong."

I want to beg him to stay with me, to help me, but he fades from view. I'm alone again.

After taking a moment to gather my strength, I roll onto my back—it takes way more effort than it should, and isn't comfortable at all with my pack in the way—and look to the night sky.

There are three moons.

My heart jumps to an anxious rhythm, drumming on my joints and sparking my brain to life. I run through all the Seven Points. Sampati and Erkir have two moons, while Yishu has just one. Pramadam, Tarix, and Neta don't have any at all.

Banak has four. Maybe I went off-course, or my brothers thought Banak was more likely to help me than Tarix . . . though the idea of getting help from the center of the Seven Points' military complex is more than a little intimidating. Officer Svarta's face flashes in my eyes. I wonder how deep Minali's connections to Banak run.

No, wait. Vic once sent me images of a trip to Banak when all four moons were in the sky. Two of them were rust-colored. One of these moons has the same silvery glow of Luna Major and Luna Minor. The other two both have a distinct bluish tinge.

I turn my head to the other side, away from where Emil was.

The portal hasn't vanished, but it's nothing like it was in the clearing. Just a tiny spark hovering peacefully between two crystal spires. Like it's asleep, but the massive power, the capacity for insanity, it's still there.

This portal is controlled. Known. Marked.

I have no idea where I am.

The tiny robot danced and waved at Liddi, making her laugh. She wanted to see what else it would do, but it turned the corner out of sight. So Liddi followed it to the next aisle of the store.

It walked on its hands, it sang a song with silly words, and it curled into a ball to roll between displays before springing back to full size. Everywhere it went, Liddi followed, until finally the routine was done and the robot went on standby. Bored, Liddi returned to the wallscreen display to ask her mother when they were leaving.

She wasn't there.

Liddi looked around. Her mother wasn't anywhere.

Panic seeped into her skin, bringing visions of a life where she never found her mother again, or her father or her brothers. Tears welled up, but Liddi wouldn't let them fall. Her brothers always told her tears just wasted water her brain might need.

Just as she was about to waste tears anyway, Anton tore around the corner and stopped, out of breath.

"There you are! We've been looking everywhere. Don't wander off, Liddi-Loo!"

He scooped her up, and she held tight to his neck. She realized her panic was silly, because she never had to be afraid of getting lost.

Her brothers would always find her.

5

THE PANIC ATTACK JOLTS a little strength into me, but not much. Enough to sit up, push myself to my feet, and immediately collapse again. My body can't take it yet.

Maybe my brain is scrambled from the journey and I've gotten confused about the moons. Maybe I have a concussion and I'm not seeing what I think I'm seeing.

There will be an explanation. I will find it, and it will make sense. I lie there on the ground some more, trying to breathe, stay calm, think, gather strength. The breathing part works, at least.

Even if I don't know what planet I'm on, I can figure out some things about where I am. It's not like the woods at home. More like the prairie parts of Erkir. Luko and Vic took me on a visit there when I was nine. Grassy with trees here and there in the light of the moons. Nothing else resembling the crystal spires of the portal, not that I can see, anyway. More hills than Erkir. In fact, I seem to be in a large bowl made of hills.

A light comes over one of those, approaching fast.

I make another attempt to push myself up, but there's nowhere to go. The nearest trees are too far and won't provide much cover. Without being able to even sit up decently, there's no way running is an option.

The light can't be a hovercar—too small, and doesn't move smoothly enough. It's more like someone running with a hand-held light, but doesn't quite match that, either. The way it jerks and jostles isn't right.

When the source arrives, I clamp my teeth down to keep from screaming. Unknown planet or not, the implant has a hyperdimensional transmitter, making distance a lot less of a factor. The continual pressure at my throat reminds me a signal could get through, triggering my brothers' deaths if I speak. Still, the figure before me makes it difficult to stay silent.

It's a person but not, like a genetic experiment gone wrong. Very wrong. The face is close, with the expressiveness and depth in the eyes to convey intelligence. But the details are off—four nostrils, an excessively prominent jaw, and a headful of shaggy brown hair that's more like a mane of fur. The rest of the body is even worse. The arms are far too long and explain the jerkiness of the light strapped to his shoulder—he runs using his arms as well as his legs.

I don't know what he is. I do know he's angry. He shouts at me with a series of grunts and clicks. I scoot myself back on the grass, getting some distance between us even if it means getting closer to the portal.

His unnaturally long arms snap out and grab me, hauling me off the ground. This time it's even harder not to cry out, because everything hurts and having my legs dangling in midair gives

me vertigo and this strange person with too many teeth is still yelling things I can't understand and I want it all to stop. I want to scream and wake myself up from this nightmare.

"Kalkig, I told you to—what are you doing? Put her down!"

I'm released, collapsing to a heap on the ground again, and find the source of the new voice illuminated by the light from the stranger's shoulder. Another person has arrived. This one is an actual person, normal-looking and everything. Well, normal enough to tell he's around my age. His skin is close to the same sienna shade of my own, if a bit darker, and he has the same dark hair, but his features aren't anything like mine. Sharper, more angular, including the shape of his eyes. His voice was that way, too, with an accent that somehow made the words themselves sharper. Then I can't see him as well, because he crouches at my side, blocking the light from his companion.

"You just came out?" he asks.

I nod. It has to be pretty obvious.

"Not feeling too great then, eh? That'll pass. I'm Tiav. What's your name?"

I think that's the first time in my life anyone's asked me my name. Even if I *could* talk, the newness of it might have held me speechless. When I don't answer, his eyes pass over me from head to toe, then return to study my face. His mouth sets in a flat line. "You're from one of the Points, aren't you?"

Another nod. If he knows what the Points are, this isn't so bad.

The strange one makes a noise, but Tiav ignores him. "Which one?"

Um, problem. That's not a question I can answer with a nod or shake of my head.

My silence doesn't sit well with him. "Maybe my friend Kalkig was on the right track."

"It doesn't matter which she's from," Kalkig says. At least, I think he does. His voice is made for the guttural language he used earlier. "We have to send her back, Tiav—she shouldn't be here. She *can't* be here."

No, I can't go back, not without helping my brothers, not back under Minali's control, which will be even tighter with my attempted escape, knowing what she's willing to do to carry out her plan. The lives she's willing to cut down. I shake my head emphatically, eyes wide.

"Are you in trouble back there?" asks Tiav. Nod. "Then you need to tell us the truth."

I don't know how to explain. I shake my head and point to my throat. The boy's expression eases, less on guard.

"You can't speak? Okay, maybe this, then." He pulls a flat-screened device from his pocket—it looks like one of our com-tablets, but different—taps a few commands on its surface, and sets it on the ground between us.

An image of light floats in midair. It's a grid, five-by-ten, filled with symbols I've never seen before. Not like icons. They're something else.

They still have written language here. We phased it out centuries ago. Only certain archivists on Tarix know how to decipher it anymore. I certainly don't.

Kalkig makes a noise that sounds like gargling his own teeth but might be laughter. "Not just a Pointed heathen, but uneducated, too."

I don't know what a "heathen" is, and I might be the least intelligent person in Jantzen family history, but I take exception to being called uneducated by an overgrown lion-monkey. We don't *need* those symbols of theirs in the Points. Enough strength has returned that I can sit up, but before I can go at Kalkig, Tiav puts a hand on my shoulder.

He does it so casually, reaffirming he has no idea who I am. The shock of it holds me in place.

"Kal, if you're not going to help, go back to the streamer. Let's try something else." He taps at the device again, and the hovering image changes. It's the Seven Points' icon, but not quite. The web is more intricate, almost like lace, and a star is in the place of the fire at the top. "Which one is your home?"

I point to the circle just right of the bottom.

"Sampati? That's a start. Until I can teach you enough writing to tell me your name, I'll call you Sam, all right?"

There are worse things to be called, so I nod. Then I point to the icon again, gesture to everything surrounding us, and raise my eyebrows.

"Where is this? You're on Ferinne. Right here." He points to the star at the top of the icon.

Ferri. The "Eighth Point" that isn't a Point. Or isn't supposed to be. That's supposed to be death. Going through the portal *felt* enough like dying, and maybe Kalkig is one of the demon servants of the Wraith.

The Wraith that isn't supposed to be real.

Panic seeps into me again. Maybe that's it. Maybe I'm dead, and maybe my brothers are, too. Except I like to think an afterlife wouldn't be this bizarre. An afterlife would have my parents waiting for me.

I know I look ridiculous, but I mime slashing my throat and slumping over dead with my tongue hanging out. Tiav

chuckles—a sound that strangely dulls my terror, bringing comfort to the madness surrounding me.

"Sorry, you lost me there, Sam."

Okay. I sit up again and grab his wrist, feeling for a pulse. Steady and strong. Then I check my own. The same, if a little elevated.

"Ah, got it. Yes, you're alive, I promise. Kalkig and I aren't delusions or hallucinations or dreams, either. At least, I'm pretty sure we're not."

Kalkig just snorts.

"We should get you back to Podra, get some rest. We'll worry about getting answers in the morning." Tiav's eyes dart to the portal but come back to me just as quickly, like he didn't want to be caught looking. "Can you stand?"

I don't actually know until I try. My legs hold me up, just barely. They still tremble and ache. Tiav notices and lightly supports me with a hand on my waist. The contact makes me shiver. I'm used to keeping a constant breath of fresh air between myself and strangers. Kalkig goes ahead of us. I distract myself by trying to think of the right word for the arms-and-legs way he walks. *Amble? Lope?* I'm not sure.

We crest the first hill only to climb a higher one beyond. Kalkig has no trouble with the hike, but it's a little much for my recently reassembled body.

"Sorry," Tiav says. "The road's just on the other side. Can you make it?"

Without bothering to nod, I walk faster, slipping away from his hand. And promptly trip. The potential media-cast plays out in my head:

Liddi Jantzen face-planted on a Periww hill today, without the excuse of Igoru heels. She's just that uncoordinated. Shame about the grass stains. Those were such nice pants.

I'm not that uncoordinated. Besides portals being the worst mode of transport ever, adjusting to another planet's gravity always takes time. But none of that changes the result of me up close and personal with the grass.

Tiav doesn't laugh. He just helps me up and we keep walking.

After the second hill, the going is easier, and it's not much farther to the road. It's not like any road I've ever seen, and the "streamer," as Tiav called it, isn't like any hovercar. The body is similar enough, and it does float a foot or so off the ground, but with no hover-struts. Instead, there's a sparkling energy field running along the bottom of the vehicle, connecting to the road. A streamer. Kalkig's already inside when we get there. One of the seats has been adjusted to accommodate his strange physiology.

So many questions, all making my inability to speak more maddening than it already was. I wonder if I can get one across to Tiav. I point to Kalkig and scrunch my eyebrows into the most questioning expression I can manage.

"Handsome devil, isn't he?" Tiav says. My stomach drops at the word *devil*, so close to *demon*—the tortured creatures serving the Wraith in the Abyss. Supposedly. Except I still don't believe that. "Kal is an Agnac."

Kalkig cuts in with an urgent series of grunts. Tiav doesn't seem bothered.

"She's here. She's seen you. And speaking Agnacki isn't going to convince her you're a genetic anomaly."

What other option is there? I settle into one of the other seats and keep question-face going. Tiav catches it, but shakes his head.

"Explaining that will take some time. And seeing will help. Let's get back to town first."

I watch his hands as he taps controls on a touchscreen. Pretty simple. A map displaying various icons. The one nearest us must be the portal. Tiav selects a larger one farther away.

The acceleration should squash us all to goo on the back end of the vehicle, but it doesn't, despite the way the world blurs by. It feels like a leisurely hovercar ride. It's not. My equilibrium can't take the disconnect, and I close my eyes in a desperate effort not to throw up. A tiny deceleration and change in the vehicle's vibrations signal the end of the brief ride. I open my eyes to find Kalkig has already gotten out. The few minutes sitting were enough for my aching body to cramp up, so Tiav helps me, and I get my first look at Ferinne's version of a town.

Podra's nowhere near the size and scale of Pinnacle, but it's nothing like the country estate, either. Most of the buildings are between five and eight stories tall. Some plain and boxy, some elaborate with decorative details. One nearby has intricate scrollwork carved into the corners, reminding me of my father's old desk. Some buildings are dark, some lit up. Almost all have colorful signs with those symbols adorning them. The names of various establishments within the building, I'm sure. Some have iconlike pictures, too, but only a few give me clues. One is definitely a restaurant, but I have a hard time believing another has anything to do with selling birds of prey.

My eyes lower to street level, and I scarcely notice the other "streamer" cars coming and going in a blur. The people—using

the word *people* loosely—walking on either side of the street demand my attention....

People like Kalkig—Agnac, Tiav called them—move along on their strange limbs. They're all larger than Kalkig, so maybe he's young, and many of them don't use their arms at all while walking.

But there are other kinds. People who are definitely adults, but all smaller than I am, fine-featured and delicate and beautiful. Others so large and muscular, they'd make Reb's laserball team forfeit on sight, all of them bald with large eyes in strange colors. Sprinkled among them, people who resemble Tiav or me. Normal people.

None of them look at me. Most of them look at Tiav.

A woozy feeling swims from my stomach to my head. I think I've forgotten how to breathe.

Tiav takes my arm to steady me and keeps his voice low. "So, it's true. The Points haven't met any aliens yet."

I shake my head. No, we definitely have not.

※ – – – ※

Tiav takes me to the eighth floor of a particular building. Kalkig comes along, glaring at me the entire time, which I try to ignore. It's more difficult than I expect. I'm used to being stared at. I'm not used to the temptation to stare right back.

The elevator lets us out into a sitting room. No people, thank the Sent—I catch myself. If "Ferri" is real in the form of Ferinne, there's no telling what roots the Sentinel or Wraith may have here. Regardless, I'm not sure I'm ready for an up-close alien encounter beyond Kalkig. Comfortable couches fill the space,

some of them clearly designed for different anatomies, and a large window overlooks the town. Tiav walks past all that to a door that opens on his approach, then through a small outer room—also empty—and into a larger one. Not empty.

A woman sits on a low couch, studying symbols being projected into the air from another com-tablet. She's tall, with skin a bit darker than Tiav's, but the same angular features. A necklace with a crystal pendant catches my eye, but I don't get a good look at it. She looks up when we come in, and any surprise she feels at seeing me is summed up in a minute raising of an eyebrow. I'm pretty sure this woman hasn't doubted herself a day in her life. Every inch of her screams self-assured and calm.

"This is what you found?"

"Yes, Mother. She came through . . . from Sampati."

That gets a bigger reaction from her as she turns off the projection. "Keep talking, Tiav'elo."

He sums up the little he knows—that I can't speak so he's calling me Sam, that I can't read or write, and that there seems to be a danger in me going back.

"Is that true?" she says to me. "You face danger in your home?"

Home makes me think of my brothers, and an aching anxiety surges through me. There's no danger from them—the danger is that without them, I have no home to return to. This woman's question isn't as simple as it sounds, but a nod is all I can give.

"This is complicated. I will inform the senior council. Do not discuss it with anyone else for now. You, too, Kalkig," she adds sternly. I'm surprised to see the Agnac duck his head, acquiescing with no argument. "Tiav'elo, this is your responsibility. What do you suggest?"

Tiav's shoulders straighten at her words. "Maybe we can teach her to write," he says. "At least enough to explain."

I nod vigorously. That's exactly what I need. My mind keeps returning to the portal in the hills, the crystal spires. If these people know enough about portals to mark and control them, I need to get that knowledge and use it to free my brothers from the conduits. Like Durant always says, if someone knows something you don't, don't be proud—just get learning, quick.

"A reasonable plan," the woman agrees before turning to me again. "You look like you could use some rest first. Show her to one of the guest rooms, Tiav'elo. Kalkig, you should be getting home."

I follow the other two out. Kalkig says something in his own language, but Tiav cuts him off with a clap on his shoulder.

"Don't start, Kal. I know. I'll talk to you tomorrow, okay?"

The response is a grunt and something resembling a shrug. While the Agnac returns to the elevator, Tiav leads me down a hall branching off from the sitting room. We pass by a kitchen and dining room, and go by a number of closed doors. This must be some kind of penthouse apartment, taking up the entire floor. Finally, he opens a door at the end of the hallway and ushers me through.

As bedrooms go, it's nice but nothing fancy. A bed, a small desk, a dresser, two paintings on the walls, and a window looking out on the city. Everything is done in neutral colors, neither especially feminine nor masculine, old nor young. There's a rustic quality to it, lacking the ever-present sheen of technology we have back home. The desk might have a computer interface built into its surface, but I can't tell for sure.

"Do you need anything?" Tiav asks.

I slide my pack off my shoulders and set it on the bed. I packed enough in there for a couple of days, so I give him a no. Then I point back the way we came and tilt my head, hoping he'll get the question.

"Kalkig?"

No, that's not it. I wait for him to try again.

"My mother? Her name's Shiin'alo, and she's an Aelo—well, we both are, but she's the primary Aelo of Ferinne. But...that probably doesn't answer anything, does it? I have more questions than I can count, so I can only imagine how *you* feel. We'll get started with writing tomorrow. Then maybe everything will make more sense."

Considering I was taught that Ferri is an afterlife ruled by two powerful beings that no one *really* believes in, I don't have high hopes for *anything* making sense.

Madness fills my dreams, the cell-tearing chaos of the portal. My brothers beg me to hold on tighter, to pull them through.

They slip away every time. I fail again and again.

I wake up with only a few minor aches remaining, but the dream of my brothers lingers. When I tried to pull Emil through with me, I wasn't ready. I was too weak. I'll have to get back to that portal with the spires, try again. Maybe once I have a better idea of this place and what's happening.

After cleaning up and getting dressed, I find a tray of food outside my door. No idea where it came from, but I bring it in and eat the provided breakfast. The fruits are different, sweeter, and the grains less refined, but it tastes good.

"Ready to go?"

I didn't notice Tiav arrive at the open doorway, yet his words didn't startle me. Maybe because I welcome any break in the silence. As for whether I'm ready to go, I don't know where we're going, but I'm ready enough, so I follow him out.

Yesterday Tiav had a cautiousness that's gone today. Now his eyes hold a distinct energy as he leads me back down to the street, like he's overflowing with the questions he mentioned last night. He sticks to easy-to-answer ones like whether I slept well (yes, well enough), whether I'll need additional clothes (yes, most likely), and whether I have any lingering injuries from my journey (no, not that I've noticed).

I don't know what other questions he could possibly have. They already know the Points exist, and they somehow control portals, which puts him at least seventeen steps ahead of me. Any details he doesn't know are insignificant next to the mind-boggling parade of *aliens* that again greets me outside.

We don't get into a streamer, instead just walk along the street. Tension I hadn't noticed relaxes from my body. Give me a hovercar over those confounding streamers any day.

Walking means weaving among the other pedestrians, including all the alien types. Again, they look at Tiav much more than at me. Like I'm only interesting because I'm with him. Whatever *primary Aelo* means, being her son calls atten-tion to him, too.

I get that.

"We're going to the Nyum," Tiav says, keeping his voice low enough that only I can hear him. "Every town and city has one. It's where the Aelo work, and sometimes representatives from the Agnacki, Crimna, and Haleian governments. Remember,

Kalkig is Agnac. That woman over there, she's Haleian." He subtly jerks his head toward one of the big, athletic-looking types. "And that one's Crimna." One of the slight, delicate people.

The building—the Nyum—isn't far. The front wall curves away from us and goes up in four asymetrical levels. It's not huge by Sampati standards, but big enough that I can't tell whether the whole building is round or just the front. Judging by the inside, I'm guessing the whole building, because the lobby taking up the entire first floor seems to be completely circular. Smooth tiles cover the floor and shelves line the walls. All the shelves are packed with similar rectangular objects, varying sizes, but I don't recognize them. To the left and right, sweeping staircases lead to a balcony overlooking the lobby before continuing on to the rest of the second floor. Several people stand near the shelves or on the balcony. A few of them nod at Tiav before returning to their conversations.

Something about this place reminds me of Tarix, but I'm not sure what.

Tiav leads me up the stairs, then to a smaller staircase leading to the third floor. It's much less grand than the lobby, more utilitarian, and I spot more touchscreens and other signs of a technological presence. We enter a small room—some kind of office, I think—with a desk in the middle and a few chairs, plus a large wallscreen.

"My mother suggested we work in here," Tiav says, gesturing for me to take a seat. I do, and he taps some commands into his com-tablet. The desk in front of me lights up, and so does the wallscreen, both with the same grid of symbols he showed me last night. He looks at the wallscreen and scratches the back of his neck. "Okay, where to start?"

He doesn't say anything else for several long minutes, until he finally turns around to find I'm staring at him, waiting.

"Sorry. I just never thought about how to teach writing to someone who's never seen it before. It's a semi-syllabic system, so there are two stages to the keypad. This is the primary stage with the base characters. When you tap one, it takes you to the secondary stage. See, each of these has different markings added to the base character to complete the syllable. The primary is in alphabetical order, but the secondary stages are a little more complicated."

I slump in my chair. Up until now, I've been reassured by the fact that Tiav speaks the same language I do—and come to think of it, that's some odd luck. But he just veered into something foreign.

Fortunately, he sees my instant hopelessness and shakes his head. "Wait. You don't know what alphabetical means, do you? Let me just show you my name so you can see how it works, then. Tiav, so I need the *t* base, which is here." He taps it, and a new grid appears. This must be what he meant by the secondary stage. All the symbols here look similar, but with minor variations in the details. "This is the specific symbol for *tee*. Then back to the main board for *ah*. And this one for *ahv*."

I look at the two symbols side-by-side, together representing Tiav's name. There's a kind of beauty to them. They're almost art. But I can't imagine anyone ever keeping enough of the symbols straight in their head to understand more than a word or two.

"You look like I've asked you to eat an Agnacki boar in one sitting." He pulls another chair around next to me. "Here, I'll tell you the sound for each base letter, and you stop me when I get to the one you want. Let's start with your name."

One by one, he names the sounds. The *l* isn't in the first row. Halfway through the second, they begin to blur together and my mind wanders. I almost miss when he gets it at the start of the third row. He's already said the next sound by the time I tap his arm and point to the one before. We continue through the secondary board until he finds *lih*. Then the whole process again from *d* to *dee*.

The two symbols line up on the queue underneath the grid. Tiav starts back at the beginning of the main symbols, but I tap his arm again and shake my head.

"That's it? Your name's Liddi?" When I nod, he smiles.

I've had a lot of nice-looking boys smile at me, not least among them Reb Vester. Tiav's is different. It's missing something. A media-cast in my head answers the question.

For the first time in Liddi Jantzen's life, a boy smiled at her with no scheming, no calculating . . . without wanting *anything.*

The realization sends a shock through me, the thrill of finding something's not so impossible.

"Nice to meet you, Liddi. What next?"

It must have taken two full minutes just to write my two-symbol name, so I need to think of something short and efficient to say. I gesture for him to restart the cycle. I think I remember the *p* sound being somewhere on the first row.

No, that was *b*. Tiav keeps going, and going, until finally he gets it in the last row. We run into a problem on the other stage, because there is no *pore*. I select the closest thing—*poh*—then circle the empty space next to the resulting symbol in the queue.

"Oh, I forgot," he says. "Some syllables cycle back to the primary stage for their end-sounds. You just have to touch this one in the corner to show you don't want it to go into the secondary stage yet."

So we go again until we find the *r* sound. Its symbol shows up differently in the queue, smaller and hovering above and to the right of the *poh*.

And again through *t* and *tah* before adding *l*.

"'Portal'? Do you mean Podra, this city? What about it?"

No, he doesn't understand. My bones feel like they've been charged with explosives. It's too slow and inefficient and my brothers are out there waiting for me. I never imagined writing would be so complicated. No wonder we got rid of it. Maybe if it were Luko or Emil instead of me—they're both sharp with visual details—but it isn't, and this isn't going to work.

I don't have time.

Silence stabs every corner of my body. I want to scream—I've wanted to for days—but that's the very last thing I can do. Instead, I jump out of my seat and start pacing, trying to burn off the frustrated, impotent energy that begs for me to cry out.

"What's wrong? I don't understand."

We're agreed on that, but I don't even know what word I could try to write to explain it to him.

"Is everything all right?"

The voice from the doorway stops my pacing. It's Shiin'alo. Tiav stands as she enters.

"Yes, everything's fine. She was able to tell me her name's Liddi. Not much else, but we only just got started."

"I'm afraid we'll have to postpone anything further for a little while," she says. "When I informed the council, Ymana pointed out something I hadn't thought of—Liddi may have inadvertently brought foreign contagions with her from Sampati. We'll have one of the doctors check you over, Liddi, just to make sure."

"I can take her," Tiav says.

"That's not necessary. You have other duties to attend to."

He doesn't make any attempt to argue. "Yes, Mother."

Shiin'alo gestures for me to follow her, but before I go, I turn to Tiav. I mimic pointing at the symbols one after another after another, drawing my face into an expression of the most mind-numbing boredom.

He nods, allowing another smile. "I'll see if I can work out something better."

That'll be good, because judging by the way his mother said "duties," I'm pretty sure he has better things to do. When it comes down to it, so do I.

Joon Elyson had been dreamed up by the artists on Yishu, as far as Liddi could tell. That was probably why so many artists and designers employed the teen. Skin as dark as her hair, tall and confident, with eyes you couldn't miss from across a crowded room. Yet at the party to celebrate Igara's new jewelry line, Joon was the one who crossed the room to where Liddi stood.

"Liddi Jantzen, right?" Joon said. "Iggy said he'd invited you."

"Unfortunately, my brothers don't think fourteen is old enough to go out by myself, so I'm chaperoned," Liddi said with a roll of her eyes toward Vic. He was talking laserball with a media-grub but had time to give Liddi a "stop-complaining" glare.

"Oh, they'll get over that soon enough. Come on, let me introduce you to some people."

Joon knew everyone important, and with her and Liddi together, there was hardly a vid-cam pointed anywhere else. Like Liddi's brothers, Joon knew how to handle the attention like it wasn't there at all, which put the younger girl at ease.

At the end of the evening, Joon gave her a quick hug. "Thanks for keeping me company. These parties can be so annoying with people who want to talk to the media-cast of you, not the real you."

It was like after years of people saying Luna Minor was the only moon, someone other than Liddi's brothers finally acknowledged Luna Major straight overhead. She felt exactly

that way, like people wanted to talk to "the Jantzen girl, heiress to a fortune" rather than just her.

"I'm going to live-comm you," was the last thing Joon said before Vic took Liddi to the hovercar.

And she did. The two of them went to other parties and openings, shopping in the fashion district, and Joon came out to the country house to visit. Liddi had something she hadn't experienced since her parents died.

She had a friend.

6

THE MEDICAL EXAM takes the rest of the day. It probably doesn't need to, but Shiin'alo didn't tell the doctor the truth about me being from off-Point. She just said that I might have picked up something unexpected in my travels, so they needed to check for everything. The doctor looked confused but didn't argue, just got to work.

Apparently "everything" includes a lot and goes hand in hand with "takes forever."

Testing is a dull process, requiring me to sit still in an isolation booth while the doctor peruses the computer. I wonder if she'll notice the implant in my throat or the "broadcasts my living-or-dead status" one in my arm, but it seems not, because she never says anything about them. From the sound of things, she's just analyzing my blood and the air I breathe out, looking for viruses and bacteria and other nasties. I'm given lunch, and the tests continue. Inevitably, my mind wanders to the dreams I had last night.

It stands to reason—if I could feel and hear my brothers while in a *portal*, they're not just in the conduit network, but in some combination of the two, or maybe a hyperdimensional space connects them. Then since I can access the boys through a portal, maybe they can escape through one. Some aspect of what Minali did to them keeps them from coming out under their own power. Before, we came through the barrier after the long journey from Sampati—at least, it *felt* like a long journey. Maybe if there's no journey, I can keep enough strength to pull one of my brothers back. And if I can free one, I can free the rest.

So it's a matter of making sure I don't go all the way back to Sampati, or any of the other Points. Of only barely going inside the portal, just far enough to find my brothers.

I don't know how the portals work, though. Are they like the conveyors in old factories, moving inexorably in a particular direction? Is it true that you just have to think hard enough about where you want to go, and that's where it'll take you? If so, I just have to think hard about going nowhere.

The idea of relying on my own brainpower isn't very reassuring. I could use a backup.

Maybe Tiav could give me some ideas. But he didn't even know what "portal" meant. They must use another name. I can probably get him to understand that. Then I need to figure out the shortest way to ask the question.

Portals, stuck, how out?

That'd take maybe ten minutes to write, if I'm lucky, but it's so vague. Tiav probably wouldn't have any idea what I meant.

I thunk my head against the wall behind me. Maybe it's worth a try.

"Is something wrong?" the doctor asks.

I shake my head. Nothing she can help with.

"Good. I believe we're done. I've found no trace of any pathogen or contagion."

The door to the booth slides open, setting me free at last. Outside, the doctor isn't alone. Kalkig stands next to her, glaring at me. It's a lot of hate from someone I've never said a word to, and my feet instinctively scoot me back an inch.

"I've sent a message to the Aelo," the doctor says, oblivious to the fiery loathing the Agnac sends my way. "Shiin will be glad to know you're perfectly healthy. Kalkig volunteered to escort you back to them."

Right, and I'm sure he did it because he's just so charitable. I need to get back to Tiav and Shiin somehow, though, and without my voice, protesting is difficult. I nod my thanks to the doctor and follow Kalkig.

It's dark outside. I knew I was in the test chamber for a long time, but I didn't realize it was *that* long. Then again, I have no idea how long Ferinne days are. We start down the street, but not toward the Nyum. At least, I'm pretty sure it's not the way I came with Shiin earlier. Kalkig's odd long-armed gait makes good time, forcing me to semi-jog to keep up. I wait for him to say something, to reveal why he wanted to walk me to wherever he's walking me. But he doesn't, just keeps barreling on in silence.

Several blocks later, the buildings look more familiar. Even without reading the symbols, I'm pretty sure I recognize the colorful sign outside a restaurant. Kalkig's taking me back to Tiav's home.

Except he pushes me into an alley two buildings short of Tiav's. Seems he wants a detour first. He tries to box me in with those long arms of his, but I duck and sidestep to avoid having my back to the wall. I should've stepped the other way, because now he's between me and the only way out of the alley. He doesn't move toward me again, so I stand my ground and wait for him to say something. I watch his lips when he does, making sure I catch every word through the accent.

"I respect the Aelo. More than that, Tiav is my friend and has been from a—" He uses a word from his own language, including guttural sounds I could never duplicate. "I would not defy Shiin'alo. But if the world cannot know how dangerous you are, *I* will watch you that much more."

He thinks I'm going to be bothered by one person keeping an eye on me? He has *no* idea what my life has been.

I may smirk just a little.

"You and your kind are poison. I do not doubt this. Whatever evil you're here to do, I will not allow it."

Evil? Words gather in my throat to defend myself, but I hold back, choking on them and my frustration instead. Too bad it wasn't Minali who came through from Sampati. She'd actually deserve this attitude from Kalkig. I can't respond and he knows it, so I'm not sure what he wants from me. I know that *I* want the conversation to be over, so I shove past him, daring him to do something about it.

He grabs my arm again, but that's as far as he gets.

"Kal!"

Tiav rounded the corner just in time to see his friend grab me, and Kalkig immediately drops my arm. I finish passing him and put some distance between us.

"I was only talking to her," Kalkig insists.

"Reminding her that she's nothing but heathen dirt, right?"

Kalkig presses both hands against the ground. I don't know what the gesture means for him. "She's from the Lost Points, Tiav."

Lost? No, lost is what I am *now*.

"Yes, I know that."

"We also know what they're like."

"So you're saying all Agnac are the same. All Ferinnes, too. I know you don't believe that. I don't believe all people from the Lost Points are the same. And we don't know what *any* of them are like, because she's the first we've met. Give her a chance before you judge her."

In that moment, Tiav holds a quiet power that echoes his mother. If I could use my voice, I still wouldn't contest him, and Kalkig seems to feel the same way. He grunts, shakes his head, and leaves.

Tiav shakes his head, too, before turning to me. "Are you all right?"

I'm fine. Other than Kalkig's hands being rougher than tree bark, he didn't hurt me.

"I'm sorry about that. He should know better, but this is so new and unexpected, and ..." He trails off, sighs. "Never mind. Come on inside, and we'll get some food. I have an idea for a program so you won't need me to read off the symbols for you, but it'll have to wait. Tomorrow's the Daglin. I'll get the computer ready the day after, I promise."

I have no idea what the Daglin is, and I don't want any kind of delay. My gut says to get back to a portal and start hauling my brothers out.

But my head, checked genes or not, knows better. One more

day to form a plan isn't a bad idea. If Minali will take until the Tech Reveal to seal my brothers in the conduits permanently, I still have time. The boys can wait.

Just not much longer.

The Daglin, it turns out, is Ferinne's version of a holiday. A very strange holiday. It's one day a year when everyone—and according to Shiin, they mean *everyone*—drops what they normally do and cleans their town or city. Literally. Cleans the city. The buildings, the parks, the streets, everything gets its annual prettification.

I don't get it. I've seen enough to know they have the technology to automate something so basic. The streamers, the crystal spires, the instruments I saw on the doctor's counter— they're different enough that it's hard to say whether they have Sampati's technology beat, but I'd say it's at least as good.

I can't ask, and my confused expression isn't enough to tell Tiav why I'm confused, so I give up on that. I've lost count of the unanswered questions piling up inside me and have never felt so resigned in my life.

"Do you mind heights?" he asks after breakfast.

No, a fear of heights would definitely have gotten in the way of all my tree-climbing as a child. All my attempts to get closer to the stars.

"Good, then you can come with me. My mother prefers keeping her feet on the ground."

He doesn't go far, just to a door by my bedroom. Behind it is a stairway going up, so we must be heading to the roof. We're not the only ones. A handful of people beat us there and are spread along all the edges, working with cords and straps and what looks like a complicated sort of pulley system. I follow Tiav's lead to one of the "stations," where we put on harnesses.

"Here, you'll need a tether—I don't know why they always have so many." After a little untangling, he hands me a coil of thin cord with hooks arranged on each end. I have a hard time believing it's going to hold my weight. "Clip it to your harness like this, then feed the other end into the winder."

We're now in matching get-ups, except Tiav adds one more thing to his—an electronic device he straps to his leg. At a glance, I guess it's a control for the winder, and that's confirmed when he taps a panel that extends the arm of the contraption over the edge of the building, leaving just enough slack in the tethers not to yank us off. Then he takes one step forward into nothing.

He hangs in midair like he does it every day, and the winder assembly doesn't even twitch. Tiav is definitely bigger than I am, so if the tether supports him, it'll support me. I take the suicidal step before he can encourage me to.

The sensation is the strangest ever. Well, not as strange as going through the portal, or even the streamers, but it's right up there. I'm hanging almost a hundred feet above the ground, but the way the harness-tether system is designed, it feels like sitting on a dining room chair. My insides flutter at the contradiction.

Tiav taps a command to lower us—I instinctively grab hold of my tether when I start to move—and scoops up two items from the edge of the roof as we pass.

"Here's your brush," he says. It's metallic, rectangular, with bristles sprouting out of one surface and two metal loops arching out from the other. "Brace your feet against the wall like this. First we scrub the walls, then later the windows. Eighth floor is ours."

When Tiav says scrub, he means it. The cleanser dispenses automatically from the metal base into the bristles, but the rest is old-fashioned work. I slip my hands into the metal loops and start working on the wall in front of me while Tiav does the same three feet to my left. My tether gets in my way at first, until I get used to how I need to position myself. It's easy to see where we've cleaned, where the dingy brown gives way to a brighter tan.

We finish our first section, and Tiav moves us six feet to the right. The winders are on some kind of track system. Halfway into the second section, the muscles in my arms begin to burn. Spending a day in the workshop may be work, but it doesn't compare to this.

I can just imagine what the media-grubs would say.

JTI heiress Liddi Jantzen got her hands dirty with the only trade she seems to have any skill at—manual labor.

They obviously never saw me have a mud fight with the triplets.

My breath hitches in my chest, nothing to do with exertion. Cleaning walls isn't helping Marek, Ciro, Emil, or any of the others. Conversely, having Vic here would help *me*. His biceps would make short work of this whole building. Imagining it, I'm not sure whether I'd rather laugh or cry.

"Are you sure Kalkig didn't bother you yesterday?"

Tiav misinterpreted my pause, but even with the frustration of silence taunting me, at least some pseudo-conversation will distract me from the ache in my arms. I nod. The Agnac may be a new species to me, but hate isn't.

He looks uncertain, but I don't think it's a matter of not believing me. "I'd say I don't know what his problem is, but I do. *You* don't."

I give him the most encouraging *go-on* look I can manage, because I really do not understand Kalkig's hate when he doesn't even have the excuse of Jantzen Jealousy.

"Long story. Complicated. But the Agnac don't trust people from the Lost Points, not like they trust us. I just wish Kal wouldn't jump to the worst possibility. You came here for a reason, right?"

Yes. I didn't exactly intend to rediscover the Eighth Point, but my brothers brought me here for a reason. That's good enough for me.

He raises an eyebrow, half-teasing. "That reason isn't to destroy Ferinne, is it?"

Is *that* what Kalkig thinks I'm here to do? For someone who doesn't know anything about my family's status, he still thinks I have an awful lot of power. My "he's-out-of-his-Agnacki-mind" expression must be enough that Tiav doesn't need a clear no from me, because he shakes his own head.

"And he wonders why the Agnac need the Aelo," he mutters. "I'll keep trying to talk to him. Maybe after a year or so I'll break through."

I point to my head and knock on the wall I've been cleaning. Tiav laughs. It's nice making someone laugh without wondering whether it's only because they want to get on my good side.

"Hardheaded. Yes, he's very. But all the Agnac are. As much as I lecture *him* about generalizing, I haven't yet met one of his people who wasn't stubborn."

Tiav makes lighter small talk through the rest of the day,

telling me about the Ferinnes who first settled Podra and an ancient feud between two architects that ended in half the town's original buildings being destroyed by sabotage. My arms get a break when we return to the roof for lunch, then it's back to scrubbing. Below us, pairs of Ferinnes work on the other floors. I worry that we'll get too close and run into their tethers, but it's like a dance. Everyone moves just where they need to *when* they need to. All the other buildings on the street are the same, people dangling like spiders on their silken threads, cleaning away.

The windows are easier—less scrubbing, more wiping—and just as the sun dips down to the horizon, we finish. Tiav takes us back to the roof one more time and helps me figure out how to get free of the harness.

"How'd you like your first Daglin?" he asks.

I rub my sore arm and shrug. I'll feel it in the morning, but really, it wasn't bad.

He laughs again and stretches his own arms. "Yeah, it takes getting used to. Do they have anything like this on Sampati?"

The idea of Reb "Lies-Through-His-Teeth" Vester scrubbing down a building is so bizarre, I can't process it. All the swarming vid-cams would get in the way, making the job impossible.

"Once we get the writing a little smoother, you can tell me a few things you *do* have, then."

Most of the others have reached the roof now, too, and many of them wave and call over to Tiav, wishing him a good Daglin, whatever it means to have a good one after you've finished your chores.

"I'll be right back," Tiav says. "Need to talk to Luo before he leaves. Just coil your tether and put it with the others."

That's fine, and he trots over to the far edge of the roof. The

 88

other Ferinnes gravitate toward him, like vid-cams on Reb at a premiere gala.

I do coil up my tether, but while no one's looking, I slip it into my pocket, hoping no one will miss it with the dozens of extras.

Super-strong, super-thin cord might be just what I need.

Liddi ran across the playground to the big tree in the corner while her classmate Zeke counted to twenty. Plenty of time for her to wedge her foot in the split of the trunk and swing up into the leafy limbs. The other kids scattered and hid behind bushes, in window wells, or at the top of the slide.

Zeke reached twenty and went hunting. Everyone knew he was fastest in the whole class. He started finding kids right away, tagging each of them out so they had to fall down "dead." Only Liddi was left. No matter how he searched, even walking right under her tree, he couldn't find her. When he went to another corner, she dropped from the tree and ran for home base at the center of the yard. Zeke turned when the other kids started cheering her on. He tried to cut her off, but she got there first, throwing her hands in the air.

"Ha, I win!"

"You cheated!"

Liddi turned to face Zeke, her hands on her hips. "I did not. I was in the tree. You're just too stupid to ever look up."

He shoved her shoulders, forcing her to stumble back a step. "Don't call me stupid."

"Then don't act stupid," she said, shoving him in return.

Words were left behind as they went at each other, goaded by their gathering classmates. Liddi had wrestled plenty with her brothers, so she wasn't afraid of a fight, especially not with someone who called her a cheater when she wasn't. Not even when he hit her in the mouth and made her lip bleed.

She was afraid of insects with stingers, though, so a

buzzing by her ear was enough to make her push off from Zeke and back away quickly.

"Stop it, both of you! Everyone inside. Zeke, Liddi, with me."

Ms. Bledsoe arrived a minute too late. It was already broken up, thanks to Liddi's fear of bees.

They weren't bees, though. A swarm of vid-cams swirled around her. They never got this close, but they refused to be shooed away, sticking right by her as the administrator led the kids into the school.

Several minutes later, Liddi sat in a chair outside Ms. Bledsoe's office, still surrounded by vid-cams. Emil's classroom was right down the hall. She wanted so badly to run straight to him, but she knew the cams would follow. That knowledge held her in place. Her parents had been contacted, so she expected her mother to arrive any moment.

The swarm of vid-cams suddenly zipped down the hall, meeting not just her mother but her father, too.

"They're not supposed to be in the school, Nevi," Mrs. Jantzen said.

Her husband glared at the vid-cams. "Leave or start shopping for new cams. Your choice."

The buzzing devices scattered.

Mrs. Jantzen knelt down to check Liddi over for injuries beyond the bloody lip as Ms. Bledsoe came out of the office. "Mr. Jantzen! I thought your wife would be coming alone. I'm sure you're very busy."

The words made Liddi's mother's lips thin, but the teacher didn't see that.

"We're both very busy, Ms. Bledsoe," Mr. Jantzen said,

"but when we learn a boy was allowed to pick a fight with our daughter, we make the time. Come on, Liddi-Loo," he added, scooping her up in his arms. "Let's go."

"I'm afraid we still need to sit down and have a talk about appropriate behavior," Ms. Bledsoe protested.

"We saw the media-casts on the way here. The boy started it, and we're going home."

There was no more arguing as the Jantzens took their daughter away. Liddi's father only spoke again when no one was close enough to hear.

"Liddi, are you all right?"

"Yes, Daddy."

"What that boy did was wrong, but you need to be very careful. Remember that you're always being watched."

"Nevi," Mrs. Jantzen cut in. "She's barely five. You really want her growing up with that kind of paranoia?"

"I know, Sav. But they're already pushing the boundaries. I'm afraid it's the life she'll have."

Liddi already knew the vid-cams were part of life. She'd seen them around and heard her brothers talk about them plenty. She knew nothing was ever secret.

Someone was always listening.

7

"HOW DOES THIS SOUND?" Tiav asks the next morning, gesturing for me to sit at the desk in the Nyum office. "I was thinking I could program the computer to read off the sounds for you.
If you wear an earpiece, whoever you're 'talking' to won't hear
anything until you have the words ready."

That seems like it'll work. I can only imagine how maddening it would be for the Ferinnes to listen to all those sounds a
dozen times or so for every sentence I try to say. Like Dom list-
ing the top-rated media-casts when I already know all of them.

"Okay, give me a minute to put the program together."

He sits with me at the desk to work, and symbols start flying
across the wallscreen in front of us. His fingers are confident as
they tap out words too quickly for me to follow. Something's
familiar in the intent focus of his eyes. It reminds me of Fabin
when he's working. Or any of my brothers, really.

Too much reminds me of my brothers. Sitting here not doing
anything makes me twitchy, but so does not being able to explain

anything. I need to communicate. I'll have to be patient, so I wait while Tiav works.

It shouldn't be a super-complicated program, but there are a few things he'll have to cover. Telling the computer to stop reading once I choose a symbol. Giving the option to start from the beginning again if I think I missed what I wanted. Piping the sound for the symbols just into the earpiece, but to read the finished words in the queue to the whole room.

For all that, Tiav finishes way too soon. He must have forgotten some things.

But no. As he hands me the earpiece and walks me through the process, pointing out the new symbols on the keypad for engaging the subroutines, I realize he thought of everything I did, and a few other things I didn't. Like creating a "word bank" where I can store words I might need later. That'll only do me so much good once I have more than a few words in there, but he even included a feature for me to draw an icon for each word, helping me remember what it's supposed to be.

He already stored his name and drew a cartoony little face for the icon. All in a very few short minutes.

Maybe *he* should go back to Sampati and take over JTI.

"What's wrong?"

I shake off the feeling. The silly icon he drew hardly looks like him, with exaggerated ears and a zigzag of spikes for hair. It makes me want to smile, so I do.

"All right, let's try it out. I'm always asking you questions. Why don't you ask me one?"

The first question that comes to mind is a random one, but I *am* curious about it, and I think I can ask in three one-syllable words, so I go for it. Tiav's program works well, reading the

symbols into my earpiece and lighting up each in turn. It takes a few minutes because I have a hard time finding the right sound for the last word—the computer predictably has a Ferinne accent—but finally I get it.

"*Tock saym wye?*"

"Why do we speak the same language? That's on purpose. Our linguists monitor the broadcasts from the Lost Points just enough to keep our language mostly in line."

I delete the first two words and repeat the last. Why?

"A couple of reasons. Back when we cut off contact with your worlds, we hoped it wouldn't be forever. If we ever reestablish the link, we want to be able to talk to your people. Then with the Agnac, Haleians, Crimna, and Izim around, we knew our language might change really quickly if we didn't keep an eye on it. All the alien races said they wanted to speak a 'clean' form of our language in case they ever run into people from the Lost Points."

There's a lot of information in there, not least the idea that Ferinne cut off contact with the rest of us, and I tuck it away in my mind. Tiav's answer about the language makes sense, I guess. If they have access to our broadcasts, though, they might know things about my family or the company. I dig back into the symbols and take a little longer for my next question.

"*Liss-en con-tent?*"

"No, I don't think so. Not for a long time now. The linguists have computer programs that monitor linguistic patterns and alert them when they start to veer too far from ours."

Too bad. No shortcuts to explaining about the Jantzen family situation, then.

Tiav coincidentally follows the same track for his own

question. "So, can you tell me why you left Sampati to come here, or *how* you did?"

I start to look for the symbols, then freeze. I'm pretty sure Minali didn't include a live audio transmitter with the implant. If she had, she'd have heard my planning with Dom. I'd never have made it out of the house.

But what if the implant *is* programmed for more than watching whether I use my voice? Voice-recognition might just mean it's programmed for *my* voice, or it could also mean it listens for certain words said around me. Key words that'll trigger the booby trap set to kill my brothers.

My ribs tighten on my lungs, refusing to let me breathe. Dom said a lot of key words when I was still home, but maybe the implant is sophisticated enough to recognize if I try to spell out Minali's whole plan. Maybe I'm becoming completely paranoid.

Maybe, maybe... maybe a lot of things, and I have precisely zero way of knowing whether any are true. Tiav's program means I just need time to write things out, but I can't risk it. Not yet, not without figuring out more first.

Tiav's hand moves to rest on my shoulder. The contact startles me.

"Are you okay? You said you're in trouble back there. Did something bad happen?"

I nod and work out the only thing I can think of that might be safe. *"How—dont no. Ack-sih-dent."*

"But you said you came here for a reason."

True, I did. *"Naht mye ree-sun."*

This little bit of conversation has taken forever. I'm not sure how long, because I can't decipher the Ferinne clocks. But between my false starts and some symbols sounding the same

at first but not really and my mind wandering off mid-alphabet when I need to be focusing, I'm pretty sure we've been in the office for at least an hour. I don't know how Tiav puts up with the waiting, but the inefficiency is making me want to punch my fist through the desk.

I have Tiav's voice and the voice of the computer, but it's still like when I'm alone at the house. Silence suffocates me.

It's worse than that. I'm alone away from home. Something I've never been. Not really. Not for more than a day. I miss Dom. Dom could find a way to speed it up. A lump of emotion adds to the constant pressure in my throat.

Tiav sees that, or sees something, because he blanks the computer. "Let's take a break. Come on."

That kind of break sounds like a better alternative than the kind I was about to put in the equipment, so I stand and follow him out of the room.

We walk down to the second floor of the Nyum, the balcony overlooking the circular lobby. Tiav leans comfortably against the railing, waiting for me to join him. Then he gestures to the shelves along the walls.

"See all those books? They hold the history of Ferinne, everything ever written by the Aelo for nearly two thousand years. It's all in the computer databases now, of course, but we keep the books. My mother has rooms full of them at home, too."

The word *books* seems vaguely familiar, and I realize it's why this place reminded me of Tarix. Old records and history. The "thinkers" on Tarix have the last remnants of our written language, maybe in things called books. I must have seen a few during a childhood visit.

"You don't use writing anymore, but you still keep history,

right?" Tiav continues. "Recordings, images, computers that can dictate it back to you?"

Yes, that's the only form of record keeping I've ever known. Talking to Dom or having him find old news-vids for me. Never had a problem with it.

"We do all that, too, but sometimes it's good to go back to the books. Quieter. Slower."

Why would anyone want to do something slower? Wasting time isn't efficient. I should know. I've wasted plenty and have zero appearances at the Tech Reveal to show for it.

Tiav seems to understand what I'm thinking, even without knowing the specifics. "Slower doesn't sound better, but really, sometimes it is. If you give your mind a quiet moment, that's when the best ideas come. Trying to write frustrates you, Liddi. I can see that. It takes a long time to say not very much. But you'll learn. It'll get easier, and it'll be worth it."

He might be overestimating the mental capacity of my checked genes. And he has no way of knowing I don't have an infinite amount of time to work in.

We eat lunch, where Tiav tells me about Ferinne's first encounter with aliens—the Crimna. How both sides had to be patient until they learned enough of each other's language to get a point across... namely that the Crimna were just looking to make friends and the Ferinnes were happy to do the same as long as everyone kept some ground rules.

I get it. He wants me to be patient. He doesn't get why I can't, and I can't explain it to him, and that just makes me *more* impatient and frustrated.

Back in the office upstairs, I still feel like punching the computer. Before that happens, an elderly woman comes to the door.

"Aelo, Shiin'alo needs you."

Tiav looks at the clock, which presumably makes sense to him. "Right, almost forgot. This might take a while. Listen, Liddi, you'll have the room to yourself, no pressure. Take the time to write whatever it is you want to say. Okay?"

I nod, and he smiles before following the old woman to wherever his mother is.

It takes several minutes, but I do take the time to write what I want to say.

"Saw-ree. Im-pohr-tent."

And I leave.

It's another of the strangest things I've ever experienced, walking down a busy street without a single vid-cam tailing me. People glance my way, but a glance is all it is before they move on. I look normal enough for a Ferinne, and with the Agnac, Haleians, and Crimna mixing it up, I'm downright boring. Tiav mentioned something called Izim, but maybe they look similar to one of the other races, or I haven't seen any yet. Either way, without Tiav, I'm background noise.

Tiav, who's busy with his mother and thinks I'm busy with the computer.

The guilt squirms around in my bones. I lock it down and shove it away. This feeling as I walk through town is too precious. It's liberating—a word I'm not sure I've ever really understood until now. Here, I can be anyone. I can be no one. I can disappear.

Except that's a lie. It doesn't matter whether anyone knows

who I am. I know I'm Liddi Jantzen. I have eight brothers, and I won't let Minali keep them trapped forever to lock in her fix of the conduits.

I came out here for a reason.

Back at the Aelo residence, I find Tiav's streamer. It has no security lockouts, just as I thought when he brought me in days ago. I may not be able to read the symbols marking most of the control surface, but I don't need to. The main control is a touchscreen, and I caught the icon signifying the portal earlier. It might take a minute to locate it on the map, but I have time.

Maybe I won't need it. I drag the map just a bit to the left of Podra's border, and there it is.

Or is it? I drag up a little bit more and find another one. Either I'm wrong about the icon, or finding a portal around here isn't that much of a challenge.

If you found a portal high, if you found a portal low . . .

One way to find out. I tap one of the icons, brace myself, and close my eyes for the moving-fast-but-slow ride. It doesn't take long, and I open my eyes again once the vehicle stops. I can't see the portal from here, but that's no surprise. Not like the road is going to run right up to it. After double-checking the map for the general direction, I get out and start walking.

I reach it easily enough. It's not the same portal I arrived at— not the same bowl of hills, and there's a small stream winding nearby. Doesn't matter. The crystal spires, the spark of energy hovering peacefully between them . . . it's definitely a portal.

It's so strange, the way the portals here are small, almost gentle-looking, compared to the terrifying maelstrom on Sampati. Part of me wonders why it's so different, if it's to do with the spires or something else, but I don't have any way of

asking the Ferinnes. Even if I had the patience to piece together the words, I'm not sure I dare. Asking for details like that could be a major mistake.

Someone's always listening. Or in this case, some*thing* sitting in my throat is listening. Maybe.

If this works, it won't matter. Once I get my brothers out, we'll go home and deal with Minali. Curiosity will have to wait until later.

The portal may *look* tame, but the feeling as I approach puts the lie to that. I thought before maybe it was because I'd just traveled through it and was experiencing the aftereffects. It's still there, though, even now. The sensation of a sleeping giant, ready with a fist the size of a mountain if it's disturbed.

And I'm about to disturb it.

First, I take the coiled tether from my pocket. One end gets wrapped around a spire and clipped onto itself. The other latches on to my belt. The strength of the portal might break it, but it's worth a shot.

The first time around, the what-to-do was obvious—run into the scariest thing I've ever seen as though I've completely disconnected from my brain. This time, it's just that little spark, and I'm not sure how to handle it. I step closer and reach toward the mote of light.

It flies to my hand, but rather than draw back, instinct spurs me to grab hold.

A sharp warmth charges from my palm through my arm and shoulder until it reaches my brain. More instincts emerge, only now I'm certain they're not coming from inside me. They're coming from outside, going through my insides, telling me what to do. I need to think about what I want.

To get inside the portal just far enough to find one of my brothers. Not go anywhere. Just inside.

The thought only has to half-form, and I'm there. Back in chaotic death, back to having my molecules wrung out, back to the most pain I've ever known in my life.

And I stay there and I stay, floating and sinking with the pain, dying and waking and waiting, waiting, waiting.

Forever. A few minutes. A little longer.

"Liddi!"

It's Marek. He's still alive, and if he is, so are the others. He's found me, and just like before, his presence shields me from some of the pain. But he looks as worn as Emil did. That was days ago, and my brothers are still weak.

It might be because of the effort it took to bring me to Ferinne. It might be because Minali's plan to make them a permanent part of the conduits is progressing. It might be both, or it might be something else.

"What are you doing here?" he asks. "You can't go home. Blake is dangerous, and she can't find out about Ferinne. The people there know things about the portals. You can't let Blake find them. Be patient—we still have time. We know what she did to you. If you don't speak, you'll be safe—just don't speak. She won't find you, and you'll be okay. We're learning things, things that might get us out."

Get them out—that's why I'm here. I don't care what he says. We don't have time for learning and deciphering and doing things carefully, and there's no point in me being safe if they're not.

I wrap one arm around Marek and reach to my waist with my other hand. The cord is still there, solid and real. With an iron grip on my brother, I square all my thoughts on going back to Ferinne and pull on the cord. Or try to. It slips along my hand. I can't get any traction.

The pain Marek was blocking from me breaks through, redoubled and retripled. Lightning strikes my body, cutting me apart at the joints. Needles sprout from my spine and pierce me in all directions. His muscles tense, holding tighter, and a new thought occurs to me.

Have my brothers been feeling this pain ever since they were trapped? Is every second I delay an eternity of agony for them?

"I—I can't," Marek forces out. "Not strong enough—others—too far. Can't push you back myself."

No, it's not about him pushing me back. I have to pull *him*.

More focus. That's what I need. I wind the cord around my forearm and yank. It slices through, cutting flesh, but we also move a little. I have no visual references to confirm that, but I feel it, so I pull again.

It's not enough. Ferinne is miles and light-years away. So are the other Points. We are Nowhere.

Marek tries to push me away, but I'm stronger than he is—a clear sign that he's hurting. "Let me go, Liddi. It won't work. You have to go back."

Not an option. I have him and I won't let go. Then I'll come back for them one by one until all eight are free.

The cord moves, tugging me. More than tugging. Like the great mouth of the universe has decided to devour me and draws me in. The barrier to Ferinne looms closer, but we don't stop. It shatters under the force pulling me, and the pressure in my throat is barely enough reminder to keep me from crying out.

The same pain but worse. The same crash to the ground but different. Different because I'm not alone. I look up to see if Marek is all right, but it's not Marek.

It's Tiav. And Kalkig. And a woman and two men I don't recognize—one a Haleian. Night's fallen, and I have no idea how long I was in the portal. About ten feet beyond the others, I see my brother reach out to me before fading from this reality.

Someone's talking, but I don't care. The Seven Points media has never caught me crying, not once, but I burst into tears in front of these strangers. Partly from the pain—my arm is a slashed, bloody mess—but mostly they're tears of failure. Of course it wouldn't be as easy as brute-forcing my brothers out, but if that won't work, what will? Something brilliant and complicated. Something that only someone smarter than Minali could figure out.

I'm the wrong Jantzen to get the job done. But I'm the only one there is.

Just like every other spring, once the snow melted and the ground dried so it wasn't too muddy, one of the Jantzens made the suggestion. The year Liddi turned twelve, it was Fabin's idea.

"Okay, guys, time for some stickball."

The twins had come by the house, which meant they had everyone except Durant. That was enough for a pretty good round, so everyone trekked out to a meadow across the river where there was enough space to play.

Liddi's brothers had the advantage in most of the games they played, being bigger, stronger, and more experienced. They always let her play, and she usually found an advantage of her own. With hide-and-seek, she was small enough to fit in hiding spots the boys might not think of. With tag, being small and quick helped her evade her larger brothers.

Stickball, however, was a hard game. She had to develop the coordination to hit the ball with the heavy stick, and she just wasn't strong enough to hit it as far as the boys did. It was the one game where they went a little easy on her. Slower pitches, less effort to field the ball, pretty much always letting her get on base. As Anton pitched to her for some warm-up hits, she saw it was going to be the same.

"Stop it," she said, lowering the stick.

"Stop what?" Anton asked.

"Going easy. I'm twelve, not two. Let me play. If I'm out, I'm out."

Anton nodded and easily caught the ball Ciro tossed back to him. "If you say so. Let's try a few more."

He really pitched it, fast enough that Liddi's swing of the stick whiffed through empty air.

"Again," she insisted.

He did, and again she missed. And a third time.

It's not that difficult, *she thought.* Just anticipate more. React faster.

On the fourth try, stick and ball connected, jarring her all the way up to her shoulders. The ball glided in a clean arc, past where Emil stood so he had to chase it. Farther than Ciro's practice hits had gone.

"That'll teach us," Luko said.

Liddi put down the stick. "Teach you what?"

"To think our little sister needs to take the easy version of anything."

8

I'M UNDER ARREST.

Those are the words I hear when I finally stop crying enough to listen. The three strangers are Ferinne's version of police—"keepers," Tiav calls them. Kalkig is furious again. That's nothing new, but Tiav isn't far behind. His eyes burn and his posture is rigid, but I think my tears make it more difficult for him.

"Liddi, you can't do things like this," he says as the keepers guide me to the streamers. "Your people may have no respect for the Khua, but when you're here, you *will* respect our laws."

I don't know what he's talking about, so I give no response, and he falls silent. The aftereffects of the portal make it hard to walk, let alone focus. My arm is wrapped but hasn't been treated yet. The keepers said a doctor would see me at the detention facility. I have only a few minutes to wonder what the facility will be like before we arrive. It's a low, wide building with glass doors leading to a simple but comfortable lobby. A standing desk with a single attendant, several chairs—none occupied—arranged artfully on the other side of the room, and even a green-and-yellow potted plant by the door.

An image pops into my head of the media-cast that would go with this.

The Jantzen girl strayed one step too far from her brothers' path today, offending several cultures and getting arrested by an alien police officer with muscles so solid, she doubts he needs bones. While Ferinne fashion leaves something to be desired, Liddi made do with the basics— functional brown pants and a blue shirt . . . nice color on that one. In related news, white arm wraps splashed with red will be available from the following designers by morning.

The female keeper speaks to the attendant at the desk. "Found her right where the alarm said but tricky business getting her out. Definitely not the usual wayward toddler. A doctor should be on the way. They can meet us at her cell."

From there it's a quick walking tour of the facility. Through a set of double-doors, down one long door-lined hallway and around a corner, then down another hall that looks just the same. Tiav and Kalkig trail behind every step without a word, until finally the Haleian keeper takes a glass chip from his pocket and slides it into a slot next to one of the cell doors. The door opens, and I'm ushered in.

The room is tiny, just enough space for a bed on one side. There's a closet-sized lavatory on the other side, and a small window on the wall opposite the entrance. My weary legs gratefully lower me to sit on the bed. There's no point in putting up a fuss. The sooner they leave me alone, the sooner I can start thinking through this mess. Besides, sitting on the soft surface feels better on my aching body.

"Someone said she was injured, yes?" says a voice from the hallway. It has a musical lilt that hints strangely at mischief.

"Right, but it's beneath your concern, Jahmari," someone replies—maybe the non-alien male keeper.

"And what precisely do you know of my concerns, Luo? Out of my way. Ah, there she is."

The newcomer—Jahmari—is a Crimna. Old, judging by the small crinkles around his eyes, but young by the light and life in them. He's small, shorter than I am, but with a willowy grace that makes him seem tall like the gallery dancers on Yishu. Juxtaposing that grace is a sharpness and precision of movement that echoes in his eyes. He sets a case next to me on the bed and opens it. Sleek equipment of some kind, probably medical devices.

"I hear from dear Tiav that I shouldn't expect a pip or whistle from you," he says. "No matter, no matter. The injury is clear enough. May I see your arm?"

I hold it out to him, and he carefully unwraps the temporary bandage, revealing the cuts. "A bit nasty, aren't they? Not to worry, mended easily."

And he does, but in the strangest way. He holds two small metal rods to either side of my forearm and nudges a switch to activate. An energy field bridges the space between them, glittering more than the clothes from Pinnacle's fashion district on a sunny day. Jahmari lowers his hands so the field rests lightly on my arm, and it sparks more than glitters. It tingles and tickles and itches and hurts but just a little bit compared to how it already felt.

My skin is stitching itself back together, all on its own. No binders or sealants, just the energy from the field accelerating the healing process. It's simple and obvious and brilliant. Effective, too. When he turns off the device, my arm is perfect, with just the itchiness left behind.

"Anything else need tending to?" Jahmari asks.

I shake my head. The pain of having my body torn apart must be mostly in my mind, not physical. That's how it was when I first came through the portal to Ferinne. I'll sleep it off.

He touches my face, an unexpectedly kind gesture from an unexpectedly smooth, soft hand. I can't help meeting his eyes. They're dark violet, startling against the glow of his pale skin.

"Communicate, my friend," he says softly. "You can't speak? Fine. There are other ways, but they will take time. I see that something is important to you. Whatever it is, you do it a disservice if you succumb to mere recklessness, I think. Informed action will serve you better."

A variation on what Tiav tried to tell me. Marek told me to be patient, too. Everyone keeps telling me to take my time when I just want my brothers safe *now*.

But they want *me* safe, and my null-skull ideas haven't helped them any.

Jahmari pats my cheek, stands, and leaves. The door doesn't close behind him. It closes behind Tiav and Kalkig after they come in. I swing my legs up to occupy the space where Jahmari sat. They can stand. Tiav is glaring at his friend, who's glaring at me.

"If I had my way, heathen, you'd be back on your twisted world right now," Kalkig says. It's getting easier to understand him through the heavy accent. I don't have to watch his lips this time.

"Kal, quiet," Tiav says. "I told you, you should be waiting outside."

Kalkig slips into his native language. I may not know a word of Agnacki, but I strongly suspect some expletives are involved.

Tiav huffs and shakes his head, clenching one hand into a fist. "Fine, then we're both leaving. Just one thing, Liddi. Is there any way you can tell us what you were trying to do out there?"

Not right now there isn't. I stare at the wall, refusing to meet his eyes.

As quickly as they came, they leave again. I get the feeling Tiav would have said more if Kalkig hadn't insisted on coming along. Maybe he would've explained why what I did is so terrible.

The lights dim, implying someone wants me to get some sleep. My body says yes but my mind says no. My mind is locked on what Jahmari said.

Communicate. Don't succumb to mere recklessness.

Be strong, Liddi.

Emil's words. I didn't listen to them carefully enough before. In this case, being strong means being more patient.

If I learn how to write, I can explain what I need. If I'm patient enough to sift through the symbols to say something so complicated. Someone here might be able to help. No matter what my brothers say, I'm the one out here. I have to help, and it *will* be worth the time.

Just not too much time.

And that's assuming a girl who can't speak can still convince the authorities not to keep her locked up.

When my door opens in the morning, I expect either a keeper or Tiav. I get neither.

I get Shiin.

Looking at her is like seeing all the facets of a jewel simultaneously. A soft maternal expression balances with a firmness, making me certain that Tiav didn't get away with white lies or troublemaking as a child. Calm while pressing. Patient with urgency. I can't wrap my head around how she's all those things at once, but she is. She stands in front of me with her hands clasped lightly, like she spends every morning talking to mute girls in detention facilities.

"We have a problem, Liddi," she says. "You clearly have some kind of curiosity or fascination with the Khua. Understandable enough, given your people's lack of knowledge, though I cannot fathom what you hoped to accomplish by anchoring yourself to Ferinne that way. You can't speak, so you can't explain it to us, and that's unacceptable. We will continue to work with you."

I look around the cell. The tiny space seems ill-equipped for writing lessons. No computer.

"No, you're being released, though I hope your night here impressed the gravity of the situation. I convinced the Agnac Hierarchy that you can't be held accountable for breaking a law you weren't aware of. And the law is that only those authorized— only the Aelo with our methods—may interact directly with the Khua. Now you know."

I guess so, except for the whole *Khua* part. Their word for the portals, I suppose.

Their word. Now that I know what to call them, maybe I can get some answers to avoid recklessness and inform my actions, like Jahmari suggested.

Shiin takes me back to the Nyum, back to the small office upstairs. Tiav isn't there. I'm not sure whether that's good or bad, but I sit at the desk and put in my earpiece. The keypad lights up across the desk surface—the "outer" symbols, the broader menu.

"Where would you like to start today, Liddi?"

She smiles, adding another dimension to my impression of her, and it brings a welcoming air to the room. She's sticking around, even though she has better things to do than deal with the foreigner. Maybe no one else is willing to after what I did last night—whatever the big problem with it is. That would explain why Tiav isn't here.

I touch the command for the computer to start sounding off the symbols, lighting each key as it does. When it reaches the *k* sound, I tap that key and get the submenu. It doesn't take long to get to *koo*. Then I repeat the process to get from *a* to *ah*. It's written, so I tap the command for it to read the word on the external sound system.

"*Koo-ah.*"

The smile fades, and Shiin sits in the chair opposite me. No smile, but I'm not sure what her expression *is*. Curious. Guarded. Conflicted.

"Yes, of course, we should talk about the Khua. The history between our peoples. We were one people once, long ago, as Tiav'elo may have told you. The Khua were discovered here, and we spread to other worlds, establishing the Eight Points on the planets most tightly connected. Your people believe the Khua are a natural phenomenon, correct?"

Yes. Certain planets are linked on a level beyond our own dimension, and portals are the energy-chains doing the linking. What else would they be?

"They're natural, yes. But they're not 'phenomena.' They're beings. Alive."

It's like she heard about my checked genes and decided I was three levels past stupid. I've known the basics of biology since I was four. Rolling my eyes gets the message across clearly enough. Shiin looks angry as she shakes her head, but not at me.

"Exactly what I expect from the Lost Points. Assumptions about life requiring certain molecules. So many assumptions. So little interest in extraordinary truth, though I can't say we're entirely innocent of that on Ferinne. Before you came here, Liddi, didn't you assume aliens were only in stories? Now you know there are Crimna, Haleians, Izim, and Agnac, and those are only the ones we've met so far, those who found us due to their own fainter connections to the Khua. If I ask you now, do you believe there are more aliens out there than those I've named?"

I haven't thought about it before, but it makes sense. As big as the universe is, it's hard to believe *all* forms of intelligent life have already converged on one planet. I nod, and my answer lights something in Shiin's eyes.

"There might be hope for you. But the Lost Points as a whole think they're the pinnacle of the universe's achievements, so they never look beyond their own borders. Seeing only what they want to see."

I make the computer say *Khua* again.

"We believe the Khua are alive, that they have consciousness and will. Your people believe they are not. We stayed here; they went to the other various Points and left us alone. Then we met people from other worlds, beginning with the Crimna, and the Agnac soon after. They knew about the Khua and believed as we did, that they are alive. Even more so. The Agnac worship the Khua, quite literally, and they take exception to the lack of belief in the Lost Points. You had erased us from your culture, relegating us to mythic afterlife, but to ensure it stayed that way, we cut you off from the Khua. We made sure your people couldn't reach us, and it worked for centuries . . . until you arrived."

So no Sentinel and no Wraith, just sparks of energy to be worshiped. I'm not sure which is worse.

Regardless of this the-Khua-are-alive insanity, the Ferinnes clearly know plenty about the portals. I feel like I do when a difficult concept my brothers try to explain finally starts to make sense. An excitement that the closed doors in front of me aren't locked after all. Locked. I can use that to simplify my question for Shiin. It takes the better part of fifteen minutes to piece it together, even with the shortcut of already having *Khua* written in front of me.

"Kon-trole koo-ah lock koo-ah how?"

A smile returns to Shiin's lips, but it's a very different one. Small, with hints of mischief, reminding me of both Jahmari's voice and Tiav's eyes.

"Oh, you're not going to like the answer to that, Liddi. Not when you roll your eyes because I say the Khua are alive."

Okay, maybe the eye-rolling was rude, but I have to go with the most efficient communication I can. I lean forward and raise my eyebrows, urging her to answer anyway.

"How did we lock the Khua?" she says. "We simply asked them not to let you in."

Facing the conduit terminal was the one thing that could dampen Liddi's enthusiasm. Visiting one of the other Points, spending time with Luko and Vic, getting away from the old routine—those things sparked all the excitement a nine-year-old could muster. Traveling by conduit made her a little nervous, though. It didn't hurt, and all she had to do was stand on a platform while an attendant entered commands. A brief disconcerting moment of nothing-everything, and she'd be there. Her brothers assured her the mild fear that she'd disappear from one world and fail to reappear at the other was all in her head, and true enough, every trip by conduit had been smooth and predictable.

It just felt wrong, and she couldn't figure out why.

She set it aside with everything else she didn't understand.

The trip to Erkir ended up being one of the best Liddi could remember. The twins took her everywhere—flying a glider over the grassland prairies, snow-shoeing in the far south, and snorkeling in the tropics. A small contingent of vid-cams followed them everywhere, of course, but Liddi was proud of herself. She didn't give the media-grubs a single negative thing to say. Not like the previous year's briefer visit to the beach property on Pramadam.

On the last day, the three of them hiked up to the top of one of Erkir's mountains. Nothing high enough to need special equipment or training, but still very high for Liddi. Her brothers offered more than once to carry her piggyback if she needed a rest, but she refused. She didn't want to let the vid-cams see her give up.

Finally, they reached the top, and Liddi lost what little breath she had left. She could see everything. And everything didn't include a single city.

"Erkir, it's like . . . it's the opposite," she said.

"The opposite of what?" Luko asked.

"Of Sampati. We have all our cities, and just a few areas like our house or the little in-between places. They have all this space and just small settlements scattered around. I bet there are more animals on this mountain than people on the whole planet."

Vic nodded. "That's true. It fits our needs. Erkir is focused on the ecological sciences, so they need space for the plants and animals to have their habitat. Sampati's main industry is technology, so we need the infrastructure to support that."

Liddi didn't know what "infrastructure" meant beyond some specific kind of structure, but she was pretty sure she understood. Something else about the situation puzzled her, though.

"It seems like when people have opposite ideas, they usually fight about it. But we don't fight with Erkir or Neta or any of the other Points."

Luko glanced at his brother. "It wasn't always that way, I've heard. People had to learn a big lesson so all the Points could get along."

"What lesson?"

Vic playfully tugged her ponytail before answering. "That just because something's right for you doesn't mean it'll be right for me."

9

WE ASKED THEM TO. The answer barely registers, it's so absurd. My mind races with a return of the maybes.

Maybe the Ferinne who figured out how to lock the Khua wanted to keep the method a secret, so he made up a story about "asking."

Maybe it was so long ago, the real event was lost and morphed into this legend.

Maybe the Ferinnes were afraid the hot-tempered Agnac would go to war if they didn't go along with the aliens' worship-the-living-sparks lifestyle.

"I knew you wouldn't like the answer," Shiin says. "You don't believe me."

No, I don't, because I've been inside, and the inside fits my idea of "chaotic hyperdimensional energy phenomenon" a lot more than "living being that'll do as you ask." There's no order, no reason, no *anything* there except a highly disturbing passage from one Point to another. Like ancient ocean crossings in a storm . . . a reality-bending, sanity-breaking storm. Instead of shaking my head, though, I start digging through the symbols again.

"Truh-bull wye?"

"Why were you in trouble yesterday?" Yes, that. "Tiav'elo tells me he hasn't had a chance to explain our role as Aelo. We are . . . liaisons with the Khua, the only ones permitted to interact with them. It wasn't always this way. Everyone used to be able to try but found it chaotic, painful, confusing. The most we could accomplish was travel between the Points. Then the Aelo developed the methods and skills necessary to understand the Khua. Later, when the Agnac came, they revered us for that understanding—they still do—and asked for a law preventing anyone but the Aelo from entering the Khua. We agreed because even without the law, it was the reality that only the Aelo went in. The law made no difference to us. But to the Agnac, the presence of one who doesn't believe or understand defiles the Khua. It's one of their deepest crimes."

My muscles tighten and I scratch my arm. The same spot where the tether sliced into me. If the Agnac find out my non-believing brothers have been stuck even partially in the Khua for this long, how far beyond "defiling" would they claim it's gone? And what would they do about it? New questions usually mean progress, but I don't like these.

Shiin isn't done. "Generally, it's not a problem. As you know firsthand, without the Aelo methods, it's painful, so no one bothers the Khua. Occasional accidental contact with small children, but that's all. The Agnac believe using the Khua for travel between worlds is also a defilement, but no one here has any wish to go to the Lost Points. Asking the Khua to cut off the Points took care of that. But then you arrived."

Right, I used the Khua to get here, somehow breaking through the age-old block, then sat around in one for several hours on purpose. That explains last night's arrest. That would also explain why Kalkig hates me. I'm the ultimate Defiler.

"Hee-then?" I write out.

Her expression turns to one of distaste. "Has Kalkig been calling you that? I'll speak to him about it. It's an old word for an unbeliever, and I'm not surprised it's fallen out of your vocabulary. It's hardly fair to call you that when all you've ever had is what your culture taught you. But you're here now and have a chance to learn more. I hope you'll take advantage of that."

Learning is exactly what I want to do. But I need to figure out what to learn, and how. Part of me says to spend the next three hours piecing together every word necessary to explain what Minali did. My own silence presses in on me, making me more alone than I've ever been. I need help.

The Agnac and their ideas of defilement keep me from finding a single word. I don't know if they'll listen, and I don't know enough about this "worship" of theirs, other than that it makes Kalkig want to drop-kick me all the way back to Sampati. An unexpected wave of sympathy for Minali passes through me. Maybe this is how she feels about stabilizing the conduits, like no one understands, like she can't trust anyone but herself to get it done.

There's a difference. I'm not killing anyone—I'm trying to *save* lives.

※ – – – ※

Shiin can't stay any longer, and I'm not surprised. In the days I've been here, she's always busy. She doesn't seem to spend all day "liaising" with the Khua—I don't think—so there's probably more to her role of primary Aelo. I also don't think for a second that she'll leave me alone. Not after what I did yesterday. It's just a question of who'll be stuck babysitting me.

Tiav arrives at the office and nods to his mother as she leaves.

He's still mad. Definitely. I wonder if he got in trouble because I broke the law on his watch. The possibility sends another shudder of guilt through my bones. Maybe I should've thought about that *before* I ran off.

Billionaire-to-be Liddi Jantzen proved once again that the rest of us are mere insects to her—

Wait, that's not fair. I don't think Tiav's an insect, or anyone else. I just wanted to help my brothers. I wanted to try.

Tiav keeps the chair on the other side of the desk, not pulling it around next to me like he has before, and crosses his arms. I've had eyes on me all my life, plenty of them judging me and plenty finding me lacking, but never a glare like this one. He doesn't say a word, so I guess it's up to me to break the silence.

"Yoo heer wye?"

"I'm the one who received the alert when you first arrived, so like my mother said, you're my responsibility... so much so that now my other duties have been reassigned."

His words bring an unexpected wave of relief, even with the anger continuing to radiate from him. I'm not sure what that relief means. It's tinged by embarrassment that I need a babysitter and he has to waste his time doing it. All together, it makes for a confusing knot of discomfort.

"You're still not going to tell me what you were doing, are you?"

I'd been considering it, really... right up until the whole

"defilement" issue. Bad enough that *I* defiled the Khua. To someone like Kalkig, my brothers might be infinitely worse. I have no idea what people here think of our conduits, attempts at artificial Khua, but I'm certain Kalkig would hate them like he hates me, and hate my brothers for their involvement with the conduits.

Tiav isn't Kalkig, but he is an Aelo. I need more time to figure out what him being an Aelo really means, and whether it'll make a difference to Tiav that my brothers didn't *choose* to be where they are. Whether someone here has the power to do something about my brothers, to pull them free, or to remove the defilement by killing them.

I need to know no one will hurt my brothers as certainly as my speaking would.

It's hard to explain without spending hours forming full sentences, but I piece together what I can. *"See-krets dane-jer dont no."*

He presses his lips together and exhales sharply. "I don't like that answer."

I need him to understand this. I don't know why, but I do, so I try again. *"Rong choys pee-pull dye."*

The battle shows like explosions in his eyes. He still doesn't like the answer but is trying to work a way through it. "If I can convince you—eventually—that telling me is the right choice, will you?"

"Hope soe. Meh-nee fak-tores."

"Other people? The ones who could die."

"And kill-er and pee-pull heer and dont no."

"You're saying you're not at the top, the one running the game."

Not even close. *"Vare-ee bah-tum."*

Something snaps in him, with a sound of disbelief huffing from his chest. "You come here, this impossible thing, from a

place we've barely heard about, and you force me to lie to almost everyone I know about who you are and where you're from, but I do it. Then you break the law, and people think *I've* lost respect for the Khua, for my mother's station, but still I'm here. You're not at the bottom, Liddi. I am, because you're the one holding answers and refusing to give them up."

He's right. I've put him in an awful position, but my choice is made. My brothers' lives come first. That doesn't mean I feel good about it.

"*Vare-ee saw-ree.*"

Tiav stares at me for a long time, like he's trying to make a decision. Finally, he exhales sharply again and rests his crossed arms on the edge of the desk. "Fine. If you're not going to answer questions, then you might as well be the one asking them."

There wasn't much snow that winter, but there was rain. Plenty of rain. Enough rain to make Liddi despair of ever seeing the sun again, and enough to drive her to more parties and clubs than usual. At least the lights there weren't gray and dreary. Then it became too much rain, with a storm that flooded the river and ripped branches and debris from the woods, blowing it all into the yard.

Afterward, though, the sun finally returned. Blue sky with a side of more blue sky. So when Emil asked Liddi if she'd help the "Triad" clean out the yard along with the garden so it'd be ready for planting, she agreed.

The four of them piled up branches and dead leaves in one corner of the yard, picked carefully through the flowerbeds, and pulled up the remnants of last year's garden plantings . . . which they should've done at the end of the growing season but hadn't gotten around to. The triplets had been very busy with their projects, so Liddi had kept just as busy in the city.

After working awhile, Liddi took a large armload of dead vines. Maybe too large. Two steps later, her foot took a squelchy slip in the mud, and she couldn't right her balance. The vines landed back on the ground where they'd started, with her next to them, chilled mud seeping into her clothes.

"Are you okay, Liddi?" Marek asked, hurrying over to check on his sister.

Just a few years ago, Marek and Ciro would've laughed at her, but now she was the one laughing. She stretched her fingers into the mud. Then she curled a fist and flung the handful of

muck at Marek. It hit him right in the cheek. He wiped it away and grinned.

"Boys, Liddi has declared war."

From there it was a mess of mudballs and tackling each other and painting mud designs on their faces and arms until every inch of their skin had gone from sienna-colored to the deep walnut of their sitting room furniture. Liddi had never been so deliriously dirty. She collapsed on the grass, letting the sun dry the mud covering her.

"Well, that was productive," Emil said, looking down at her.

"Yes, it was," she countered. "It was fun. You guys are leaving soon, and we won't have many more chances for fun like this."

"Sure we will. We'll visit." He reached down for her hand and pulled her to her feet. "Come on, let's get cleaned up."

10

I CAN ASK QUESTIONS, pretty much any questions I want. Tiav says he might not answer them all, either because he won't know or won't be allowed, but I should ask. It's hard to choose where to start, but the immediate past makes the most sense.

"Owt uhv koo-ah how?"

Maybe talking about that isn't a good idea, because his expression goes a little stormier again. "How did we get you out? With you using that tether to anchor yourself, we weren't sure what to do. No one does that. You're lucky it wasn't any worse than those cuts on your arm. Crossing the physical world with the Khua . . . strange things can happen."

"How?" I repeat.

"Wasn't that complicated in the end. There's another Khua less than a mile from there. I went in and asked your Khua to pull you back and push you out. Still took some time."

Something pulled that tether, no question. I thought it was the people on the outside. Maybe it was. Maybe while Tiav was coming back from the other Khua, the keepers or Kalkig pulled me in.

"*Yoo theenk koo-ah ah-live?*"

"Don't think. Know."

Right, he couldn't be an Aelo if he didn't believe it, I suppose. "*Wer-ship lyke Ag-nak?*"

"No, not like that. I can't exactly say I'm friends with them, but I respect—no, that's not the right word, either. It's like . . . how you feel about your parents, but different. Looking up to them, learning from them, and realizing as you go along that they respect you back." His pause is full of having something more to say, so I wait. "I know I said you could ask the questions, but I hope you can answer this one. Do your parents know where you are? Aren't they worried about you?"

I hunt down the single syllable I need. "*Ded.*"

Tiav's stance has been defensive since he arrived, his expression hard and immovable. Now it softens, just a little, and he uncrosses his arms. "I'm sorry. How?"

I did *accident* once before, so I scroll through my list. It was a lot of words ago, and I'm not sure what icon I put with it. The computer reads my first guess to me in my earpiece. Wrong. My second guess is right, and I have the computer read it to Tiav.

"Recently?" he asks.

I shake my head. Sometimes it feels like it hasn't been that long, but ten years is not recent. The turn in conversation brings up another question of my own.

"*Yore dad?*"

"My father? He lives a few provinces from here, rehabilitating sick and injured animals. I don't see him as much as I did when I was younger, but that's just because I've been busier. It's not . . . my mother's not exactly typical, in anything. She wanted a child. My father obliged. So we're not a family, exactly. But he's a good person, and he's there when I need to talk to him."

The situation is hard to fathom. My parents were always two halves of a whole to me, a perception solidified when they died together. Then again, if I could choose between my situation and Tiav's, I'd take the two very separate but very alive parents over the together but very dead ones.

I stare at the grid of symbols, fighting the impatience that rages at using it. So slow. So incomplete for expressing myself. I can get basic messages and questions across, but not what I'm really thinking. Not what I'm feeling. Silence still wins.

"Liddi?"

Tiav's expression has changed again, like he's been studying me while I studied the symbols. Like what he sees worries him.

"Whatever your trouble is back home, it's bad, isn't it?"

Definitely. *"Bad fore mee."*

As soon as the computer says it, the words pierce through. If my brothers die or are even just stuck in the conduits forever, *my* world will end. A few friends will mourn them, but we've always been closest to each other. And if Minali's plan succeeds in stabilizing the conduits, that's a *good* thing for everyone in the Seven Points. She'll explain away the disappearance of the Jantzens, that we gave our lives preserving the connection between the worlds. No one will suspect her in Garrin's death.

I wonder how many people would put the conduits before my brothers' lives, but the number doesn't matter. *I* can't. But I can't pretend the conduits' demise means nothing, either. Shiin said the Agnac requested a ban on using the Khua for travel, and that asking the Khua to cut off the Lost Points took care of that. But it didn't. Shiin said the Khua cut us off centuries ago, but even with the conduits, we used portals to travel between the Seven Points. Not easily, not often, but people did sometimes because they didn't trust the conduits yet. And then there were the vague sightings after the conduits were perfected.

Sort of perfected. Their current state of destabilization shows definite flaws. Maybe it's time to risk trusting Tiav with some information and see what happens.

"Koo-ah still inn lost poynts."

Writing that took forever, but as soon as the computer reads it, I have Tiav's attention. He leans forward, his muscles tense. "What? What do you mean?"

This will take even longer, but I stick it out. *"Nott saym. Kall pohr-tahls. Hard but kan yooz trah-vuhl."*

Tiav keeps his eyes on the desk, running a hand through his hair as he absorbs what I've told him. "So you didn't somehow break into a Khua from your end. One was already there."

That's accurate as far as I know. *"Look diff-rent. Skair-ee."*

Finally, he drops his hand and looks up at me again. "This ...I don't know what this means. If the Khua didn't cut your people off, but told us they did...I don't know. There's a reason, an explanation, has to be, but... we should keep this to ourselves for now. Definitely don't mention it when Kal's around, or any of the other Agnac."

I was hardly planning on it, but that brings up a very different question. *"Yoo dont hayt mee lyke Kal wye?"*

It might be a bold question considering Tiav's anger, but that seems to be fading. "Kalkig...His regard for the Khua runs deep. It does for all the Agnac, and it makes them very protective. They're quick to judge. As an Aelo, I can't be. Or I'm not

supposed to be, at least. It takes time and patience to understand the Khua, and I've always assumed the same is true of people. So I tried—*am* trying to give you a chance."

"*Wye frends?*"

"Why am I friends with Kal?" Tiav pauses and shifts in his chair. "I wasn't always sure I wanted to be an Aelo. When I was younger, I was pretty sure I *didn't* want to. Other people said I'd grow out of my resistance, learn to embrace my role. Kal and I were already friends, played *gedek* together all the time. He told members of the Agnac Hierarchy right to their faces that if I didn't want to, I shouldn't have to. I should do whatever I want with my life."

"*Still Ay-loh.*"

"Yeah, well...I grew out of some things and grew into others. Kalkig was right about me doing what I want. That 'relationship' with the Khua I told you about—as I discovered that, what I wanted changed. And I learned how to cope with the responsibility."

I lean onto the desk and rest my head in my hands. It's so unfair. Tiav sounds like one person who could understand the pressure of being "the Jantzen girl." But thanks to the implant in my throat, there's no way I can tell him. Explaining what JTI is, its importance to the Seven Points, my utter failure to live up to familial expectations...it'd take days to tap out. More time than it's worth.

For now, I'm still on my own.

✳ – – – ✳

Silence has had a vise on my chest for days, and it's tightening again. Like it's pushing me further into myself, separating me from the people of Ferinne. It's even tight in my sleep, giving me dreams of suffocating at the top of a mountain or drowning in an ocean.

I wake with a start, gasping for breath that comes easier than it should. Easy breath isn't enough. I need fresh air.

The apartment is silent, no sign of movement from Shiin or Tiav. After being arrested, I know better than to think I can go out the front door without an alarm going off, but there's a chance I have another option. The door to the roof is right by my room, and it doesn't have anything resembling a lock-panel.

I open the door—sure enough, unlocked—and wait. When nothing happens for two full minutes, I head up the stairs.

The night air is cool and clean. It helps. The complicated winch assemblies from the Daglin are gone, so I sit against the low wall edging the roof. Then I close my eyes and just let myself breathe in, trying to loosen the vise. Trying to relax, because being tense and anxious never helps *anything* in my life go better.

I think of home. The workshop. The night phlox. The river. The portal.

The ball of energy on Sampati whirls in my memory, snapping and sparking. Then the little mote of light here on Ferinne, hovering peacefully between two crystal spires. I went in one and came out the other. They have to be the same thing. The in-between felt like both and neither, all contradictions and chaos.

Two ends of a string. One end tethered to the spires on Ferinne. The other free to roam. Sampati. Banak. Neta. Anywhere.

If you found a portal high . . .

Except if I'm right, the Sampati end of my portal—my Khua—wasn't free. My brothers held it in place long enough for me to reach it. Maybe.

A picture half forms of something that *must* move but can't because it's restrained. What would happen? Violent vibrations, probably. Maybe that's what I saw on Sampati.

Minali trapped my brothers in the conduits, but I've been with them in the Khua. So for them to be in both, the two networks must be different, but somehow connected. Like... different frequencies trying to send the same message.

"Liddi?"

I know that voice, so I open my eyes.

Emil stands a few feet away, and he's not alone. Marek and Ciro are with him, the whole Triad. Their faces tell me they're still in pain but trying to hide it, working hard to appear here. I can't ask. I can't say anything to them, and I can't stop my own tears from falling.

"Don't cry, Liddi," Emil says. He crouches in front of me, but he's not solid enough for me to reach out and hold his hand. Even with three of my brothers here, I'm still alone, choking on my tears. "We can't stay long. Marek told us what happened, how you got hurt. You can't do that again. You have to be safe."

"That's the most important thing," Ciro says. "More important than us."

"We're starting to understand some things from this side," Marek adds. "Things that might help, how it's all connected. What Blake's doing. Leave it to us. You stay out of trouble, try to fit in. *Be safe.*"

They fade away. Gone. Busy.

I leave the roof and hurry down to my room. I can't shout or scream, but I have to do *something*, so I kick the desk, thump a fist against the wall. It doesn't help, and I do it again, harder. And again. And eight more times, one for each of my brothers.

Wherever Shiin's and Tiav's rooms are, they're far enough not to hear me, because silence is the only company to my impotent rage. Finally I collapse on my bed, knowing I can cry in peace and knowing one other thing with certainty.

Even my brothers have realized I'm useless.

Liddi and the likewise mud-covered triplets had to promise Dom several times that they'd definitely and absolutely clean up the mess they tracked into the house before he'd open the back door and let them in. As soon as they were inside, though, Dom had something else to say.

"Someone's at the front entrance."

Ciro was closest, so he checked the ID screen and opened the door. Reb Vester stood on the other side, tall and muscular, his shiny hair looking like they'd frozen it perfectly in place at an expensive salon. He ignored the Triad completely and stared at Liddi—her muck-crusted hair and skin darkened from minerals in the soil that would take ages to wash away.

"Liddi, I, uh ... hi." Reb seemed flustered by her appearance, but then she noticed the way Emil glared at him. All three of her brothers did. Maybe Reb wasn't ignoring them after all. Of course, even at his best, Reb wasn't the most eloquent person she'd ever met.

"Hi, Reb. What brings you out to the country?" Liddi asked.

"There's a new club opening in Edgewick, supposed to be ten times as good as Syncopy. Wondered if you wanted to set the trend opening night."

Liddi was sure the club owners would be thrilled if she did. Then she wondered if those owners had any affiliation with Reb's laserball team. She'd been friends in passing with Reb since he was the top recruit in the junior leagues, but she

knew better than to trust his motives. Before she could say no thanks, though, Ciro jumped in.

"Edgewick is two hundred miles away. A bit far for a club opening."

"Just a couple of hours in my hovercar," Reb said.

Marek stepped up to Ciro's shoulder. "Liddi has more important things to do with those hours. Be on your way, Vester."

Reb considered arguing for about three seconds, then gave Liddi a nod and left.

She whirled on her brothers. "Thanks a lot!"

All three looked startled. "What, you wanted to go?" Marek said. "That guy is trouble, Liddi. He only cares about your status."

"Like I don't know that? But you think I'm such a child that I can't handle one laser-addled jock. That I can't handle anything."

Emil nudged her arm. "We don't think that. You know we don't. We just know that you have to handle more than the rest of us combined. So when we can handle something for you, we do."

She pushed him away and stomped upstairs. They handled the things they could, leaving her only the things she had to handle on her own . . . but couldn't. And that was the problem.

11

"ARE YOU OKAY, LIDDI?" Tiav asks the next morning after breakfast. "You look tired."

I am. Every attempt to sleep after seeing the triplets was met with nightmares about my brothers dying and my rescue attempts doing nothing but getting in the way. Hardly restful.

"Let's not bother with the Nyum today, then. We can stay here."

I can't help noticing Tiav's anger has cooled, so at least that's an improvement. He leads me to one of the book-filled rooms—there are a few—and I sit on a couch. It's definitely more comfortable than the office. Then he sets his com-tablet on a low table in front of me, complete with a holo-projected keypad hovering in midair.

I have nothing to ask, nothing to say. My brothers don't want my help, even if I had any to offer.

Tiav, as usual, does the talking. "I went to a Khua early this morning and asked about what you said. How they're still in the Lost Points, but different. If I understand correctly, what you have is a sort of 'echo' or tail end of the Khua, but I couldn't make sense of why they were there. Still, they seemed to be saying they'd been left alone for ages until you came along. Does that sound right? You were the first to travel through them in a long time?"

As far as I know. That probably explains the improved mood, knowing the precious Khua have been left untouched in the "Lost" Points.

Since I have nothing better to do, I halfheartedly indulge my curiosity. *"Tock koo-ah how?"*

"I'm not sure 'talk' is the right word for it. The Agnac and Izim call what we Aelo do 'communing' with the Khua, but that never felt right to me, either—too rooted in the worshiping they do. It's watching and listening to everything inside, keeping your mind quiet and focused on what you want to know, then trying to make sense of it. It's still confusing—lately more than ever, like nothing even the oldest Aelo can remember. But we're chosen because we have a knack for it."

The Aelo definitely have some special skills if they can make sense of the migraine-inducing mess I've been privy to twice. Or maybe they're deluding themselves, convinced information comes from the Khua when it's really their own subconscious.

Maybe it doesn't matter. Why should I care what the Ferinnes believe?

Tiav studies me while I try to avoid looking at him. "Something's wrong. Are you homesick?"

Among other things. I shrug.

He deactivates the com-tablet and tucks it into his pocket. "We keep telling you to be patient, but then we push you to work all day. A break might help loosen our brain cells a little. There's a regular game of *gedek* over at the athletic park, should be starting soon. If we go, you won't try to run off to a Khua, will you?"

I shake my head. An empty space in my chest echoes my brothers' words from last night. There's no reason to go to the Khua.

"Okay, then let's get going."

The park is far enough to take a streamer—definitely not something I'm in the mood for, but a short enough ride to tolerate. Once there, I'm glad to have Tiav guiding me through. I'd get lost for sure. Several fields cover the space, each with different markings, some with equipment. A blend of mesh fences and energy fields keep the areas separate. A ball the size of my head crashes into one of the fences and bounces back, so it doesn't interfere with the neighboring games.

Vic would love this place. He'd want to try each game in turn. The empty space inside me manages to both grow and shrink at the same time.

Tiav leads us to what I assume is a *gedek* field. A few Ferinnes and several Agnac are playing around and warming up, and watching them gives me some idea of the particulars. The field is arranged in a triangle, complete with painted lines, and a strange bit of framework draws my attention to one corner. Its base rests well behind the triangle, its body rising up and over, with a horizontal bar hanging above that corner.

A Ferinne girl stands in the middle of the triangle with an eight-inch ball. She lobs it toward the main point, where an Agnac boy grabs the horizontal bar, swings with those ridiculously long arms, and kicks the ball to the outer edge of the field.

"What do you think?" Tiav says. "Do you want to watch or play?"

It's a low-tech game and looks a *lot* like stickball, other than the number of corners and using feet in place of the stick. Probably an Agnacki game, judging by that swinging apparatus, but nothing I can't manage, and I could use the distraction of something physical. Beating up the walls of my room last night wasn't enough. I point to the field.

Tiav smiles. More like the way he smiled before I ran off to the Khua two days ago. I think he's forgiven me, at least mostly.

The others spot him and stop what they're doing to come over. They're all around our age, but in two seconds, I can see the respect they have for Tiav. Kind of like how people look at me in clubs, emphasizing my separateness, but also kind of not. No one here wants to use Tiav to advance themselves, to take advantage. A twist of something almost like jealousy pinches me.

"Everyone, this is Liddi," he says. "She's visiting from Sedro, so it's her first time playing. Oh, and bizarre accident, long story, but she can't talk. No big deal, right?"

He carries off the lies more smoothly than I expected, but then I remember what he said about lying to almost everyone he knows since I arrived. The others nod or grunt their agreement that my muteness is immaterial. Except one person. I didn't see Kalkig before, but here he is, glaring at me as usual. Tiav doesn't seem to notice until we split into teams and his friend chooses the group opposite us. Then he looks both hurt and annoyed at the same time.

While everyone gets situated, Tiav quickly tells me the essentials of scoring and penalties. Definitely enough like stickball for me to follow. I nod my understanding, but he lowers his voice for one more thing.

"Kal plays rough," he says. "So do all the Agnac, and so do we, but Kal especially. And you know he doesn't like you, so watch out for him, okay?"

His eyes say he's worried about me. So does his hand on my arm, which is still as distracting as it was the day I came through the portal, but not the same way. It's not the touch of a stranger anymore. Doesn't matter, because he doesn't need to worry. I'm not a delicate flower that can't take a few bruises.

Our team starts in the field while Kalkig's is up to swing. I do all right, fielding the ball when it comes my way and throwing it back in to the corners. One of the Agnac girls on our team says, "Good arm." Given the efficiency and power of her own arms, I'm pretty sure that's a high compliment among her people.

It feels nice to do something right.

The opposing team scores a couple of points before we give them enough penalties to switch sides and it's our turn to swing. During the first round, I noted a difference between the Ferinnes' and Agnac's techniques. While the long-armed aliens just reached up to the bar and swung themselves, the Ferinnes stood on a rung above the base and jumped forward to grab the bar. My team insists I take a couple of practice swings, which I do without any trouble.

The first few players on our team get good kicks, including Tiav, and then it's my turn. Before I can get to my place on the framework, Tiav touches my shoulder, startling me.

"Don't think too much," he says. "Just follow your instincts."

Good advice, since overthinking has never done me much good.

Then the other team changes up positions so Kalkig is lobbing. Great.

Liddi Jantzen was knocked unconscious by a deliberately misthrown gedek ball, much to the amusement of the alien who hates her guts. One can only hope the head trauma knocked some of her neurons back into place.

I'm definitely not letting that happen, with or without neuron-knocking.

Kalkig's first lob is high. Not enough to hit my head, but the ball slams at high speed into my chest, knocking the air out of me. I barely keep from making a sound.

"Come on, Kal," Tiav yells. "Since when do you lob like a yearling?"

The Agnac grunts and glares as I drop down and take my position on the rung again. This time the ball comes straight to where I need it, and my timing is perfect as my feet make solid contact. I don't wait to see where the ball goes. I hit the ground and run for the first corner. Judging by the cheers from my team, it's a good kick, and I get to the corner safely.

This feeling…it's familiar, but old. Camaraderie with people who offer it without even knowing me. Like playing games with other kids when I was little enough that none of them knew or cared about the Jantzen family. When things were simple and obvious. A bright energy charges through me. I wonder how long it'll last.

Our next player kicks well, too, getting me to the second corner. If I get back to the start, I'll score a point for our team. Next up is a Ferinne boy, and his kick is only okay. I'm already running, but Kalkig fields the ball quickly. He runs toward the same corner to go for the penalty.

Tiav told me the rules. If Kalkig can't stop me, I get the point. I see his confidence, and why not? He's definitely bigger and undoubtedly stronger than I am. Faster, too. He'll beat me to the corner, so my only chance is to knock him down.

I know something he doesn't. I've been knocking down my bigger, stronger brothers for years. They taught me how.

Don't break stride. Stay low. The arm holding the ball means he leans to the other side slightly—exploit the weak point in balance.

Most important, what Vic always told me, again and again. Don't be afraid of the hit.

And in this case, *do not* make a sound.

The impact jars from my shoulder to my toes, but it doesn't stop me. I push through, using my legs to shove Kalkig up and back. A noise I have to assume shows surprise escapes from him as we both tumble down.

Then it's drowned out by cheers and laughter from my team.

I reached the corner. I got the point.

Some are asking if I'm okay. I untangle myself and get to my feet, but when my teammates try to pull me away and congratulate me, I shrug them off. Instead, I offer my hand to Kalkig, with no idea whether he'll accept it or not.

His eyes lock with mine for a long heartbeat, like he's not sure whether to take it either. In the end, he does, his rough hand gripping mine to pull himself up. He also lets go as quickly as possible. One grunt, and he heads back to his position.

The rest of my team pat my back and shoulder, telling me what a great hit it was. It takes a minute for things to settle down so the game can continue. When it does, Tiav pulls me aside.

"You're okay, right? I know for a fact how hard-boned Kal is."

I'm fine. Might have a few bruises, but nothing major.

Tiav smiles. "Looks like you didn't need that warning after all. And now Kalkig knows something. You may be a 'Pointed heathen,' but you're also tough as any Agnac."

If I am, it's because my brothers taught me to be. Always the youngest and the smallest, but I had eight people telling me not to let that stop me.

Something clicks in my mind like I can feel my own synapses firing. It didn't take a blow to the head to knock some neurons into place after all. Just a blow to every other part of my body. My brothers told me to leave things to them and stay out of it because they're scared for me. They've never in my life told me I couldn't do something because they thought I was incapable.

They're the ones always telling me I *am* capable.

They might not like it, but those are the words I'm going to listen to. Because they can't possibly be as scared for my safety as I am for theirs.

☀ — — — ☀

I can't sleep—again—so I go back up to the roof. My gut tells me I won't see my brothers, but they're not what I'm looking for. What I'm looking for is nearly as hard to find, it turns out. Some stars show themselves, but it's not that much better than Sampati. Just too much ambient light. Still, I study the ones I can see, looking for familiar patterns. I know I won't find any, but I look anyway, and make new patterns.

"I didn't realize there were stargazers on Sampati."

Tiav's voice startles me as much as his statement irks me. It's true, though. I got my stargazing from Mom and never met anyone else with the habit.

"Then again, I don't know much at all about Sampati," he continues. "So that was probably rude. Sorry. Have something to say?"

He offers me his com-tablet, and my posture slumps. I'm too tired, and writing takes too long. Every time I think I remember one of the primary symbols, I realize I've mixed up five of them. They're all so similar.

I need to talk. Each day, silence adds another weight to my heart.

"Okay, we'll try without," Tiav says, replacing the device in his pocket. "The view here is awful. Want to see a better one?"

After looking down at myself and at him, I pinch the material of the loose shirt and shorts I'm wearing to sleep in and raise an eyebrow.

"It's fine—no need to dress up for this. It means taking a streamer, though, which you hate. Right?" I shudder, which makes him smile. "See? I guess pretty well. So, do you want to?"

I do. Streamer or no streamer, a better view of the stars sounds like what I need.

As usual, I close my eyes for the length of the streamer ride, and it's definitely lengthier than usual. Wherever Tiav is taking me, it's farther from Podra than I've been since I arrived on the planet.

"We're here," he says, signaling me to open my eyes.

I'm not sure where "here" is. We're in front of a circular building with a rounded dome. Nothing else is around for miles as far as I can tell. The sky is punctuated with several times more stars than I saw from the roof, far more than could be seen from anywhere on Sampati. Much better. But Tiav leads me to the door of the building. He runs his hand over some kind of lock-panel off to the side, and the door opens. I tap his arm and point to the lock.

"Being an Aelo has advantages, including access to observatories anytime. Come on."

The interior is simple—beautiful stonework on the walls in swirling, organic patterns, and a staircase spiraling up toward the dome I saw outside. Tiav opens another door at the top, leads me up a set of stairs through the floor above, and shows me what he brought us here for.

All the stars surround me, more of them than I've ever seen, even on Erkir where there are hardly any cities. I don't know if the dome is some kind of special glass accentuating the night sky or if the whole thing's a computer projection. Whichever it is doesn't matter to me, because it's perfect and it's beautiful and it's right there. Reclined chairs in the center of the room are arranged carefully to allow the best viewing, but they're not all the same. Some are designed to accommodate the odd Agnac physiology, some are reinforced to support a Haleian's mass, and some are smaller for a Crimna's stature. Like everywhere else on Ferinne, there's a place for everyone.

Tiav leads me to an adjacent pair of normal-people-shaped chairs and we sit down. At first I'm happy to just stare at the whole sky, but then I get the feeling I should be looking for something in particular.

"Here, I think you'll want to see this," Tiav says. He taps on his com-tablet, and a ring appears on the inside of the dome, highlighting a single star. "There's your home. That's Sampati's star. You can see the others, too. Pramadam, Erkir, Yishu, Neta, Tarix, and Banak."

I stare. These stars belong to the Seven Points. In all the time I've spent looking at stars, even in some silliness of looking for Ferri as a child, it never occurred to me to wonder where the other Points were in the larger sky. Shiin was right. We stopped looking beyond our own borders ages ago. "Other worlds" meant the other Points, places just steps away through a conduit.

With all of them highlighted, I see something else. The way they're arranged in a large ring, spaced almost perfectly. Kind of like in the Seven Points' icon.

"Over there is Agnac, and Halei's not far from it," Tiav continues. "Crimna's closer to us, and then there's Izima—you can just barely see it."

After that, he starts pointing out constellations. The farmer. The swan. The three ships. I imagine the people who first named these pictures in the sky, wonder what made them see that shape in the stars instead of another. Then I start making up stories about each one. The farmer made a bargain with a sorcerer to save his crops, but the price was being frozen where he stood, watching over the Seven—the *Eight* Points. The three ships were the only ones left of a convoy that passed through a devastating storm. One called the frog met an unfortunate end thanks to the swan.

"See how close the frog is to the swan's beak?" Tiav says. "When I was little, I always said the swan was going to eat the frog someday."

The way he says the exact same thing I was thinking makes me laugh.

Out loud.

I clap a hand to my mouth, but I can't force the sound back in. It was a tiny one, so brief, but it might have been enough.

Tiav sits up, startled by the sound. "So you *do* have a voice?" Incredulity weaves through every word.

He may be startled, but he has no idea that eight people might be dead because of that laugh. I don't have time to make him figure it out.

"Hey, where are you going?"

Where I'm going is outside. I get to the spiraling stairway before Tiav catches up, but I don't let him stop me.

"Liddi, wait. You have a voice but don't talk because you don't want to? Or something else? Just slow down and help me understand."

No, slowing down would mean taking longer to get outside, and outside is where it's night, where the moonlight is.

Where I might have a chance of seeing my brothers if I haven't just killed them all.

Nothing has changed outside the observatory. The streamer waits for us, and everything else is still and quiet. I move away from the building, searching the fields in every direction. All three moons are out, which helps, but I don't see anyone. I do see something else—a sparkle in the distance. One of the Khua, maybe.

My brothers have been at their strongest and easiest to see near portals. It's worth a try, so I start running.

"No, Liddi!"

Tiav sees the Khua as well as I do—he probably knew it was there without seeing it. He's fast enough to catch up, and he grabs my waist to stop me. Tries to, at least, as I keep pulling.

"We talked about this—you can't interfere with the Khua again. The Agnac won't let it go anymore. You have to stop!"

I twist to look up at him. His eyes are stern, but they also hesitate. He doesn't want to be angry with me again, but he will if I force it. I plead with him to read my eyes back. To see that I don't want to interfere with anything—not this time—that I just want to get closer.

The sternness melds with confusion. "Is it something else?"

I nod, encouraging him to follow the line of thought.

"Is it something that will get us both in trouble?"

No, not unless seeing a ghostlike version of one of my brothers is cause for trouble. Which it might be. Or it might be a good thing. If Tiav can see one of the boys, it would end my indecision on whether to tell him. He'd start to understand what's going on, and maybe if he *sees* them, maybe if he could even talk to one of them just for a moment, he wouldn't see them as defilers. He'd see they're just trapped and need help.

If they're not dead.

Tiav thinks it over for a solid minute, and I force myself to wait calmly, not struggling. That's not easy, because I'm definitely not used to being this close to him, and I'm not sure how I feel about it.

Finally he decides. "Don't make me regret it."

He lets go, and I continue toward the portal again, taking it a little slower and willing my brothers to show themselves. Just one of them. Just one glimpse. They can't be dead. I can't have blown it like this, in such a small moment of distraction.

A boy succeeded in making Liddi Jantzen laugh, leading to the utter destruction of everyone who means anything to her—

Thinking like that isn't helping, so I shut it down.

Less than halfway to the portal, a flash of movement draws my eye to a stand of trees off to the left. Durant is there, his posture uneasy, but he waves before fading away.

He's alive.

I turn to Tiav, looking for his reaction. There isn't one. He's been keeping an eye on me and the portal the whole time. He didn't see Durant at all.

It doesn't matter. The important thing is that my momentary slip didn't cost my brothers their lives. My laugh could've been deadly, but it wasn't. The implant's listening for more than a laugh. A single word might still be enough.

I have to be more careful. I can't slip again. Not once.

Not ever.

Liddi didn't make it to the new club in Edgewick opening night, but when she live-commed Reb later, he said it was only a soft opening anyway. The real opening was in a few days. Still annoyed with her brothers for making the decision for her, she told Reb she'd be there.

The boys weren't happy, Emil especially. Luko even showed up to talk her out of it. When she reminded him that she had only a few years left to have any kind of fun before taking over the largest, most important corporation in the Seven Points, his argument lost its fire.

She got her way. As usual.

And she lived to regret it.

The club had half the flair of Syncopy, and Syncopy wasn't even her favorite. Tired music, lighting effects that the better clubs had tried and given up a year ago, and Liddi's only company was Reb Vester. Him and about a hundred other people who wanted an excuse to become her new best friend. She hated retreating to the Exclusive Zone on the upper level, but eventually she had to have some breathing room.

"There you are," Reb said, a drink in each hand. "Come on, let's get down there and dance again."

He was a good dancer, but it wasn't any fun with people constantly sidling up to offer phony compliments or ask inane questions. It made Liddi want to feign clumsiness and accidentally throw an elbow toward their noses.

"Sorry, I think I'd better get home," she said. "My brothers were against me coming in the first place, so the least I can do is get back before morning."

Reb set his drinks down and took both her hands in his. They were still slick with condensation from the glasses. Less than pleasant. "Liddi, those brothers of yours want to keep you locked up. They don't want you to have a life, so who cares what they say?"

She pulled her hands back, wiping them slightly on her skirt. "I do. Yeah, they're annoying and overprotective some-times, but . . . they're my brothers. They have their reasons. And I want to go home now."

"Okay, I get it. Let's go."

It took strategic maneuvering that'd do the military grunts on Banak proud, but they finally got out of the club. Leaving the music behind felt good, except it was replaced by a buzzing swarm of vid-cams. Not a big deal, since once they were in the hovercar, they'd leave them behind, too.

"Hey, Liddi, hold up a second."

She stopped and turned to Reb. He took her face in his hands and kissed her.

His lips were too wet, he held her head too tight, the buzz of the vid-cams turned into a roar as more swarmed to catch the action, and there was absolutely nothing romantic about it at all.

Liddi pushed him away and glared at him for two seconds before deciding she couldn't trust her voice, because even with her glare, he was grinning at her. Without a word, she strode to a for-hire hovercar and got in. Her brothers definitely wouldn't mind if she spent the credits, and there was no way she was spending two hours alone with Reb after that.

As she rode toward the borders of Edgewick, a few frustrated tears fell. Her first kiss would be seen by millions on a media-cast. They'd probably think her storming off was staged for more attention. Every moment would be analyzed and argued about. No one would care about the truth, except her brothers, and she'd have to keep them from getting arrested for killing Reb Vester.

Just like everything else, Liddi couldn't get it right, and she couldn't have it to herself.

12

THE NEXT DAY, TIAV IS unusually quiet, nearly as silent as I am. He's got to be puzzling out what happened last night, trying to make sense of why I panicked and why I calmed back down. I stare at the keypad trying to think of something safe to say while he's probably doing the same thing.

"You said people could die if you do something wrong," he finally says. "You almost did something wrong last night. Because you laughed?"

I nod. Pretty much, that's it.

"Are you worried about more people breaking through from the Lost Points? Like an invasion?"

Not remotely. The only people with any chance of coming through are my brothers. At least, there'd better be a chance of that. Given how awful Durant looked last night, though, I need to make some progress. Soon.

Tiav sits back with a frustrated sigh. At least he's sitting next to me again. "You realize this makes no sense, don't you? And every day it makes even *less* sense?"

I swipe through my word bank for a word I nearly have memorized, but Tiav gently takes my wrist to stop me.

"Don't go hunting for 'sorry.' I already know you are. You'll tell me when you can tell me?"

I hope so. I hope it'll get to the point where I can, because Tiav sounds almost as sad as he does frustrated. My heart beats in equal frustration, the pulse of it warming against his palm where he still holds my wrist. His touch lingers a moment longer before releasing.

"I should tell *you* something. Or ask—I don't know. It's something I've thought about for a long time, before you came. That maybe we've kept the Lost Points closed off from us for too long. Maybe both sides are missing out on something. The Aelo back then said it wouldn't be forever, but then it started feeling like nothing would ever change it. Until you showed up."

That's a pretty big proposition. Tiav has to know that, too. I imagine what would happen if the Ferinnes revealed themselves to the Seven Points after so many centuries apart.

The Jantzen girl finally had something to show at this year's Tech Reveal—an entire planet. Turns out those children's stories about Ferri are true, sort of. In other news, mass hysteria has broken out pretty much everywhere as deformed friends of the Ferinnes have cropped up throughout the Seven Points.

No, the Points could cope with the idea of aliens, if handled properly. I only freaked out a little, nowhere near hysteria. There would be bigger problems, though. Like the conduits. I still can't tell if the people here would be glad we found a way to get around without bothering their precious Khua. Or if they would take our (admittedly failing) attempts at Khua substitutes as a major offense.

Actually, I think I know the answer to that, at least for a certain segment of the population.

"Ag-nack wood naht lyke. May-bee yoo too."

"I don't know. If they came up with you, Sampati at least can't be as bad as they say."

His smile holds a teasing hint of mischief I haven't seen before, and I turn back to the computer as heat blooms in my cheeks.

He made me blush. Something Reb Vester on his best day can't dream of accomplishing.

I have a sudden urge to know how long until lunch, but as usual, the symbols of the Ferinne clock make no sense. That's really starting to annoy me. And it shows, because Tiav sees exactly what I'm thinking.

"Want me to explain the clocks?"

No, I want one that'll make sense to me, that I won't have to decode and decipher every time I look at it. Explaining it in words will take forever. *"Want draw."*

"That's easy enough." He shows me how to switch to a blank screen that'll let me draw on it.

I draw a simple landscape with a sun at sunrise, midday, and sunset. Above each position, I add a clock face with tick marks and the two indicators in the approximate place for that time of day. Underneath, I draw the landscape again, this time with the three moons. It's not exactly accurate, since they don't all orbit at the same rate, but I draw them similar to the sun's positions anyway, showing how the clock face cycles again overnight.

"I've seen something like that in old artwork. Different

though. We probably stopped using them about the same time your people stopped writing."

"*Mayk mye-sellf.*"

"Of course, Sampati, land of the technologists. You can put together any device you want in about five minutes, right?"

If only he knew. But a clock is simple enough. A clock is innocuous, too. A clock is a good excuse to find out how technology around here works without getting myself in more Khua-related trouble. Maybe a little tech focus will spark an idea for helping my brothers.

I need *something* to work on.

"Okay, I know a shop that should have whatever you need. Let's go."

He stands and guides me out the door first with a hand at the small of my back. Again, his touch lingers maybe a second longer than it has to. I don't mind. There's something comfortable about it.

The shop Tiav mentioned is just down the street, and he was right. It has everything I need. Parts for a Ferinne wristwatch with its symbolic readout, first of all. But also various shapes and sizes of casings and display screens. Everything looks different from how it would back home, but most still make sense when I look at them. Tiav only has to tell me the purpose of a couple that are too small for me to see functional detail.

Just as I finish gathering the components, I freeze. I don't have a single credit to my name in this world. Tiav just offers one of his easy smiles and takes everything from me, setting it on the counter for the shopkeeper to tally.

"My treat," he says.

He's been "treating" me all along. The only reason I haven't starved is because Tiav and Shiin took me in immediately. Fed me, gave me extra clothes. Given where they live, I guess it's nothing they can't manage, but this is the first time it's occurred to me that I'm a financial burden to them.

After years of having designer clothes sent free of charge and dinners comped at the hottest restaurants, you'd think Liddi Jantzen would be used to such treatment.

But my mental media-cast lies. It's not the same. I never asked for those clothes, and more than once I tried to pay for dinners. Everyone gave me things because they wanted the prestige of having my name attached. Tiav and his mother have taken care of me because I needed help. Because they're good, charitable people. Even when I don't deserve it, when I've broken their laws and may very well do it again.

That thought sets the guilt twisting in my bones again, but something else loosens it, just a little. Tiav buying these things so I can build a timepiece that makes sense to me, that's not charity. That's something else.

Like a real gift.

We get back to the office in the Nyum, lay everything out on the desk, and get to work. Tiav starts by drawing a more careful clock face on the wallscreen, noting I'll need a different arrangement of tick marks than I drew on my sketch. That makes sense. Different planets have different day lengths due to rotation. We always have to adjust when we travel to other Points, and it's certainly one of several reasons I haven't slept too well since I arrived.

Once I figure out how the tick marks should be, Tiav has me draw it exactly how I want it on the desk. I give it a blue background, black tick marks, and two silver indicators for the

hour and minute. He shows me how to label the indicators as "moveable" with an anchor point in the center.

"Then just slide the drawing to—never mind." He stops because the face is already showing up on the tiny round display screen. "You got it."

I'm not sure exactly how I did it. I noticed the underside of the screen had what looked like a data receiver and used one of the tools Tiav gave me to activate it, then slid the drawing to a part of the computer display that my gut said meant transmit.

That sounds good in retrospect, but I still don't know how I recognized the data receiver. The Ferinne technology is an odd mix of metallic and crystalline parts like I've never seen, and I've seen all kinds of technology in the workshop back home. But when I looked at the back of the display under the magnifier, the tiny little bits in that area seemed like they could only do one thing that made sense. Receive data.

Something making sense. That's a new feeling.

I keep following what makes sense, connecting the regular chronometer to the display in a way that tells the indicators how to move. That takes some trial and error, but I get it eventually. I find one of the standard watch pieces that I'm pretty sure uplinks to some kind of central computer clock to coordinate the time, and I get that incorporated, too. Once that's done, it's just a matter of fitting everything into the casing and attaching a wristband.

It's finished, so I put it on. I can see that we're just past midday. As soon as I get used to the slight differences in hour and day measurements, I'll be able to estimate how long I've been doing something or how long I have until something is finished.

Once again, Liddi Jantzen single-handedly set a fashion trend, bringing back wristwatches, which have been out of style for, what? Nearly a century?

Forget fashion. This is something I made, and it works. I catch my reflection in the surface of the desk. A tiny smile plays on my lips.

"There's something I've always wondered," Tiav says. "Is it true that whichever of the Lost Points you're from, that dictates what you have to do with your life? Like because you're from Sampati, you *have* to be a technologist?"

Yes, *I* have to be, but that's not why. I sweep the drawing program off the desk so Tiav can bring the keypad back. This'll take a while. I keep making the computer read parts back to me to remember where I am, to make sure it sounds close enough.

"Dont haff too. Eetch haz strawng theeng, muh-jore-ih-tee. But uh-ther theengs, kan goe uh-ther poynts."

"So there are things like bakers and merchants on Sampati, or computer technicians on Erkir. Makes sense. What's that look for?"

I've been glaring at the keypad, because I paid attention to my new watch while I pieced together my explanation. It took ages to create an inelegant, incomplete statement. These broken bits of language are so much work for so little, and I'm sick of it.

"Sownd stoo-pid."

Tiav puts his hand on mine, startling with the surge of warmth that comes with it. This time I notice his hand isn't rough like Kalkig's or shockingly soft like Jahmari's. Somewhere in-between.

"I know you are nothing close to stupid, Liddi." The confidence in his voice draws my eyes to his. I knew they were brown, like mine, but now I notice they're a more golden shade.

"Maybe it's not ideal, and I know you hate how long it takes, but it's what we've got."

It is, and so long as Minali effectively has my throat tied off, it's all I'm going to get. Instead of taking my hand back to write some more, I use my right. This one is short enough.

"*Moor tek. Pleez?*"

He smiles and squeezes my hand. "Okay, sure. I'll see what I can teach you, but I'm no technologist."

Neither am I, really. I'll learn whatever he can give me. Maybe whatever my brothers are doing on their side will solve everything. But maybe it won't.

I'm not going to leave that to chance.

*— — — *

We keep working on technological things, building some gadgets and taking others apart. Tiav continues to be surprised when I manage things without being able to read, and sometimes without waiting for him to explain. I can't figure out the words to make him understand, probably because I don't understand, either. I just know that the way Ferinne technology is designed flows for me. It does what I want it to do, like it knows, the way I always wished my projects would work.

I don't know whether I'm making progress. There's something about the crystalline components we work with. The way they align energy patterns. Since the Khua-spires are made of crystal, too, there might be a useful connection there, something that can help free my brothers. Even if I'm wrong about that, the experience of things making sense and *working* tickles my brain. I have to believe if I keep chasing that feeling, eventually the right idea will spark. My extreme focus on building assorted gadgets must seem strange to Tiav, but he doesn't question it. If anything, his smiles and patience hint that he finds it amusing with a side of fascinating.

At the end of another day of nonstop tinkering, I'm ready to keep going for a few more hours like we have the past few nights. Tiav has other ideas, because he clears the screen and picks up my tools.

"Jahmari once told me an old Crimna saying about obsession," he says, tucking the tools away. "It's fine to feed one, as long as you starve it once in a while, too."

I raise my eyebrows. That kind of talk would make me hungry, except we just ate.

"It's called taking a break. And I'll apologize in advance, because it means another ride in a streamer."

That changes my expression in a hurry. The only interest I have in streamers is taking one apart to see how it works.

His own expression is a combination of relaxed and eager as he offers me his hand. "Please? I want to show you something. I think you'll like it."

My resistance melts, and I take the offered hand. The work will wait.

The streamer ride is what it always is, if a little longer than usual, and I'm glad when it's over. Upon opening my eyes and getting out, however, I have no idea where we are. No sign of the buildings of Podra, and no sign of the usual hills and woods surrounding it, or the mountains in the distance. This place is flatter. I turn, and maybe I do see the mountains, much farther away than before. I can only see them at all because one of the smaller moons is peeking over the edge.

Tiav takes my hand again and guides me in the opposite direction. "Over here. Come on."

Several steps away from the streamer, I'm able to see enough to know the ground ends just ahead of us, because there's something else out there. The ocean. We're on a cliff above it. Tiav tries to lead me right to the edge, but I hold back. It's hundreds of feet down if it's an inch. His grip on my hand tightens as his thumb gently runs along mine, sending a shiver up my arm.

"It'll be okay, Liddi, I promise," he says. "And it's worth it, but you have to see only the ocean and the sky."

He's never lied to me yet, so I take the last few steps and carefully lower myself to sit with him, our feet just inches from the edge. A mix of vertigo and euphoria slides from my stomach up to my head, but then it settles, and I see what he means. Just the ocean and the sky, one reflecting the other, going on and on to the edge of the world.

It silences the constant "I-should-be-doing-*something*" in my head.

My hand is still in his, and neither of us makes any move to let go. I watch the waves undulate, lightly rippling the reflected moons and stars. The saltiness in the air carries all the way up here, and I imagine during the day the sounds of sea birds would surround us. It's beautiful, and I'm glad Tiav brought me. We have nothing like this on Sampati, nothing so peaceful and big. Maybe the view is old and boring to Tiav, though, because he's watching *me*. I don't have to check to know it. Being watched is familiar . . . but there's something less familiar in this.

The break in the silence is gentle, his voice just loud enough for me to hear. "I have to tell you something, Liddi. I want to kiss you."

That's enough to pull my gaze from the ocean. I look at him and try to figure out why he would say that. He doesn't know who I am. He doesn't know anything about me.

The corner of his mouth turns up into half a smile. "I'm getting pretty good at this game. You're thinking that I can't possibly know enough about you to want to kiss you. Other than how you look, maybe—which doesn't hurt, by the way—but there's more. You haven't needed your voice to show me who you are. The way you played *gedek*, how you light up when you're working on tech, even your frustration with writing... You also don't need your voice to tell me to back off if that's what you want."

Maybe all he doesn't know is a good thing. He doesn't know I'm set to be the richest girl in the Seven Points. He doesn't know I'm a disappointment to the Jantzen family name. He doesn't know how completely I'm failing my brothers. He wants to kiss me anyway.

I want him to kiss me.

So he does.

It's a blanket wrapping around me and a fire searing my veins at the same time. Sharing a breath, like his voice could be both of ours. His hand releases mine so it can find its way to my back, teasing my spine with its light touch. As I grip the front of his shirt, his other hand brushes against my cheek, then slides down to my neck. He's gentle, careful, like he doesn't want to break me. I draw him closer, but then his thumb slides over the implant in my throat, adding to its everpresent pressure, and I wince.

Tiav pulls back, his eyes overflowing with both curiosity and concern. "What's that?" He traces his fingers over the implant until I shy away. "Is that why you won't talk?"

I nod. Finally, I'm able to give him a bit of truth.

A smile breaks across his lips. "Then we can go to Jahmari. He'll know how to remove it, or one of the other doctors will."

No. No, we can't do that. Minali's no null-skull. She'll have some kind of fail-safe if anyone tries to remove or tamper with the device. I shake my head and ease Tiav back, but he catches my hands in his. They're warm and strong, tempting me with the lie that everything is okay when it isn't.

"Something bad will happen?" My nod brings a twist of despair to his eyes. "I hate this, Liddi. Not understanding. I'm good at the game, but I can't guess this. You're in danger at home and can't tell me what kind. You can't speak—someone's done something to you to make sure of it—and you can't tell me why. All I want is to help you, to fix it. To find who did this to you and make it right."

I wonder if he'd feel the same way if he knew how much the Khua are entwined in the situation. If he knew what it would mean to the Agnac. I remember what he said after I was arrested, how some people questioned his respect for the Khua. This would be much worse.

Tiav would have to choose the Khua over me. His duty, his life, his world. Just like I'd choose my brothers over him... if I had to.

He tangles his fingers in my hair, bringing me close. "Whatever it takes, I'll help you. I'll find a way to understand. I won't stop until I can hear your voice."

I take his face in my hands and kiss him again, hoping he hears the words.

I know.

When Fabin's warning about being late got no response from Liddi, he went to her room to see what was keeping her. His little sister hadn't even started getting ready for their evening at the theater. She sat on her bed, staring at the open closet, though it was unlikely she could see anything through the flood of tears.

"What's wrong?" he asked.

Liddi said nothing, just pointed to the wallscreen where a media-cast was queued.

Fabin started the playback but still didn't see the problem. Just a standard fluffy report on Liddi attending a fashion show with Anton.

Then he saw Liddi had enabled the chat-line tagged onto the end of the report, and the tears made a lot more sense.

"How could any designer let her come into their show looking like that?"

"She always looks like that. All the designers in the Seven Points together can't save her from those stick-arms."

"You'd think she'd learn something after thirteen years of being spoiled rotten."

"She's such a fake. I wish she'd just die already like her par—"

Fabin deactivated the screen and sat with Liddi, letting her cry a little longer. "Don't listen to them," he finally said. "Seriously, chat-lines are useless, and those people are jealous and full of hate. They think it's okay to hurt you because they don't know you—you're not a person to them."

"But the other kind is just as bad!" Liddi protested. "Pretending they like me but they don't. They don't know anything, they just want the attention. They don't know me, either."

A sigh was Fabin's only answer at first. "The Jantzen family legacy. People fawning over us on one hand, then celebrating every misstep on the other. And you have it worse than the rest of us. Since you inherit, they've decided you're fair game."

"There's nothing fair about it!"

He gave her a squeeze. "No, there's not. But there are good people out there who'll see past the flashy media-casts. I promise. Just keep being yourself, and they'll find you."

13

GOING BACK TO TIAV'S HOME is a little strange. Not that I don't have my own space—I've still never figured out exactly where his room is in the labyrinthine penthouse. But the one time Reb Vester made the mistake of kissing me, we didn't have to sleep under the same roof. And this wasn't a mistake, and my brothers aren't here, and I just don't know *what* it is.

We run into Shiin as soon as the elevator doors open. Tiav is still holding my hand. His mother's reaction is difficult to read.

"How did today go?" she asks.

Tiav glances at me before answering. "Good. Liddi definitely has a knack for electronics."

"I'm sure she does," Shiin says with a small, distracted smile. "I'm going to the Khua, but I'll be back soon. Sleep well."

Once she leaves, I turn to Tiav with the question in my eyes. Maybe a few questions.

"It's an Aelo thing. We can't sleep if something's bothering us. Especially my mother—she's the one who started the practice of really *asking* the Khua things beyond 'Do you mind blocking off the Lost Points?' Before that, Aelo were more passive 'listeners.' Not that asking always leads anywhere, but it's better. Feels more like moving forward."

I point to the door Shiin just went through.

"What's she going for now? Could be anything. Remember I told you the Khua have been more confusing than usual lately? My mother's set on unraveling it." He must catch the look in my eyes, because he quickly adds, "Don't worry, nothing to do with you. It started before you arrived."

That's a relief, but I was right—that's not the only question I have. When he figures out the other one, he slides an arm around my shoulders to hold me close. I'm surprised at how easily I relax into his embrace.

"She trusts me to make my own decisions. And I'm pretty sure she likes you. She'll be fine."

I hope that's true. I didn't make the best first impression. Shiin probably prefers her son *not* get involved with girls who get arrested.

Tiav still hasn't let me go when he sighs. "I should probably let you get some sleep, shouldn't I?" I glare up at him, remembering he was the first one to yawn before we headed back, and he laughs. "Okay, maybe you should let me get some sleep."

He walks me to my room, and I find myself lingering in his kiss good night before letting him go. For once I sleep without nightmares of my brothers. Silence doesn't suffocate me, and I'm not alone.

✳ – – – ✳

The next day is full of normal-but-not. Tiav and I work on my latest tinkering endeavor, but he sits a little closer to me. He talks and I write, but his patient smiles distract me from what I want to say.

After I've built my own live-comm unit—for no particular reason, because I certainly can't speak to use it—Tiav asks his usual question.

"What do you want to make next?"

"Vid cam. Lyke on Sam-pah-tee." Actually, I have an idea how to make my worst nightmare, one that's even smaller and doesn't buzz. I get a perverse sort of pleasure knowing the media-grubs will never see it.

Tiav looks at the few bits and pieces left on the desk. "We definitely need more parts, and probably better tools. I know a good place to look. Let's go."

We've been on shop runs before, sometimes all the way across Podra. This one is close enough to walk, which means an excuse for Tiav to hold my hand again.

People notice. Unsurprising since they always notice Tiav, but now they start to notice me. Some look curious. Some just smile. A pair of Haleians look like they can't be bothered to care, as long as we make space for them on the walkway.

The shop Tiav pointed out is just ahead, but so is something else. A large group of Agnac. They've seen us, and even with the differences in alien expressions, I can tell they're not happy.

"There she is!"

"I see her!"

The second shout comes from behind us. More Agnac approach from that side.

Approach very, very quickly.

In the time it takes for the shock to register in Tiav's eyes, they're on us. Too close, pressing in, I can't breathe. Tiav's arms lock around me as he demands to know what's going on, but the Agnac voices drown him out. Most of them use their own language, but I make out a few words.

"—trespasser—"

"—must stop—"

"—Lost Points—"

"—heathen!"

They know! They found out where I'm from, and their reaction is just as bad as I feared.

No, worse.

They grab at me, their rough hands scraping everything they touch, but I cling to Tiav. He's one of their Aelo. They'd never hurt him. With him I'm safe.

Someone behind me gets a grip on my arms and pries us apart. Someone else pushes Tiav away from me.

"Liddi!"

I want to call his name back, I want it more than anything, and the tightness in my throat barely stops me. Already I've lost sight of him in the mob of Agnac with their shaggy manes and odd noses, shoving me and shouting at me. Others on the street have realized what's happening, Ferinnes and Haleians and Crimna. Some shout for me to be left alone, while others hear what the Agnac say about me coming from Sampati and join in their outrage.

One of the Agnac takes a swing at me. I block and swing back, making contact and setting blood streaming from his four nostrils.

It was instinct, what my brothers taught me to do. But it wasn't smart.

Fists fly from every direction, and I can't block them all. One to the stomach, one to the back, then one clips my head and I can't count them anymore. Some keep hitting me, some hit each other. I bite my lip because I can't speak, I can't cry out, not even a little.

"Stop! Liddi!"

"Leave her alone!"

"Heathen!"

I spot an opening in the mob and break for it. Something clamps on to my ankles, and I go down hard. No more worrying about fists—my world is a sea of feet. Agnac kick better than they punch.

Do not cry out, Liddi, just don't cry out, not one noise, not one sound—

A weight crashes onto my leg. I bite down on my fist as a bone snaps.

Pain burns through me, I have to let it out but I can't I can't I can't.

I'm not sure if it's the strain or if someone kicks me in the head. Either way, I'm grateful when blackness creeps in.

The gratitude doesn't last long. I come around, still enveloped in chaos, but with a breath of space. That breath is getting bigger, too. No one's hitting or kicking me anymore.

Good thing, because the pain I've already got is enough to make me want to throw up. I fight back the tears, afraid if I let them go, my voice will go with them. Every place a punch or kick landed throbs with its own beat, and my leg...I'd rather have my leg cut clean off than this.

In all my years of dealing with media-grubs and crowded parties, nothing like this ever happened. No one on Sampati would dare. They can gossip about us all they want, they can lie about us and call us names, but the penalty for physically attacking a Jantzen would be too severe.

I don't know what the penalty here will be, but as I writhe in agony, I do spot some keepers hauling people away. Then I spot something that makes me want to give in to my urge to cry—Tiav's face when he sees my state.

"Liddi?" He rushes over and crouches by me, taking my hand. Finally I have somewhere to direct my desire to scream, though it might result in his hand getting crushed. "Sparks... what did they do to you? Can you get up?"

Oh, so definitely not. I point to my leg. I've broken it before, so I know this feeling.

"Sparks," he says again. The way he says it sounds like the kind of word my brothers tell me not to get caught saying on vid-cam. Tiav looks around desperately, his eyes lighting up when they find something. "Jahmari!"

"On my way, on my way. Liddi! Oh, dear. This is more than a few scratches, isn't it?" The Crimna doctor settles on my other side and begins to assess the damage, but Tiav interrupts him.

"Painkiller first. Now. She can't hold her voice in forever like this."

Jahmari's head tilt reads as curious, but I'm just glad Tiav

figured that much out. My bone-splitting grip was probably his first clue.

For the painkiller, I expect an infusion or maybe injection. Instead, Jahmari takes a tiny device from his kit and attaches it to my temple. The edges soften instantly. I still know I hurt, and I have no intention of moving, but I don't have the desire to perform my own amputation anymore.

The doctor returns to cataloguing my injuries. I'm not sure what exactly he's doing. Or what anyone's doing. The motion around me is different. Everything is. Slower and faster and hard to understand.

That device "fuzzied" more than just the pain, Liddi.

One corner of my brain keeps enough sharpness to stop me from speaking, which is good, because I'd really like to say "What?" a lot, but I shouldn't. Things move. I move. Jahmari and Tiav are still with me, though, in some kind of vehicle. Probably a form of streamer, but I can't see outside, so I don't care. The two of them talk, and their words swim over me.

"I was on my way to the Nyum when I saw the unpleasant-ness. What happened?"

"The Agnac found out where she came from."

"How? Your mother was very clear about the confidentiality of that information."

"Oh, I'm pretty sure I know how."

Silence, then more moving. The vehicle roof turns into the sky turns into a ceiling. It flows past my eyes like a river, then stops. Hospital? Blinking lights and energy beams, Jahmari looking over everything on his scanners, Tiav looking at me. Just me.

"What's this?" Jahmari asks.

Tiav squeezes my hand again. "I don't know, but it's why she won't talk. She seemed afraid something bad would happen if you removed it."

They found the implant.

"Ah, she may be right." Jahmari sounds disappointed. "Quite a complicated little thing, may have all kinds of triggering mechanisms. Shame, shame. And look, here's another one, quite well hidden."

"What's that one for?"

Reporting my death to Tarix, should it happen, but I can't tell them that.

"No idea. There, that bone should be finished mending. Let's see."

Jahmari ticks off a list of other injuries I don't want to think about, particularly since he's saying they've been fixed. No use worrying about them now.

"Aelo, we brought him, as requested."

I don't know that voice, don't know what it means, but Jahmari ignores it. "You shouldn't need this anymore," the doctor concludes, removing the device from my temple.

The returning sharpness of the world jars me like being dunked in ice water. Not entirely pleasant, except the pain's down to a dull ache. That's good. I can also see clearly enough to notice Tiav has disappeared from my side.

"What were you thinking, you—!"

There he is, or his voice at least. Not that I've ever heard anything like that tone coming from him before, not even when he was angry with me. And if I'm not mistaken, the last word was in Agnacki. I push myself up to see what's happening.

What's happening is Tiav standing nose-to-nose with Kalkig, who has a pair of keepers flanking him.

"You know what I was thinking," the Agnac counters. "She's dangerous, and you've become a fool."

That's the same old argument, but Tiav doesn't have the same old response.

He punches his best friend.

What follows is so interspersed with Agnacki words on both sides, I can't make sense of either of them. I don't really have to. Kalkig obviously wants to strike back at Tiav but doesn't dare with the keepers on him, and Tiav obviously wants his taunting shoves to goad the Agnac into tangling anyway.

The room is a bomb, and the little parts are clicking into place for a massive explosion.

I don't like explosions—they're Ciro's territory. I grab a piece of equipment from a bedside table, hope it's as sturdy as it looks, and drop it. The resulting thud does its job, silencing the boys and drawing attention to me, but I can't say anything. It seems unlikely Tiav will be able to guess what I'm thinking when *I'm* not sure what I'm thinking in the first place.

Then behind the boys, Shiin steps into the doorway.

"Liddi's right," she says. "That's quite enough."

Sure, that's probably what I was thinking. It gets Tiav to back off a few steps from Kalkig, but his temper hasn't cooled much.

"I don't think it's anywhere near enough," he says.

"Kalkig defied my instructions, betraying my confidence," Shiin says. Kalkig ducks his head like he did before, clearly more comfortable defying Tiav than the primary Aelo herself. "He will face consequences for that."

Tiav's jaw is so tense, it's a wonder he can form words. "He did more than defy an Aelo, Mother. Liddi could've been killed."

Shiin puts both hands on her son's shoulders. "I know, Tiav," she says softly. "Please."

It's such a maternal gesture, a tone I haven't heard in her voice before, not calling him by his whole name . . . like they should be alone, just family. The empty spaces next to me pull with an ache for my own parents like I haven't felt in years.

The words work. Tiav returns to my side, and the keepers take Kalkig away again.

"I'm sorry," Tiav says, touching my arm. "How are you feeling?"

I point and flex my toes, testing the formerly broken leg. It feels like someone fastened the bone together with rivets, but several days ago. Not perfect, but not terrible.

"She'll be fine," Jahmari supplies, picking up the instrument I dropped. "Sore for a few days, certainly, but fine."

"I'm glad to hear that, but I'm afraid Kalkig's actions have had a deeper impact than just Liddi's well-being, Shiin says."

I don't like the sound of that, and neither does Tiav, judging by the sharpness in his eyes. "The council?" he asks.

"Yes, the council. The senior councillors have kept Liddi's origin secret, but now that it's widely known, they feel they must address the issue officially. Liddi's been summoned to the capital."

By the time Liddi was thirteen, she'd visited all the Seven Points except one. Concerts on Yishu, mountain climbing on Erkir, the beach house on Pramadam . . . she'd even been to Tarix and Banak. The former had been a day trip with Fabin to hear a lecture on ethics versus necessity in the modern age, and the latter a week to help Vic install a new set of training simulators at one of the military academies.

But she never went to Neta. The boys did sometimes when new laws that would impact the company were being considered, but that was rare. As Durant said, there was nothing to see on Neta except people arguing in circles and skillfully dodging questions by weaving minimal truths into their answers.

Definitely nothing to interest Liddi. She got enough of all that from the media-casls.

14

MOST EVERYONE INVOLVED in the riot has been rounded up and taken to the detention facility, and the hospital has an underground parking area so we don't have to go outside. That doesn't stop a team of six keepers from escorting us to the streamer we'll take to the capital. I'm not sure whether they're more concerned with someone attacking me or Tiav. As long as they're shielding both of us, I'll take it.

Shiin can't come with us. There has to be at least one Aelo in Podra at all times, so it's either her or Tiav. I'd be a lot more anxious without him with me, so maybe that's half the point.

Tiav tells me Podra is the center of all things Aelo- and Khua-related, and the capital—Chalu—is where the actual government sets up shop. Seems sensible enough. After all, Neta is where the Seven Points government is located, but no one bothers with them unless we have to. Sampati's year is the standard for all the Points. Government power versus cultural power.

Jahmari, however, does come along, ostensibly to make sure he didn't miss anything in patching me up. Shiin tries to tell him it isn't necessary, but he insists.

It's the second time someone's said Jahmari doesn't need to bother with something. Just like when Luo said the cuts on my arm were beneath his concern. Jahmari's more important than just a doctor, but no one's ever said why.

And he knew about me from the beginning. When Tiav said the Agnac found out where I came from, Jahmari knew Shiin had made it confidential. It wasn't news to him.

Thoughts about Jahmari aren't enough to keep me distracted during the lengthy streamer ride to Chalu. The gut-churning contradiction of what I see and what I feel is even worse with the lingering echoes of being trampled. Tiav stays close, stroking my hair.

It's something my family would do, but Tiav definitely isn't family. The mix of familiar and new burns through me, but it still isn't distracting enough.

I haven't seen my brothers in days, I haven't made real progress in helping them, and now I have to worry about government officials and being attacked in the street. It isn't good. That's the real distraction from the streamer ride, as the anxiety tightens on my lungs.

We reach Chalu, and I learn something new. The vehicle *can* move at a normal speed. Jahmari slows it down as we enter the city.

And it really *is* a city.

Buildings stretch like fingers reaching for the clouds, lights and signs and symbols decorating them like jewelry. Streamers dance along the streets, far too many to safely zip along as usual, even with the computers managing traffic. And people—all Ferinne's different types of people everywhere.

Except Izim. I've heard the alien race mentioned but still haven't met any, and everyone I see still fits the races I *have* met. I take Tiav's com-tablet and put in my earpiece.

"Eye-zimm?"

"No, there aren't any here. We communicate with them, but they mostly keep to themselves."

We wind through the streets, arriving at a particular building, but Tiav puts a hand on my arm to keep me in place. Only Jahmari gets out.

"Good luck, my friends," he says. "Tiav, keep me informed, yes? I'll see you soon."

The door closes, and Tiav taps a command for the streamer's next destination. I take his hand so he'll look at me, and he guesses the question.

"The council wants to see you at the Nyum right away. No delays."

I want to ask what to expect there, but I don't think he knows. The ride to the center of the city isn't long enough for me to form the question anyway. We arrive, and the door opens.

I can't get out.

People crisscross along the walkways, a sea tangled in conflicting currents. I can't go out into it, can't get pulled under, kicked and crushed and buried alive. Again.

"Liddi, what's wrong? Slow down and breathe."

My panic's grip is too tight to do as Tiav says; it constricts my lungs so the more I try to breathe, the less air I get.

He takes my face in his hands, forcing me to turn away from

the potential nightmare outside and look at him instead. His eyes are steady and strong as they lock on mine, and the warmth of his hands battles the cold terror inside me.

"I'm so sorry. You shouldn't have to do this so soon, and I wish we could've said no. But I promise, no one will hurt you again."

Something in his words eases the vise on my lungs. I tap one finger against his chest.

His expression relaxes. "No, they won't hurt me, either. Come on, it's not that far to the door. You can do it."

Kalkig isn't here. He's miles and miles away in a detention facility. With that realization, my fear dissipates and I finally breathe. We get out of the streamer, and nothing terrible happens. No tidal wave of people trying to crush me. I feel silly for letting panic paralyze me like that, but as Tiav takes my hand and squeezes it, he doesn't seem to think so.

He's worried, and not just about my emotional state. He doesn't want me to see it, but I can read his face almost as well as he can mine—and much better than I can read Ferinne writing. In just the short walk from the streamer to the Nyum, I feel another difference. Not from Tiav—from everyone else on the street.

They're watching me. They know who I am. Word has already spread.

It's like being home, but there's no comfort in the feeling, even with these onlookers seeming distinctly more apprehensive than violent. I spend the last few steps mourning my anonymity. It was nice being just another face, one people might look at because they liked my eyes, or look away from because they thought my nose was ugly, but nothing more. For a while,

I knew what it was like to be a person others could take time to get to know. Not that it stopped Kalkig from forming an instant opinion of me, but Tiav has kept a pretty open mind all along.

Now it's different. Now I'm a very particular face, but one without a voice.

The Nyum in the capital is much different from the one in Podra. Tiav explains it softly as we walk in. There's a senior council with one representative from each species, then a larger council with more delegates. Each of the five species—even the ever-absent Izim—has its own chamber for meetings surrounding the much larger hall where they can all meet together. We go to the main hall, and while it's not full, it's also nowhere near empty. At least, the sections for the Ferinnes, Agnac, Haleians, and Crimna aren't. Each holds a handful of very different people.

And those people are already arguing. Even if some of the aliens weren't going at it in their native languages, I wouldn't be able to understand. Too many voices, too much emotion.

Tiav won't let go of my hand. Good thing, because I don't want him to. Unless it's to let me run back the way we came. Rooms of powerful people aren't my strong suit.

What is *your strong suit, Liddi?*

The members of the senior council sit on the stand at the front of the hall. They're not arguing. They're not saying anything. The Ferinne lifts his hand to signal someone, and a chime sounds from all around us. Immediate silence follows.

"Tiav'elo, thank you for bringing our guest," the Ferinne says. A few Agnacki grunts follow his use of the word *guest*, but the man ignores them. "I'm sure you have things to attend to, so you may go."

"No, thank you, Voand," Tiav says. "My mother has assigned

me the duty of watching after Liddi, and I won't leave her here alone. She can't speak for herself."

"Ah, Shiin'alo didn't mention that. Why can't she?"

His hand tightens on mine as he glances at me. "I don't know." A limited truth, since he knows what keeps me from speaking, but not why it's there.

"We can arrange a computer for her to write her thoughts."

The Crimna chairwoman cuts in. She's a lot like Jahmari—old and young, graceful and sharp all at the same time. "Your Lost Points forewent written language many years ago, did they not?"

"She's been working on learning it," Tiav says. "But it's not easy, and it takes a long time for the computer to read off the sounds until she finds the ones she wants. Time I'm sure the council doesn't have."

Voand sighs. "Very well. Both of you have a seat over here. Questions will be difficult."

"Questions are unnecessary." The voice comes from the gallery, one of the Agnac. "We know the truth, that she comes from the heathen worlds. She has been told too much, and she endangers the Khua."

"And I do not like the course of action you suggest," Voand says. "Ymana?"

"Nor do we," the Crimna confirms. "Berk?"

The Haleian heaves his shoulders in a shrug. "I'm not sure we know enough yet to like or dislike anything."

Tiav doesn't ask what the Agnac have suggested. He probably knows already. After what happened in Podra today, it's not hard to guess.

A flame of anger kicks through my chest. I don't like all these people talking about me without being able to answer. Don't like their words bouncing back and forth between them as though I'm not here. Tiav's going to have to speak *for* me, and I don't like that any better than when my brothers did it. But there's no better alternative. So I sit with Tiav, the center of attention yet virtually sidelined. He still has my hand, and I *am* glad for that. Being alone in this would be too much.

"We've managed to contain some of the specifics of Liddi's arrival and *activities* since," Voand says, "but we have to think about what will happen when others find out. They will eventually."

"By 'activities,' you mean her violation of the Khua?"

Tiav's voice startles me, so strong and clear, more than before when he was simply stating why he would stay. Even if I *could* speak for myself, my voice would probably shake in front of these people.

Voand looks down, consulting notes on a com-tablet, maybe. "Yes, she remained with a Khua for several hours before she could be retrieved, correct?"

"She didn't know what she was doing. She's from Sampati. We all know that the Lost Points don't understand the Khua as we do—that's the whole point of them being lost. But just because they don't believe doesn't mean they can't learn. Since we told her the law, she's respected it. As this regards the Khua, the situation should remain in the purview of the Aelo, *not* this council."

The Agnac senior councillor leans onto the table in front of him with his long arms. "We are not satisfied with Shiin'alo's handling of 'the situation' thus far and cannot leave it to her any longer." Tiav flinches, so slightly I doubt anyone else sees it, but otherwise doesn't falter. "She has given us no information on the only questions that matter—how the heathen got here, and why she has come."

All evidence of flinching is gone as Tiav finally releases my hand so he can stand, but he doesn't stop there. He strides across the space separating us from the council, staring down the Agnac.

"We will not answer any questions so long as you keep calling her that. Just hours ago, she was nearly killed in an unprovoked attack instigated by *your* people, Oxurg. That's exactly the type of action we've been taught to expect from the so-called heathens, not our own friends, so I will not stand for the use of that word anymore."

That quickly, my anger at my own silence cools. Tiav knows these people and their cultures, and young as he is, he has authority I don't grasp. He can advocate for me in ways I couldn't for myself.

A familiar gesture answers Tiav's outburst—a slight ducking of Oxurg's head, though he certainly doesn't look happy. "My apologies, Aelo."

Ymana raises a finger to call for the floor. "I can't help but notice, Tiav'elo, that you hardly seem objective."

No, he's not objective. And I'm glad he's not.

"It isn't my duty to be objective. It's my duty to observe and to use both my head and my heart. And it's been my duty to get to know Liddi despite the fact she can't speak. I don't know everything, but I do know she is not the evil the Lost Points are meant to be."

"Naturally, we respect your insight on her character," Voand says. "The questions raised, however, are good ones. Why is she here?"

Tiav returns to my side, and I see the tiniest cracks in his confidence. Not doubts. But maybe anxiety. He knows I haven't told him all I could, and while he accepts my reasons—for now—it's another matter when it comes to world leaders.

"She's in danger on Sampati. I don't know what kind, except that other people are also threatened. And I'm confident that anything she's done—or not done—has been her best effort to keep people safe."

"And we are to be satisfied with such vague reasons?" Oxurg counters.

I read the question in Tiav's eyes—can I explain now, suffering through the effort of writing it out? The answer is no way. Not after what happened in Podra, not here with the Agnac already certain I'm the embodiment of evil, not when they know more about the Khua than I do. Not even when it's putting Tiav in such an awful position. I can't risk them taking some kind of action to hurt my brothers, and I don't know that Tiav could stop them.

"For now, it's the best she can offer," Tiav says. "And if lives are in the balance, I won't question it. The Khua haven't been clear, but they point toward trusting her, too."

I didn't know that. Neither did anyone else, judging by the murmurs that rumble through the hall.

The senior council members turn to confer with each other, and the various delegations continue their own deliberations. It seems to take forever. Long enough that Tiav takes my hand again. Finally, Voand waves the others off.

"This is simply too complicated a matter to take action in such short order. Liddi will remain in the confines of the primary Aelo quarters here in Chalu until we can determine the best course. Tiav'elo, again, thank you. You are both excused."

As Tiav takes me back out of the main hall, his eyes stay resolutely straight ahead. A twitch in his jaw tells me he's holding something back. I wait until the door to the hall has closed behind us, then rub my thumb along his. He looks down at me and exhales some of the tension.

"It could've been worse, Liddi. A lot worse. They could've forced the Aelo out altogether, sent me home. But this still isn't good."

I keep the question in my eyes, asking him why.

"Because you can't leave Chalu until the council makes a decision. How efficient is the government for the Seven Points?"

Now I know what he means.

I could easily be stuck here for the rest of my life. And that really isn't going to work for me.

Liddi knew she shouldn't have pitched a fit when it was time to leave their vacation at the beach. And she shouldn't have been surprised when she turned on a media-cast the next day and found herself headlining it.

"Eight-year-old Liddi Jantzen was not happy about leaving the family's Emerald Coast property yesterday."

"And Vic Jantzen has the bruises to prove it."

"This childish display certainly makes one wonder how she'll handle the pressure of an entire—"

The voice-over cut off when Luko deactivated the screen. Liddi was going to tell him off and get him to turn it back on, but the look in his eyes stopped her. Sad and worried. So she stayed calm and asked a simple question when he sat next to her.

"What pressure do they mean?"

"Vic and Durant won't be happy if I tell you," he said. A long pause left Liddi thinking Luko wouldn't risk his brothers' wrath. Then he sighed. "But better me than the media-grubs. Dad's company . . . when he died, he left it to you."

His words twisted into an indecipherable knot in her gut. "Me? But Durant's the oldest. I thought the oldest was supposed to get things. Or all of us."

"We do all have a piece, but you have the biggest, the controlling share. The rest of us make a committee that'll run things until you're eighteen."

She hugged her knees to her chest. She was too little to run

a company, and she couldn't conceive that even at eighteen she'd be big enough. "I still don't get why."

"Dad worried that if we all had an equal part, we'd compete for control, fight with each other. Or if he put one of us in charge, the others would resent it. He was probably right— you've seen how we go after each other."

"You won't resent me?"

"No, we could never resent you. You're the one person we would all just want to help. And that's what we'll do."

15

THE PRIMARY AELO QUARTERS turn out to be in the building where we dropped off Jahmari. It's not quite the penthouse in Podra, but spacious and comfortable as temporary prisons go. Jahmari asks for the blow-by-blow as soon as we walk in. Tiav gives it to him while I work on spelling something out.

"Dee-sih-zhun kood bee wuht?"

"What could the council decide to do with you? Sparks, Liddi—argh, Jahmari, I know. 'An Aelo shouldn't use such language.' Sorry."

So I was right. *Sparks* is definitely swearing. Maybe a derogatory word for the Khua.

Tiav can't stand still. He paces, runs a hand through his hair, a caged tiger ready to attack anything that gets too close. An instinct urges me to calm him down, but I don't know how.

"They could force you back to Sampati," he finally says. "Or keep you in confinement forever. Or leave you free, but never allow you to go home."

The world turns to a winter freeze around me. Never go home? I don't want to go *now*, with Minali threatening me, with my brothers trapped. But it's always been in my mind that *eventually* I'll go back. My brothers and I will find a way to free them and stop Minali and I'll go home.

But Tiav's home is here, and the thought of never seeing him again is almost as cold.

Nothing fits.

Jahmari sits calmly, the only calm thing left in the universe, I'm pretty sure. His eyes explore mine, find what they're looking for. "There's someone you care about on Sampati, someone you couldn't bear to leave behind forever."

Tiav's tiger-trance breaks. He stops, looks at me with terror radiating from him. "Someone like...?"

Like Reb Vester wishes he could be? Definitely not. I shake my head, but Tiav and Jahmari both know there's something. I can give them the tiniest piece of truth I dare.

"Bruh-therrs."

"Liddi...you have family? They must be so worried about you."

Not as worried as I am about them. I can't keep that worry from my face, and Tiav can't miss it.

"They're the people in danger. The ones who could die if you don't make the right choices."

I glance at Jahmari, but if Tiav trusts him, so can I. I nod.

"How many?"

Eight fingers, and Tiav can't completely hide his surprise. It's a big family, I know. Explaining that a set of twins and one of triplets boosted our numbers would be too complicated.

He chooses not to say anything about it. Instead he crosses

the room and wraps his arms around me. Steady and warm and safe. All the lies I need to tell myself to keep going another day. He doesn't bother making empty promises. We both know there are no promises to be made. I can't go home now; he doesn't want me to leave. I can't stay on Ferinne forever; I don't want to leave him.

The contradictions and paradoxes tie themselves in knots around my gut.

"There's another option the council could go with," Jahmari says softly.

Tiav's muscles tighten through his arms and back, holding me closer, and his voice matches. "They wouldn't." I look up, willing him to explain, but his eyes are locked on the Crimna physician. "There hasn't been an execution in ages."

My breath catches. I knew my life might be on the line with Minali, but not here.

"Yet the laws permitting them remain," Jahmari says.

"She hasn't done anything to warrant it."

"If we can't determine how she reached us from the Lost Points, an argument could be made."

"Only by the Agnac. The others won't allow it."

Jahmari nods. "I hope you're right."

So do I. As little good as I'm doing my brothers now, I'll do even less if I'm dead.

✹ – – – ✹

Waiting for the council to make up their minds means we have nothing better to do than continue working on gadgets and making small talk at the rate of three questions and answers per hour if I have to spell things out. Tiav generally sticks to things I can answer easily, or lets me ask my own questions. If I don't, his anxiety returns. Then silence is Tiav's companion as much as mine, the only words passing between us coded in the way he holds my hand.

I'm not sure what Tiav thinks about when silence fills the room, but I keep thoughts of the council far from my mind. If it comes down to it, I'll escape, find a Khua, get back to one of the other Points. Somehow. Letting the council stand in my way isn't an option.

I keep trying to find something in the gadgets, in the way the crystalline tech works, that'll help free my brothers. The connections seem to click in my head one by one, but I can't see where they're going. Mostly I get distracted by the watch on my wrist, reminding me how time is ticking away. Time for Minali's plan to move closer to completion, time for my brothers' imprisonment to become irreversible.

Those things are much more important than anything the politicians might be saying.

He doesn't say so, but I'm pretty sure Tiav has bigger things on his mind, too. Especially after a live-comm with Shiin. The conversation happens in another room and takes a very long time. When he comes back out, he makes a bigger effort to hide the stress. He fails. I distract him with a wave scanner I took apart.

Jahmari, meanwhile, is much busier than we are. He flits in and out of the apartment several times. Most of his time with us is spent tapping away on a com-tablet of his own. While he's gone again on the second day, I decide to take the time to ask Tiav a question.

"Juh-maw-ree im-pohr-tent wye?"

Tiav sits back in his chair and smiles—the first smile I've seen from him since before the street attack. "Ah, you noticed that. There are a couple of answers. He's the top physician on all Ferinne. They'd like him to live here in the capital, but he chooses to live in Podra because our province has the largest concentration of Khua. He likes being close to them, and he's supported my mother and her work for a long time. Without his influence, she might not have been chosen as primary Aelo. He travels wherever he's needed, but he always comes back to Podra."

That makes sense with what I've seen. The cuts on my arm definitely didn't need the best doctor on the whole planet. Tiav said there were a couple of answers, though, and I'm pretty sure all that was just one of them.

"That's why he's important to Ferinnes, but for the Crimna there's more. I don't understand all of it, but I'm told if he stayed on their homeworld, he'd be their leader. He chose a different path. They call him something in their language, which is much more difficult to learn than Agnacki, by the way. The best translation they can give me is 'Khua in Crimna form.' Because he sees the heart of things, beyond the medical."

I think back to my cell in the detention facility. The way he sat with me for just a few minutes and seemed to understand my impatience. My recklessness.

A man that perceptive, and he's on my side. Yet it also sounds like he reveres the Khua. I wonder where he would stand on the "defilement" issue.

Maybe I'm better off not knowing.

Almost in answer to that dark thought, the door opens and

Jahmari enters. He doesn't go far, though, just stands there as the door closes behind him again.

"Tiav, the Izim are coming to Ferinne."

The gravity of his statement is obvious, but I don't feel it as much as Tiav does. He stands and approaches the doctor. "What do you mean? The Izim never come here, not in person."

"Not never, but rarely," Jahmari says. "You're too young to remember the last time they visited."

"Does my mother know?"

"Yes, she contacted me so I could relay the message to you."

I get up and join them. Tiav looks down at me, and I try to make my questions clear. He takes a moment to make his guess, never in a hurry.

"Why don't they ever come here? Besides not having much need to, the environment doesn't suit them."

"Indeed," Jahmari adds. "Even when they do visit, they don't typically come to the surface. They do better on planets like Crimna."

Tiav's still studying me. "You have another question. Why are they coming now?" I nod. "Good, because that's my question, too."

The doctor stretches his arms straight down. I think the gesture is the Crimna equivalent of a sigh. "Because of Liddi, of course. Don't make that face, dear. You arrived, that event had consequences, which led to other events, so on and so on. You can't help that."

"But what do they want with Liddi?" Tiav asks.

"I suppose you can ask them yourself. They want to talk to you once their ship's in orbit."

"When will that be?"

"Any minute now, I believe."

That soon? No, that doesn't make any sense. None at all. I go back to the computer and activate the drawing program. I think I can draw this faster than I can piece together all the words. I slide the program to the largest screen on the wall, drawing a quick Eight Points icon on one end, then a general planet-looking thing on the other end. I look to Tiav and gesture at the distance between the two. He glances at Jahmari before answering.

"Yes, Izima is a long way from here, but their technology makes the distance less of a problem. That technology is how we're all able to travel between planets. It...I'm sorry. I don't think I'm allowed to talk about how it works."

That makes sense. Someday I'll return to the "heathens"—hopefully—and the Ferinnes don't want me helping them get off Sampati and the other Points.

Sense or not, it stings. Because it means Tiav knows he can't completely trust me, no matter how much he wants to.

The computer chimes, and Tiav taps some commands. My drawing disappears from the screen, replaced by a person's face. I can't say if it's a man or woman. Maybe the Izim don't even have gender the way we do. Either way, the suit the person wears obscures any hints. It's metallic and includes a dark face shield, yet it doesn't seem bulky or cumbersome. It's sleek and beautiful, almost like an exoskeleton, fitting every edge and curve perfectly.

"You are the Aelo who found the visitor?" the Izim says. The voice is smooth and calm, a voice that could chase away nightmares.

"Yes. I'm Tiav'elo."

"A pleasure, Tiav'elo. I am Quain. And this is the visitor?"

Tiav takes a half step closer to me. "Her name's Liddi."

"Liddi. An honor."

Jahmari draws a sharp breath. I'm not sure why. Quain's easy voice draws me back to the screen.

"We are very anxious to speak with you. To know of your life on Sampati and what brought you to Ferinne."

"We're all anxious for that, Quain," Jahmari says. "But Liddi can't speak. Working with writing frustrates her and takes a great deal of time."

A gentle hiss comes either from Quain or the suit. "Unfortunate, indeed. Perhaps if you come aboard, we can find more efficient means."

Just as I think that there's something off in Quain's extremely good manners, Tiav's hand snaps around my wrist, too tight, like a reflex he isn't controlling. I check his expression. Difficult to read. Maybe he's anxious at the idea of going on an Izim ship. Maybe his heart just jumped at the idea of finally being able to communicate, to get answers.

Mine did. Actually, my heart split in half and jumped in two directions. One half leapt at the thought of finally getting around this barrier, this restraint. The other plummeted. Without the excuse of my silence, secrets will be much harder to keep. All this time, and I'm still not entirely sure what I should and shouldn't tell Tiav. What might condemn my brothers and what might save them.

Instead of stinging, the thought aches. I guess I don't trust him completely yet, either.

"I'm afraid it's not an option," Tiav says. "Liddi isn't allowed to leave. House arrest, you could say."

Quain's faceplate is irritating. No eyes to read, no expression

to decipher. The voice remains smooth, offering little. "Why is this?"

"It's a condition of the Agnac Hierarchy."

"Unacceptable."

Two heartbeats pass, and suddenly the screen splits—Quain on one side, Oxurg from the Agnac on the other. Before anyone says anything, it splits again, bringing Voand and Ymana. No sign of the Haleian leader. Maybe he's busy. Maybe no one cares because he never has anything to say.

"Oxurg, why are you punishing the visitor?" the Izim asks.

"She broke the law repeatedly, not least when she violated the Khua to come here in the first place. She has made continued attempts to interfere with them. We must protect the Khua from her, and if I had my way, we would kill her and be done."

"Violated the Khua? How do you mean?"

Tiav uses his hold on my wrist to pull me a little closer. I remember one of the few things he's said about the Izim so far, that their regard for the Khua is more like worship, the same as the Agnac. Oxurg's intent is obvious. He wants Quain to take his side, to try to persuade the others that it's dangerous to keep me around.

If *two* races push for my execution, I'm not sure I like my chances.

"The Aelo ensured the heathens would be kept far from us, barred from the Khua, many years ago. This girl attacked the Khua, breached the seals. Her mere presence is an assault."

Quain's head tilts. "That is your interpretation? It is a puzzling one."

Voand and Ymana have been silent, but the Ferinne leader speaks now. "How so, Quain?"

"Because it presupposes anyone could defy the Khua in such a manner, through sheer force."

"She is not supposed to be here, yet she is," Oxurg protests. "What other explanation is there?"

"A very simple one. The Khua allowed her to pass."

Several months after meeting Joon at the Igara party, Liddi got an itchy, irksome feeling in her gut, like something was off. She'd hardly spent any time in the workshop lately, she was always so busy going out with her friend. At this rate, it would be another year with nothing to debut at the Tech Reveal. Anxiety gnawed at her, but no matter how she tried to set aside time to work, it just didn't happen.

Then Liddi realized what it was. Every time Joon live-commed, she talked but didn't listen. If Joon wanted to go shopping, they went. If Liddi said she was busy, Joon talked her out of being busy. If Joon came over, they spent all their time watching media-casts and trying on everything they'd ever bought during their shopping trips.

Being Joon's friend was exhausting.

With the next live-comm, Liddi decided to put her foot down. "Sorry, I can't," she said. "I have to spend some time in the workshop. You should come over, though. I'll show you what I'm working on."

"Are any of your brothers home?"

Emil was just passing through with a sandwich from the kitchen, out of the live-comm's visual range. His eyes widened and he shook his head.

The gnawing feeling twisted into a sharp-toothed growl. Liddi didn't know how she'd missed it before. Joon always asked if her brothers were home. If Emil wasn't, she didn't bother coming.

"If all you want is to flirt with my brother, live-comm him, not me."

"Oh, come on, Liddi, you know it isn't like that."

Joon's mouth said one thing, but her eyes said another, and Liddi didn't miss it this time. "Find someone else to leech off of, Joon. Good-bye."

The end of the live-comm signaled the end of the so-called friendship.

Two days later, the media-casts started. *The Insecurities of Liddi Jantzen.* Things only Joon knew, because Liddi hadn't told anyone else. Things that made the Triad worry because even they hadn't known. Her infatuations and fixations, her anxieties and fears . . . the fact that she still dreamed about her parents sometimes and woke up crying.

It was clear what Joon had gotten from the friendship. Her profile was at an all-time high.

All Liddi got was a vow never to trust anyone outside of her family again.

16

I LOSE TRACK OF the conversation at that point, because all four leaders talk at the same time. Technically, I think that makes it not a conversation anymore. Oxurg shouts over everyone, half his words in Agnacki, something about Quain's assertion being "blasphemic," whatever that means. Voand's and Ymana's words are lost under his, and I can barely make out Quain's calm voice at all.

This is certainly government productivity at its best.

Tiav must have a similar thought, because he taps something on his com-tablet. The mouths on the screen keep moving—other than Quain's—but no sound comes out. The muting must affect everyone, because after a moment, true silence extends its arms to all of them. No more talking.

"It's bad enough Liddi can't speak for herself," Tiav says. "We don't need to argue as if she isn't standing right here. Personally, as an Aelo, I think Quain's theory sounds possible. Liddi, do you remember anything about your passage that might mean the Khua let you through?"

I remember the barrier, how we pushed through it. All the pain and effort it took. If anything, it felt like we broke it down through force of will. If the Khua really were some kind of self-aware entity that could say, "Sure, come on in, can I get you something to drink?" then what it offered me seems less than hospitable.

That's not the answer Tiav wants, though. It's the answer giving credence to the Agnac argument, that I somehow tampered with the Khua. It's what Kalkig's been saying all along. And maybe what I felt was because I was trying to bring my brothers through with me. Maybe. Maybe not.

So I tell half a lie with an uncertain shrug.

The leaders have calmed enough for Tiav to un-mute them, and Voand has something to offer.

"I don't know if Quain is correct, but I do believe something complicated is at work here. Shiin'alo has inquired of the Khua several times, trying to find answers about Liddi. She's been unable to make any sense of what they tell her. If they allowed Liddi through, they've not made that apparent, nor have they indicated she somehow overpowered them. Not clearly, at any rate."

Tiav's posture shifts and his eyes falter for just a moment. I remember what he said about the Khua being extra confusing lately; I get the impression his mother doesn't fail to make sense of them very often.

"The Aelo told us you are keeping Liddi under 'house arrest,'" Quain says. "If we are correct that the Khua have a purpose for her, she should not be confined."

Ymana nods. "This will take time to unravel, and we cannot treat her like a prisoner without cause. Jahmari?"

The physician has been silently attentive through all of this. "Yes, yes, I quite agree. Once Liddi was informed of the law, there have been no further problems. Nothing warranting this type of treatment at all."

"Then I'm taking her back to Podra," Tiav says. "You can contact us just as easily there."

Oxurg grunts. "I still say it is a foolish theory, and we will watch closely. If she violates the law again, we will demand action."

It strikes me—*I'm* not like Minali, knowing a particular truth that others won't listen to or understand. The Agnac are. Single-minded, blind, and obsessed when new information threatens to change what they *thought* was truth.

I'm not sure whether that makes me more angry at both Minali and the Agnac or just sad for anyone who lives like that.

The screen goes black, and the tension drains from Tiav's body. "The Izim, Jahmari, really? I don't like them having this much interest in Liddi."

"You're welcome to talk to Quain again and say so. See what kind of response you get."

Tiav groans and collapses onto a couch. "No, thank you."

He looks exhausted and I don't understand why. I get his attention, gesture to the part of the screen Quain appeared on, and point to Jahmari while imitating the way he gasped earlier.

"Ah, yes," Jahmari says. "My apologies for not controlling myself better. You see, Quain said it was 'an honor' to meet you. I've been around a long time, and I've never heard the Izim use the word 'honor' except when referring to the Khua. It startled an old man, that's all. Given the theory that the Khua granted you passage, it makes some sense."

That's one question down, but there's still another. I cross to where Tiav sits and clamp my hand onto his wrist the way he did mine, raising my eyebrows to convey the question.

He shifts my grip to hold my hand instead, pulling me down onto the couch next to him. "The Izim, Liddi . . . they're not like us or the other races. They're older, more advanced, and communication . . . They'll discuss things, but in the end, they do what they want. And we can't stop them. So when they suggested you go aboard their ship, it worried me. If they decided you're better off on Izima than here, they'd just leave."

Heiress Liddi Jantzen fell into the worst cliché of heiresses throughout history, getting herself kidnapped.

Well, no, that's not an option. I need to stay where I can get to my brothers.

Jahmari shakes his head, mostly to himself. "I need to have a few more conversations. Maybe an hour, then we'll return to Podra."

The Crimna leaves, and I take Tiav's com-tablet so I can write something. His arm curves naturally around my shoulders as he waits. I like Podra better than Chalu except for one thing, and as much as I hate to bring it up with Tiav, I have to.

"Kal-kigg and Ag-nak?"

Sure enough, that brings all the tension back to Tiav's body. "They won't hurt you again. Kal's in the detention facility, and any who aren't . . . they won't. The keepers are on alert, and with the Izim in orbit, Oxurg will warn his people not to interfere."

That's good, but I realize my own discomfort goes deeper than that. *"Kal-kigg had see-kret wye tell now?"*

His fingers trace small circles on my shoulder. "Because I'm not very smart. The night before the attack, I told him how I feel

about you. He's been my friend for a long time, he *knows* me, so I hoped he'd see I couldn't feel this way about someone who's as terrible as he thinks you are. Stupid. Instead, he decided I'd betrayed my people and the Khua both."

I feel the ache extending from his own heart to mine. He trusted his friend, and his friend repaid that trust with fire. I know a little of how that feels. And now I know how it feels for it to be my fault.

As usual, Tiav sees what I'm thinking, and he gently lifts my chin to face him. "Hey, I wouldn't change it. It's not easy, but my mother taught me anything worth doing takes work. Kal's my friend, and I told you how he's been on my side. But I think sometimes being a real friend means knowing when to be *against* him. I hope he stops being so blind, but even if he doesn't, I don't regret my choices."

When I wrap my arms around him, holding him tight, I hope he knows that despite it all, I don't regret mine, either.

There's a familiarity in returning to Podra, almost like coming home despite the shortness of my time here. But it's also like returning to a home that's changed entirely in my absence. Wariness cloaks every eye that meets mine, and Agnac go out of their way to keep their distance. We hardly see Shiin, she's so busy meeting with citizens who have questions about the Khua and me . . . questions that don't have answers.

The wariness and suspicion of the city begin to press on me as much as my silence. It makes me jumpy and tense, and it doesn't help that every time I look at the streets, I remember what it was like to be under the crushing feet of a mob. I barely hold back further panic attacks, and only because we're never out on the streets for very long.

I don't say anything, but Tiav knows. So one night, he takes me out of the city.

It's not quite the observatory, but the view of the stars is still beautiful from the top of the hill. Admittedly, I'm not spending much time looking at them. Tiav has me too distracted. His lips in particular. And his arms as they keep me close.

You don't have time for this, Liddi. Kissing a boy does less than nothing to help get your brothers back.

But that's a lie, because even my brothers say our brains can't do anything decent if they don't stop and recharge a little. Besides, this is about more than kissing a boy. This boy has stood up for me against leaders of different worlds, against his own people. He cares about me and I can't imagine why when he knows so little about me. Except he says he knows *me*, and when he says it, I believe him. He's a good person, good in a way I've rarely seen, and besides wanting him, I *need* good people to help me free my brothers. If I can ever find a way to help, and a way to tell Tiav.

When he pulls away, one hand continues to stroke my hair. "Liddi, we're going to do something we should've done a long time ago, even if it gets me in trouble."

I shake my head. I've been in enough trouble myself—I don't need him getting into any. But he takes my chin in his hand to stop the movement, and his touch melts thoughts of protest from me.

"You don't get to stop me. The risk is my choice."

Arguing is pointless, so I give him my "what" face.

"You'll see. Come on."

He pulls me to my feet and leads me down one hill and up another. From the top I can see where we're going; one of the Khua sparkles ahead. I tug on his hand and give him a repeat of what-face.

"The Khua aren't answering the Aelo's questions, and I think it's because we're not the ones they want to talk to. So I'm going to ask again, but I want to bring you with me. Technically, it's allowed, but it'll be my responsibility if the Agnac want to complain."

My last two experiences in the portals flash through my mind, especially the pain. More pain than should be physically possible. I don't want to do it again.

But going with him, seeing the Aelo way of handling a Khua and the chaos inside, maybe even figuring out what interaction convinces Tiav and others that the energy phenomenon is *alive* ... that's the kind of information I've been looking for all along. Like Emil once told me, it's not just that mimics aren't as good as originals—secondhand reports aren't as good as firsthand experience, either.

Even if that firsthand experience feels like getting trampled by a mob of Agnac ten times over.

I sigh and keep walking, silently agreeing to Tiav's request.

Like the others, this Khua sends off waves of dormant power, shrinking me to nothing by comparison. Only it's different this time. Tiav makes it different, because his stride doesn't hesitate. I wonder how it feels to him. Welcoming instead of intimidating? Is it a matter of upbringing, his Aelo training, or is it a perspective he chooses?

I wish I could ask him.

When we reach the crystal spires, Tiav doesn't immediately step between them or reach for the mote of energy. Instead, he uses his free hand to pull something from under his collar—a flat crystal disk with a complex design of curves and flares etched onto it, surrounded by a ring of platinum that hangs from a black cord around his neck. Similar to the one Shiin wears, but I never noticed Tiav's. I assumed it was either a mark of her rank as primary Aelo or just a piece of jewelry.

"This is how the Aelo do it," he says, pulling the cord over his head. "As long as we use this, the Agnac consider it 'authorized.'" He dangles the disk near the spark of light, and it gravitates toward the crystal. Tiav releases the cord just as the two meet.

The collision is the most breathtaking sight of my life. The Khua explodes like a supernova, showering the countryside with the light of midday. When I can see again, it's formed a coherent energy field suspended between the two spires, rippling like fabric spun from starlight. Every time the field moves, the colors shift, sparkling and shimmering with red, then violet, then yellow, spreading from the spot where the disk is suspended.

Tiav releases my hand only to put his arm around my shoulder, pulling me tight against him. The warmth radiating from his body seeps into mine, and that's when I realize how cold I am. As beautiful as the Khua is right now, I'm still afraid to go inside.

But when he steps forward, so do I.

The expected maelstrom of chaos doesn't come. No rending of my neurons, no shattering of my bones, no pain. Just piercing heat from all around and pure light, like we're *inside* the

little spark of energy. Everything here is too clear, too sharp, too strong. It's hard to make sense of it.

I hear Tiav ask a question, or maybe I feel it. Asking the Khua if they have answers, and if they're willing to share. Focusing on me as the subject of his questions. Tiav is so calm, so relaxed here. He's used to it, knows how to pay attention to the right things. It's what his family does.

The family business, and he's good at it. Not like me with mine.

It may not be the swirling insanity of my previous portal adventures, but images and thoughts and feelings crash into me. I'm pretty sure it's in my head, clear as a memory but with a skewing twist. It's everything I'm afraid to tell Tiav but desperate for him to know and understand. The scene from the clearing back home plays out, with the raging violent portal—nothing like the Khua here—and my brothers surrounding it until I ran in.

Next is something that's definitely not a memory, at least not mine, because I never saw it. My brothers in different places, but always at a conduit terminal, working on the mechanism with tools I don't recognize. Each of them disappearing in the midst of their work with a snap of light—the moment Minali trapped them, however she did it.

I have the sensation of opening my eyes, except I don't think I ever closed them. If what I saw before was in my head, what I see now is real . . . or as real as anything in the Khua is. My brothers approach, but not too close. They stand in an arc in front of us, speaking words I can't hear. Emil reaches toward me, but something blocks him, forcing him back like an invisible wall.

Still, their presence curves my lips into a smile. I look up to Tiav to see if he understands now, if it's all right.

There's no understanding in his eyes. There's only horror.

Either Tiav pulls or the Khua pushes. Whichever it is, the bright, perfect fire surrounding us snaps and breaks, leaving us under the moons of Ferinne. No sign of my brothers.

Tiav isn't looking at me. He presses his palms against his eyes, his muscles so tight they're shaking. When I touch his shoulder, he shrugs me off and steps away, leaving me behind him.

"Kalkig was right," he mutters.

I freeze. Not good.

"Liddi, how can you do this? I don't care about the not talking, but all this time being my friend, being . . . and the whole time Kalkig was right. You and your brothers, you've done something to the Khua. Is it some kind of attack on us? Trying to destroy the Khua or use them because you don't believe they're alive? What is it?"

No, not us! He saw something different than I did, or he misinterpreted it. I grab his arm and force him around. He has to look at me, look in my eyes. I have to make him understand, because what he's thinking is much worse than Agnac ideas of defilement.

His eyes meet mine for half a breath. For that half-breath, I see the familiar spark. The spark that made me trust him, the spark that gives me hope. Then his eyes dart down several inches.

"How did you get that?"

I follow his gaze. The crystal disk hangs from my neck. I have no idea how it got there. A spark of light glows in the center—a familiar spark of light—and I instinctively turn toward the crystal spires.

The Khua isn't there. Tiav sees it at the same time I do. Fear and fury vie for domination, contorting his face.

"What have you done? Give that to me, now!"

His anger at Kalkig was nothing compared to this. It's nothing I've seen in him yet, and it scares me. I reach for the cord—of course he can have it back, I didn't take it, I don't know why I have it—but my hand freezes halfway.

DO NOT TAKE IT OFF.

It doesn't come in words—it comes in feelings. But that's ridiculous. Why wouldn't I? It's not mine.

DO NOT GIVE IT BACK. DO NOT TAKE ME OFF.

Even without words, I get the clear sense of a "me" in there. I feel it, a sense of self emanating from the disk, as strong as my own awareness and individuality. Any remaining doubts that the Khua are alive are eradicated in that moment.

Instead of taking off the disk, I take two steps back from Tiav. He takes one step to close the distance again, grabbing my arm. No tenderness with a light touch, no answering tingle across my skin. Just pressure clamping down.

I break his grip and knock his arm away. Between the media-grubs and guys like Reb Vester, my brothers made sure I wasn't defenseless.

"It's not a game, Liddi. Stop this."

No, it's not a game, but I don't know what it is. I don't know what's happening; I only know my heart is pounding, throbbing through my head. And I know I hate how Tiav is looking at me.

RUN.

He takes out his com-tablet, taps something on it. "The keepers are coming. They'll have to sort it out."

RUN.

More than the anger, the hurt in his eyes burns into me. "The Agnac may get what they wanted after all. And you'll never tell me why, will you?"

Because this Khua might have answers . . . which means this might be the only way to save my brothers. That's why.

I mouth the words, hoping he can read my lips. *I'm sorry.*

Then I run.

"Liddi!"

I ignore him. I don't know where I'm going—where I *can* go—but I run anyway. He'll catch me. He has longer legs and knows the territory. My only advantage is that I caught him by surprise. It gave me a head start, but it won't last. My feet nearly fly out from under me as I run down the far side of the hill, but after that, there's a long flat stretch before the hills rise up again.

Tiav still calls after me, but there's another sound, this one from my left. Heavy footsteps, too heavy for Tiav. I glance to the side and find a silhouette in the moonlight. A very large silhouette. Haleian. He's running a path that'll converge with mine in moments. Maybe he's a keeper who was already nearby when Tiav called. He'll catch me with zero effort, but I have to try. I'm about to adjust my course to move away from both him and Tiav, but my gut stops me.

JUST KEEP GOING.

Having a crystal disk talk to me without a voice is freaking me out, but the conviction of the impressions keeps me moving.

As expected, the Haleian quickly reaches me, and I brace myself for impact, but it doesn't come. He doesn't tackle me to the ground. Instead, he grabs me by the arm and waist, slings me across his back, and continues without breaking stride. If anything, he goes faster.

I'm clinging to the back of a stranger who feels like he's made of solid rock, except rock could never move so fluidly, with such speed. He climbs the next hill like it's level ground, and I know without looking that Tiav is falling behind.

"Don't—Liddi, stop! You can't—you can't hide. We'll find you!"

They probably will. Even if they can't follow the broken heart I'm trailing, they can probably follow the Haleian's huge foot-prints. As the alien cuts toward the low mountains rising in the distance and Tiav's voice fades, I wonder if I'll ever hear it again. If I do, it will never sound the same, never have the same care and life in it. I stole that from him when I stole the disk.

Not that I intended to steal it.

I have to think about something else. The Haleian helps on that front.

"If you're wondering, my name is Yilt. Quain sends his regards."

My first thought is that I didn't know Quain was a him. My

second thought is to wonder how Quain knew to send a Haleian to help me tonight, and why he did it. The Khua around my neck tells me the answer by way of my gut...maybe...or it's just my own best guess:

I'll find out when we get to where we're going.

Like every other day that week, Liddi's friends decided to play skip rope during lunch. And as usual, the bossy ones declared Liddi would be last. She didn't mind. She was fine watching the others.

If you found a portal high, if you found a portal low,

Where in the Eight Points would you go?

Sampati was always a popular choice, even though no one was very good at jumping that fast. Some of the kids said picking Sampati showed you liked your home and had proper technologist pride. Others chose Yishu because they could make everyone laugh with their silly dancing, and Pira always chose Erkir because it was easy.

Finally, Liddi's turn came around. She ran in under the rope and started jumping.

"Ferri!"

The twirlers dropped the rope, but everyone was already running like they had a head start. Which they did.

Liddi always chose Ferri.

17

I RUN. WELL, YILT DOES, MOSTLY. He put me down for a while in a small slot canyon where it was hard enough for him to fit through on his own. As soon as we came out, he picked me up again.

I hide. Flyers have been passing overhead at least once an hour. Every time they do, Yilt hears them coming. He stops and covers me with a length of super-thin cloth from his enormous pocket. Something to keep heat sensors from seeing me, I guess. While I peer from under the sheet, Yilt just stands close to the nearest tree, concentrating like he's trying to name his ancestors from shortest to tallest. He doesn't say anything about it, but when the flyers clear and he picks me up again, I notice his body is cooler. It makes me wonder if he can consciously control his own temperature.

I think about taking off the disk with the Khua hitching a ride. It would be just as safe in my pocket. But my hands are busy enough clinging to Yilt most of the time. When they're not, it just seems easier to leave the disk where it is. Silly as it feels, I try thinking questions at it. *Who are you? What's going on? Why did you do this?* No response. Nothing to say now that I'm running like it wanted.

And it definitely wanted. Energy doesn't want, so I have to accept that Tiav and Shiin and Kalkig and everyone were right on at least one point. The Khua are alive. They're aware and they want and they communicate and they decide . . . they just don't do it in anything resembling the way we do. I can't wrap my head around it beyond accepting that it's true. That must be what the Aelo spend their whole lives doing, trying to make sense of it.

The knowledge both fills me up to bursting and leaves a gaping void of uncertainty. I don't know what the Khua being alive is going to change, but I do know I don't have a lifetime to figure it out.

After uncounted hours, as the sun finally teases the horizon, we arrive at a road with a streamer waiting for us. Yilt and I both get in. He doesn't know how much I hate the streamers; I'm not sure he'd care if he did. He's been careful enough about keeping me safe, but I can't exactly say he seems concerned about my mental state. Or the fact that I'm exhausted.

Just like every other time I've been in a streamer, I close my eyes. I can't stomach the warped rushing of the world outside the windows. The upside is that the trips are so brief.

Except not this time.

It keeps going. Maybe twenty minutes. Possibly longer, because there's every reason to believe I doze off. I open my eyes with a start when the sudden sensation of non-motion returns.

Night's approaching again, with the remnants of dusk holding on a little longer, highlighting that we've traveled a *long* way with the crazy speed of the streamer. We've stopped on a street with nearly identical single-story buildings. I don't see any larger buildings in the distance, so we're probably not in a big city. There's something strange about these buildings, though. Their single story is a little too tall, and so are the doors, which are also a little too wide.

Yilt is about to get out of the streamer, but I tap his arm to stop him. A gesture at our surroundings with raised eyebrows is enough to communicate the question.

"This is Cim. A Haleian settlement for when we get tired of bumping into things in the cities."

Fair enough. If I were as big and solid as they are, I'd probably want a little more open space, too.

We go inside, and I discover the building is a house, furnished in a way that's both simple and comfortable. Comfortable for Haleians, anyway, which means everything's a few inches too tall for me. Yilt gestures for me to sit on a cushioned chair, so I do, but my feet don't reach the floor. I feel like I'm eight years old again.

"There you are, Yilt. More eventful than we expected?"

I turn at the voice, but we're alone. It comes from a computer screen on a nearby table, displaying Quain's shielded face.

"You could say that," Yilt replies. "Something happened at the Khua, and the young Aelo turned on her. Look."

He gestures to the disk dangling from my neck. As always, Quain has no expression for me to read, but he—if Yilt calls him a "he," I guess I can, too—makes a slight hiss.

"Unexpected. And intriguing. Liddi, you are still unable to speak?"

Yes, obviously, nothing's changed on that front. I may have a bizarre energy-based being around my neck, but I also still have a hyperdimensional transmitter implanted in the same vicinity. Worse, I no longer have access to Tiav's symbol-reading program, and I only have a couple of words locked in my memory.

"Are you able to commune with the Khua as the Aelo do, now that you have the disk?"

The weird feelings and impressions I had before come to mind, but I don't know if it's the same. Tiav said what some of the other races called communing was just watching and listening to what the Khua "said" inside, then trying to make sense of it. No deep understanding, just gut instinct and guesses.

My only answer is a shrug.

"If you can communicate with them as you cannot with us, it is important you do so. And soon."

I open my expression to look as curious as possible, hoping Quain has enough experience with Ferinnes to read it.

He does. "Unlike the others on the planet with you, we detect the energy of the Khua in much finer detail. Since before your arrival, the energy has been changing. Either the Khua are trying to tell us something, or something is very wrong."

That weird feeling comes again, the instinct-from-outside, telling me the answer.

PROBABLY BOTH.

※ – – – ※

Yilt informs me this is a safe-house, but without the program to read off the symbols for me, I can't easily ask why they have one, and Yilt doesn't volunteer the information. Despite hours of being carried across the countryside by the guy, I'm not sure what to make of him. At least Durant's age, if Haleian life spans and aging patterns are anything like ours. Built like Reb's laserball-playing friends, only more. Maybe that's what gave me the impression that he's not too bright. He got us all this way without being caught by the keepers, so he can't be completely stupid.

I just don't know. It's hard to get to know someone when you can't talk.

Somehow Tiav and I managed. Only now he thinks all my non-words were lies.

"Liddi, are you listening?"

I push the sudden surge of emptiness back to my toes. Yilt's trying to explain the safety protocols in the house, and no, I haven't been listening. I lower my eyes, apologetic.

"You're probably too tired to remember anyway. Go on and get some sleep. We'll try again in the morning. And hopefully the Khua will tell you something."

I've been "thinking at" the Khua all I can, trying to get it to respond to me, with no luck. But sleep sounds good. At least it's something I know I can succeed at. I curl up on a too-large and too-high bed and close my eyes, emptying my mind and allowing it to float.

I do float. I float out of the room and away from the safe-house, up and out until I'm surrounded by white light. The same white light. The light inside the portal, like with Tiav. Only Tiav isn't with me. No one is.

Wait. Someone is. One of my brothers?

No.

My brothers don't come, but someone's still here.

Yes, I am.

The Khua is here, somewhere.

Not somewhere. I am here. "Here" is me.

Not helpful. Dreams rarely are, but maybe this one will be. I want to ask a question, but the words don't come. The Khua waits, circling me. I feel her motion, without any visual clues.

Her. Why do I think of the Khua as a her?

If we were male and female, I would choose female. That is why.

She answered that question, but I wasn't asking her. That means something, and I try to work it into something useful, but an image of Tiav emerges instead. The aching emptiness swells, and I can't focus on anything else. I hurt him, the most solid ally I had on this planet. The first person to care about me without knowing about JTI and wealth and fame, my fate and my failures. And it's because of this Khua, because she stowed away in the crystal disk and made me run away.

I didn't force you. You had a choice.

It didn't feel like a choice.

That's because the right choice feels like no choice at all. Would you choose differently?

No, I wouldn't. Thinking back on that moment, I realize she's right. I *did* choose. When I realized it was my first real hope of helping my brothers, the choice was made. It might break my heart all over again, but I'd choose my brothers every time. I just hate that I had to choose in the first place.

The Aelo is skilled, but he didn't understand, and we don't have time to wait for another to come to us. You are the one who's been to both sides. You understand what's happening.

No, I don't. I've been bumbling and fumbling ever since my brothers went missing.

You know who puts us in danger, you know those she's using to do it, and you know catastrophe will be the end of it all.

Minali. Yes, I know about that. But the Khua talks like I'm some kind of chosen one meant to save everybody. I'm not. My family tried that. It didn't work.

No, you are not chosen. You are the one who chose. And you are the one who still chooses.

The teacher showed the children a new game. New for the other kids, anyway. Anton had taught Liddi before she started school. He also told her it wasn't just a game. It was to teach kids the basics of circuits and resistors and switches.

As much as Liddi liked playing with her big brothers, running around with six-year-old kids who didn't really care about keeping the rules was a different kind of fun.

She chased Pira through half of a double-bind—a parallel circuit—and caught her before a teammate could throw the switch. Pira hated to lose, so she wrenched her arm out of Liddi's hand and screamed.

"Cheater!"

"Liddi."

Liddi whipped around at the teacher's voice. She hadn't cheated—she'd been following the rules better than anyone— but the teacher glared at Pira before turning back to Liddi.

"Come here, please."

She followed the teacher to the door and out into the hall. Luko stood there waiting. Shaking.

Everything went cold, like winter had come and the environmental controls failed.

He swept his sister up in his arms, hugged her too tight. She started crying before he said a word and didn't know why.

Then he told her why. Something about an accident. The details didn't make sense. Only the bottom line mattered.

Liddi would never see her parents again.

18

THE NEXT DAY, I OPEN my eyes and commence staring at the ceiling. I have a problem, and it's bigger than the fact that I've just slept until midday. The "conversation" with the Khua is only as clear as a dream. Something about making choices, I remember that much. At the time, I thought I had an idea what choices she meant, but that's slipped away.

Slipped through my sieve of a brain, just like everything else important. I rub my temples, trying to come up with anything useful. Nothing. Whatever she tried to tell me, it's gone.

It would be nice to have a name to call her other than "the Khua."

SPIN-STILL. THAT'S HER NAME.

The name is too strange for me to have made it up, but I don't hear and feel her voice the same way I did in the dream. Seems like the key to getting answers from Spin-Still is not to ask directly, but that makes it awfully difficult to get the right questions asked. Maybe that makes sense for an energy being, not bound by the limits of physicality, existing in a hyper-dimensional state. Makes sense but doesn't, because I'm still limited to a simple set of three dimensions, plus the fourth—time.

A bang on the bedroom door interrupts my efforts to ask without asking. "Are you awake?"

The only way to answer Yilt is to open the door, so I do. He's alert, tense, yet I get the feeling he hasn't slept. Maybe Haleians don't need as much sleep.

"There's something you should see." Without another word, he turns back to the main room, so I follow.

Ferinne doesn't have media-casts, but their news-vids put Sampati's to shame. One's frozen on the screen—an image of my face with text symbols along the bottom. Yilt taps a command to resume the playback.

"Liddi went missing sometime yesterday. The Aelo are concerned for her safety and ask that if anyone sees her, they contact local keepers immediately."

I look to Yilt, confused. He's glaring at the screen.

"They're not talking about the incident with the Khua. Not labeling you a criminal . . . yet. They haven't mentioned me. I don't think that will last."

His statement confirms he's smarter than I initially thought, because I think I know what he means. People might panic if they know I'm wearing a Khua around my neck and deliberately ran off. The idea that an unbalanced Haleian took me might be easier to swallow. If they identify him and word gets out, Yilt will be in trouble, maybe even here in Cim.

There's a single-symbol word I've used enough times that I remember it. I pull up a keypad and hunt the symbol down. *Why?*

He starts to say what I've already figured out about why the news-vid isn't reporting everything, but I shake my head to cut him off. I point at Yilt, then point at the word again.

"Why am I risking myself?" he guesses. "You heard what Quain said. Something may be wrong. That Khua chose to contain itself, to travel with you for a reason."

It chose. I choose. I understand, supposedly. That's what it said. But Yilt hasn't really answered my question. What he said explains why *someone* needed to help me, but not why *he* did. I try one more time, pointing to the word before poking him in his boulderlike chest.

He doesn't guess so quickly this time. Despite their large eyes, Haleian faces haven't seemed very expressive to me, but I see the change in Yilt's when he understands.

"Why me? Some of us feel the Agnac have surrounded the Khua with so much ritual and reverence, they've forgotten that the Khua live and change. Too many laws and regulations surrounding them. Shiin'alo was wise when she began the Aelo practice of active questioning. Asking new questions seems more important to me than maintaining old answers. When I heard of a visitor from the Lost Points, I thought it might be the jostling we need. Quain knows my views, so he asked me to keep an eye on you once you returned from Chalu. I thought perhaps the Agnac would cause trouble again, so I would bring you here for safety—the Aelo, too, I thought. I didn't expect this."

I'm pretty sure no one expected it except maybe Spin-Still. The thought that Yilt might have seen what Tiav and I were up to before visiting the Khua brings a threatening blush, quelled by the resurging ache. Maybe it's not quelled enough, because Yilt sees something.

"The Aelo are good people. Your friend especially—his mother has broken new paths for all Aelo and has taught him well. But I'm sure he didn't expect this, either."

Regardless of my conflicted feelings, I can't give the Haleian much more than a nod, but that's enough. Crumbling into a tear-soaked mess doesn't sound good, so I distract myself with the basics. Yilt goes back to scanning news-vid feeds, and I get something to eat—some kind of pastry holding meat and vegetables. Once I'm not starving, I go to another room where I can think. I've got to figure out *what* exactly Spin-Still is so sure I understand.

That night on the roof, when the Triad told me to stay out of trouble, to let them handle things, I had an idea. The Khua are like strings, one end anchored to the spires, the other—or others—roaming on various planets. The conduits are the same but different.

The conduits have always been anchored at both ends. They take a lot of energy to maintain but they're still breaking down. Maybe some of that energy goes into dampening those violent vibrations I saw from the Khua on Sampati. Minali thinks they need a biological catalyst to stabilize the conduits. Why don't the Khua need a biological catalyst to be stable?

Because they're already alive.

Whether she realizes it or not, Minali's trying to make the conduits into more than artificial portals. She's trying to make artificial Khua—artificial life. But it's not what she's really doing. It's not going to work that way. What it's doing is bringing the faulty non-Khua closer to the real Khua, making contact with them. That's why I can interact with my brothers inside—at least, I could when I was inside without Tiav's disk.

The disk makes it different, controlled, cleaner for the Khua. But the rest of the time, they and the conduits are more intertwined, like the same family of frequencies, overlapping.

That contact with the conduits isn't good.

IT HURTS.

All the questioning and theorizing in my head definitely felt like my own, but that last bit, that certainty that the conduits are hurting the Khua, that has to come from Spin-Still.

It's information, and I have to make Yilt understand. He's still watching news-vids, but it doesn't look important—they're talking about a summer festival in some city or another. I'm familiar enough with the computer interface to pull up the drawing program, but I have to stare at the blank wallscreen for a minute. How can I get the idea of conduits and biological catalysts and a bad interaction across in a picture?

I can't, so I shouldn't try. All I need is one word, more abstract, that'll tell Yilt enough, and he can pass it along to Quain.

First a mouse eating food. Then a dashed line to show the mouse's path as it walks away. Finally the mouse unquestionably dead, and I go back to add a bunch of arrows pointing to the food for emphasis.

Yilt takes it in, thinks. "Poison?"

Yes, that's it, exactly. What Minali's doing to the conduits is poisoning the Khua.

"Have *you* been poisoned?"

The sudden urgency in Yilt's voice startles me, and I shake

my head quickly so he won't get ideas about force-feeding me antitoxins. I point to the disk hanging from my neck, then back to the mouse food.

"The Khua have been poisoned? Did the Khua tell you this?"

I'd say no, because it came from my own thought process, but Spin-Still confirmed it. It's the same thing, so I nod.

As I hoped, Yilt immediately contacts Quain and fills him in. If it's possible for an Izim helmet to frown, that's definitely what it's doing now.

"If this is true, then we cannot waste time," Quain says. "We must discuss this in person, but I cannot reach the surface without drawing attention. Yilt, do you have any contacts who could get Liddi into orbit?"

The Haleian shakes his head, but I'm barely paying attention. Spin-Still can get me there. I'm certain of it. I get Quain's attention and point to the disk.

"Has the Khua offered to bring you?"

If that kind of gut instinct can be called an offer, sure.

"Very well. Yilt, keep the location secure. Liddi, I look forward to your arrival at the Khua's convenience. Safe journey."

I can't help remembering what Tiav said about the Izim. How anxious the idea of me going on their ship made him. I get the feeling the journey isn't what I need to worry about.

✳ – – –✳

Spin-Still wants to wait until evening, which I don't bother arguing with. She's in charge. When she decides it's time to go, she gives me next to no warning.

None of my portal experiences compare to this. Like being

fired from a slingshot or a cannon, hurtling through the white chaotic nothing-everything. No pain—I'm cocooned by Spin-Still's energy—but I wouldn't call it comfortable. At the other end, I'm thrown to the ground, crashing to my hands and knees with a jarring force that echoes along my bones.

Not ground. Smooth metal, but white. I'm in a hallway made of the stuff, the floor curving perfectly to the walls, then ceiling. So much white could blind me, but fixtures on the walls aim light upward, dim and indirect enough to work. A familiar smell teases my nose, tickling my memory. It smells like the workshop back home, only different. Brighter.

Homesickness surges through my chest, filling my lungs until I force it away. I don't have time for this.

The floor vibrates underneath me, accompanying the clank of metal-on-metal. I get to my feet and turn around. Quain approaches. At least, I think it's Quain. If all the Izim have identical suits, I have no idea how I'd tell them apart. He stops a few feet away. No handshakes for greeting the Izim, I guess.

"Welcome, Liddi. Please follow me."

As we walk down the corridor, it occurs to me that I could hand over Spin-Still so she and Quain could figure it all out directly. That'd be easier.

NO IT WOULDN'T. SPIN-STILL CAN'T COMMUNICATE WITH THE IZIM THE WAY SHE DOES WITH ME.

Great. These two can't talk to each other, and I can't talk at all. This should be fun.

The room Quain takes me to is more white on white—white walls, white chairs, white table. The instruments built into the table and walls break up the monotony, at least, not that I can understand anything on the screens. Lots of flashing lights and diagrams. Ferinne symbols and totally different symbols.

I sit in a chair I assume is meant for someone like me—like on Ferinne, others are clearly designed for different alien species. Quain doesn't sit. He walks around the perimeter of the room, looking over the different displays. Some change while he's looking. Enough to convince me it's not a coincidence of timing, but he never touches any controls. Never gives any voice commands.

Like maybe he controls it with his mind.

That's serious technology. Tiav said they were advanced. He even seemed a little afraid of them.

Maybe coming here was a bad idea.

IF IT TURNS BAD, SPIN-STILL WILL TAKE ME BACK.

But how do I know Spin-Still is on my side?

BECAUSE THE LIVES OF HER KIND ARE AT RISK, AND I'M THE ONE SHE BELIEVES WILL FIND THE WAY TO FIX IT.

I rub my temples, pushing back a burgeoning headache. The only way to communicate with Spin-Still is to wonder things to myself, and then my own gut tells me the answer. It's confusing, and I don't really like it.

"Is something wrong?" Quain asks. "Are you unwell?"

I shake my head. What's wrong is nothing Jahmari could treat, much less Quain.

"You told Yilt that the Khua are somehow being poisoned.

I need to know more about this. As you cannot speak and do not have skill with the Ferinne writing system, I prepared one of our old ways."

A panel on the table in front of me slides over, revealing a hidden compartment underneath. A hidden compartment full of pearly white goo.

"Before we learned each other's languages, we used this to communicate. Your neurolinguistic signals are sensed and transmitted by the gel, then interpreted by the computer. It took some time for the computer to learn initially, but now that the full language is programmed in, the process is nearly instantaneous."

If he thinks I'm going to smear this stuff on my head, then I think I'm leaving right now.

"If you place your hand in the gel, we can begin."

A hand sounds more reasonable, but I'm not ready to dive in. If this thing is going to read my brain waves, it could spill everything. Most of "everything" would make things easier, but I don't have any reason to trust Quain with the entire contents of my brain. I fold my arms and look up at him, waiting for more information and bracing myself in case he decides to force my hand, literally.

My suspicion must read clearly enough. "It will only detect focused linguistic thoughts. Ferinnes have described it as the words you hear in your head, heard by all."

I'm not ready just yet. I pretend to put my hand in, then jerk it out quickly, keeping my eyes as questioning as possible.

"The moment you remove your hand, the process will cease," Quain says. "You may do so at any time."

That'll have to do. I submerge my hand—the goo is cold and

slimy and really gross—and think the focused kind of thought that doesn't work at all on Spin-Still.

"I get to ask questions, too."

So easy. So perfectly what I was thinking. It could actually be me speaking, except that the computer's voice veers more male. I think of all the time and effort to piece together broken sentences, how hard Tiav worked to understand me, and I want to scream or cry. Maybe both at the same time. All we needed was something the Izim had all along—something they call old, yet all the Jantzens together couldn't have invented it.

"Certainly," Quain says. "But first, could you please explain the 'poisoning' you mentioned?"

I'm very careful. I keep my brothers out of it. Just describe how technology being developed by my people involves energies similar enough to interfere with the Khua and different enough to be damaging to them.

"Could you not explain this to your people, have them deactivate this technology?"

"I didn't know when I was there, and now ... there are complications."

There's that hiss coming from his suit again. "The Khua must be preserved and protected. Does the one you carry tell you anything more?"

I don't know, I guess she's told me a lot of things, but what does she want me to share with him?

ONE THING.

"She's worried about the anchors. That both people and Khua will get hurt because of them."

"How would this happen?"

It took until I heard the computer say my words to understand. Anchors mean the crystal spires. Just like I saw in my mind, held in place here, but free to move around in the other worlds.

Minali is tying the Khua to the conduits—intentionally or not—and every conduit is locked in place by seven terminals, one on each Point. The Khua are only meant to have one anchor point, but the connection to the conduits is restraining them. Like my brothers temporarily restrained one so I could use it. If the Khua are locked down, the vortex I saw on Sampati could happen on both ends—all the ends. Or even worse.

"The Khua have to move, right? It's like breathing for them. If they're held in place everywhere, not just on Ferinne, what would happen?"

Another hiss. That's definitely his not-happy sound. I don't need more answer than that. The vibrations would turn destructive.

There has to be something we can do. I still don't know how to undo the conduit interference, what to do about Minali. But Ferinne is the one Point the conduits *aren't* connected to. Only the Khua are. If the Khua are loosened here, maybe that'll relieve some of the tension temporarily. And keep eight planets from getting torn apart.

"So the Khua need to be untied from the anchors, at least until I can get things worked out back home."

Quain stares at me, or at least his helmet stays pointed directly at me, like that's not unnerving. So is the way he's been standing perfectly still through this whole conversation. Not fidgeting, not shifting his weight, nothing.

"The Khua chose to bind themselves to the anchors, to make

this the one home they always return to," he finally says. "But they cannot unbind themselves as freely."

That's a lie. I use my un-goopified hand to hold up Tiav's disk with Spin-Still nice and cozy inside.

"Yes, the sempu disks of the Aelo could be used. However, you have only the one, we do not know how to fabricate them, and I do not think the Aelo will share that information with either of us."

SPIN-STILL THINKS I CAN FIGURE OUT WHAT TO DO. IF SHE GETS ME TO AN ANCHOR, WE CAN SOLVE IT TOGETHER.

Her confidence is nice, but I can't help wondering if it's misplaced. The Khua and their anchors are still so new and foreign to me. And Ferinne isn't as friendly a planet as it used to be.

"You need to tell the council what's going on, what we need to do. If they catch me—"

"I am sorry, but I cannot do that."

"What? Why not?"

"The council is very slow to make decisions, particularly when there is arguing, as there would most certainly be in this case. According to our energy readings, which we can now interpret better with your information, the Khua do not have that much time. If I speak to the council, it will only warn them of your intentions, making your task that much more difficult."

Quain is starting to seem severely useless, and a particular word he used sparks my anger.

"My task? You're not going to help?"

"I will do what I can from here, but I cannot help on the surface, no."

"*Why not?*"

"It is difficult enough being in proximity to the Khua you carry. I could not be even this close to one still tied to a planetary core."

He's telling a truth that still hides something, and I don't like it. "*Why? If you want me and Yilt to do this alone against a whole planet, no help from anyone, tell me why.*"

Quain hesitates. His posture slumps and his head dips forward like he's fallen asleep standing up. I wonder if it's another alien gesture. Maybe their version of crossing their arms and looking defiant.

Something rises from the back of his neck, through the suit. Floating. If a Khua is a tiny knot of whirling energy, a star in miniature, this is a single point of light, like a star light-years away.

This is what Quain really is.

The tools were heavy and unwieldy in Liddi's little hands, but she didn't care. She was going to make something like her brothers. Something to make their father proud. Something better than what the triplets were working on. Liddi was pretty sure they were just rigging ways to destroy each other's projects. Their mother said being eight years old made you want to destroy everything because that was the quickest way to see how it worked.

"Marek, Ciro, Emil," Mr. Jantzen said from behind them, making them jump. "Those signal converters aren't cheap. Try using them for something a little less destructive. Liddi, dearest, what's that you're working on?"

"I don't know."

He came around to her end of the workbench and put a hand on her shoulder. Big and strong. "Sometimes we don't know what it is until it puts itself together, so keep at it. You'll need to set up pathways to and from the power source, though. The energy needs to know where to go."

"That's stupid," Liddi said.

"Why's that?"

"Because the energy should know what I need it to do and just do it."

Her father laughed and gave his youngest a squeeze. "If only technology were so cooperative rather than making us fight it every step. We could just ask it to kindly do its job and be on our way."

Liddi wasn't sure why that was so funny, but she liked making him laugh...even if it meant her machine wouldn't work.

19

THE SUIT ISN'T A SUIT AT ALL. It's a robot controlled by the energy being that's actually Quain. Between this and the Khua, everything I thought I knew about defining life is moot. Good thing I don't have to use my voice, because I don't think it would work in the face of this revelation.

"Does everyone know you Izim are like this and just forgot to tell me?"

He rejoins with his mechanical body to answer. "The Crimna know. The others do not. We found it easier to interact with species like yours in this form. When we saw how the Agnac elevated their respect of the Khua to the point of religion, we chose not to discuss our true nature."

They didn't want the attention that comes with being worshiped. I can't argue with that.

"What does this have to do with why you can't get close to the Khua? Aren't you the same?"

"We were once, long ago. Our originators were Khua who

left the core worlds—what you call the Eight Points—to explore others. While the Khua's energies bind with the biological, ours adapted and changed, more in tune with the technological. That is the best I can explain using your words. After these ages, our energies became too different. We cannot communicate with the Khua, but they came before us. They are ancient and have power we do not, so we honor them."

They don't worship the Khua—they honor their ancestors. Different energies, so being near them probably causes interference, especially with the robo-suit. Interference ... something about that tickles my brain, and I stow it away for later. The bottom line is Quain can't help. Not in person, at least.

"You said you don't think there's much time. How long, do you think?"

"I cannot be precise, but in the Ferinnes' measure, no more than one moon-cycle. And I suspect the conflicting energies will significantly damage the Khua before that, if they have not already begun to do so."

I run the numbers quickly, accounting for Ferinne's and Sampati's slightly different day lengths. A moon-cycle from now lines up closely with the Tech Reveal. If something bad is coming before that, Minali may be entering another stage of her process. If the Khua are running out of time, so are my brothers.

Quain can't help, and just about everyone else is against me, but Spin-Still is right. I'm the one who knows what's happening. It's up to me, and a fugitive Haleian and rogue Khua will have to be enough help to get it done.

My brothers told me to stay out of it, to stay safe and leave it to them. Whatever plan Spin-Still and I can come up with, it's not likely to be safe at all.

I've spent a lot of years doing what my brothers told me. I think now is a good time to stop.

It might also be a good time to get back to Ferinne's surface. A *really* good time. A time so good, I'm pretty sure it's Spin-Still's idea talking to me, and she doesn't want to wait for me to say good-bye to Quain.

The metaphorical slingshot pulls back and releases, catapulting me through everything and nothing until I crash-land on the ground.

Ground, not floor. Grass. Stars above me.

Not the safe-house.

Even better, a thin layer of the neurolinguistic goop still covers my hand. All I can do is wipe it off on the grass and hope it isn't toxic.

"Liddi!"

I sit up to find the source of the voice, because I recognize it. Fabin, standing between me and a Khua-and-anchor combination just a few feet away. Still ghostly and only half-here, but he's also exhausted and terrified. It seems ages since I've seen any of the boys, and more than ever I wish I could hug him.

"Where were you?" he demands. "Are you all right? We felt it—that you were gone."

I point straight up. That's the best I can do to explain I was on an orbiting spaceship, and he can see from looking at me that I'm in one piece.

"Okay, never mind. I don't know how long I can hold myself here, but I have to tell you, I have to explain. Liddi, I'm so sorry. It's my fault, all of it."

The anguish in his voice chills me. I reach for his hands, even though I can barely feel them.

"I didn't mean to," he continues. "We were all working on the conduits, and I was studying energy signatures. I thought I saw something, so I kept looking, and it seemed like there was a gap, something keeping the signature from being complete. The missing piece reminded me of a biological energy signature, but a little more complex. So I mentioned that to Minali. It was just an observation, I never imagined she'd use people, or any living thing. Not like this. It's madness. She's so convinced it's the solution, locking us in here. And the portals, the conduits are hurting them, and we're stuck partly in the conduits, partly in between the two. We thought maybe we could force a bigger separation, keeping them apart—we've tried, but we can't. We can't. There's nothing we can do to stop it."

Fabin is ranting, something I've never seen any of my brothers do. I can't speak to calm him. I can't put my arms around him. I look at the Khua hovering between its spires. Then I look at Spin-Still in the sempu—the crystal disk.

Interference. If the disk can only hold one Khua, I wonder what would happen if I tried to put another in.

SPIN-STILL HAS NO IDEA.

No time for research and bench tests. I'm going to have to jump straight to the full-scale experiment.

I hold up one finger to tell Fabin to wait. Then I take Spin-Still from around my neck and loop the cord on my hand several times so the disk rests against my palm. A few steps carry me to the other Khua, and it's only on my approach that I realize something's different.

The Khua's power, I still feel it, but it's no longer a sleeping giant waiting to crush me on a whim. It's a power bound, a being in trouble, crying for help. Like it's too large to help itself. With a silent hope that I'm small enough, I raise my hand to the mote of light.

It doesn't join with the disk and form the energy field like I saw with Tiav, but the two do collide. The impact sends hundreds of tiny needles into my hand—at least, it feels like it—and I bite the inside of my cheek to keep from crying out. I blink through tears and see the Khua pressed against the face of the disk.

Now that I have a physical connection, I need to break it free from the anchors. In theory.

All I can do is follow my instincts, pushing it away from myself. Or I try to. It's like it weighs twice as much as Yilt. So I bring my other hand behind the first, using both arms to push.

The needles burrow deeper. Every fraction of an inch takes all the strength I have. Half the exertion is from the effort not to scream. I couldn't scream if I wanted to. I can't breathe.

Finally it's enough. The Khua breaks free from the anchors, floating off to who-knows-where, and I stumble forward a few steps.

It worked.

"Setting it loose on this side," Fabin says. "Clever girl."

He hasn't called me that in years. The words bring a Khua-sized glow, even if Spin-Still is really the clever one.

IT WASN'T HER IDEA. IT WAS MINE.

It's getting a little easier to separate Spin-Still's gut-speak from my own gut instincts, so I guess the idea of how to free the

Khua *was* mine. I unwind the cord and find my hand is bleeding. Dozens of pinpricks, tiny but deep.

"You're hurt!"

Fabin saw, but it doesn't matter. I shrug. It has to be done.

His jaw sets, acknowledging he doesn't like it but can't do anything about it. "All right. I'll let the others know what you're doing. We'll try to find a way to help. Be strong, Liddi."

Always, I'm trying. Fabin disappears, leaving me alone with Spin-Still. The other Khua has either wandered out of sight or disappeared as well. There are alarms of some type to detect Khua-tampering—I know that from the night I was arrested—so I'd better get going before the keepers arrive.

Or the Aelo. When I first arrived on Ferinne, Tiav responded to the alarm. I can't begin to guess what assumptions he and Shiin and Jahmari will make about what I've done, what betrayal they'll read into it, what possible explanation they'll come up with. It's unlikely to be anywhere close to the truth. Knowing that brings a fresh surge of heartache.

I have to get out of here. I wonder if Spin-Still can slingshot me back to the safe-house.

SHE CAN'T. BUT I'M NOT FAR FROM CIM.

Time to run.

The summer got unbearably hot, beyond what the weather modulators could handle. So hot, Luko threatened to make those modulators his next project, upgrading them so they could truly control the weather, rather than just smoothing out most hurricanes and the like. The Jantzens could have stayed inside—Dom kept the house perfectly comfortable—but it was summer. Summer was not for being locked up in the house.

Liddi wasn't allowed to go swimming on her own, which she hated. The triplets were definitely allowed on their own when they were ten. Fabin didn't like her going with just those three, either, convinced they would get too distracted to notice a river snake strangling their little sister. That was ridiculous—even Ciro wouldn't be that irresponsible, and Emil would never let anything hurt Liddi—but with Durant, Luko, and Vic out of the house, Fabin was in charge. The rule wouldn't have been so bad, except Fabin was spending more time in the city with the older brothers. Anton was gone almost as much, usually spending time with various girls, according to Marek.

Every time one of Liddi's brothers got old enough to oper-ate a hovercar, it was like another thread loosened in the seams of their family.

Finally, though, Anton stayed home one day and agreed to take the younger kids swimming. They hiked out to the widest part of the river—the hike itself was almost too much in the heat—stripped down to their swimsuits, and cannonballed in.

It was the Sentinel's paradise. Just cool enough to be comfortable, and deep enough to test Liddi's swimming skills. The triplets took turns jumping into the water from a tree branch high above. Anton shook his head at them a few times, but didn't make them stop. Liddi kept busy swimming back and forth and flipping under the water.

When she got tired, she went to lean against a tree on the bank, just long enough to rest. A moment later, she felt something on her head. She reached up and touched it: cold and wet. Before she could panic, Marek was laughing.

"Careful, Liddi, toads will make you ugly."

A toad. Liddi tried to grab it so she could take a look, but it hopped down to her shoulder. Good enough. It was red with yellow and black markings along its back.

"Something pretty isn't that likely to make me ugly," she retorted.

"Maybe that's how it gets pretty," Ciro said. "It steals the 'pretty' from little girls."

Anton splashed water at all three of them. "Grow up, you null-skulls. Liddi, you can be as pretty as you want. And you look like Mom, so you probably will be. But you're a Jantzen. Make sure that toad doesn't steal the brains from you, and you'll be fine."

Liddi took the toad from her shoulder, kissed it just to make the boys shout with disgust, and set it on the bank to go on its way. The triplets had their first time at the Tech Reveal when they were Liddi's age, but she hadn't come up with anything to show this year. Not a big deal—the rest of the boys didn't debut until they were eleven or twelve. Liddi knew she wasn't just a

Jantzen—she was the Jantzen. The one who would take over the company. For her, a clever debut wouldn't be good enough.

It had to be amazing. And amazing would take time.

Hopefully that toad hadn't stolen her brains. And if the kiss gave her a little luck, that wouldn't hurt, either.

20

I KNOW ONE THING FOR SURE. As long as I have Spin-Still around my neck, I don't have to worry about getting lost. She has a super-solid sense of direction. That shouldn't surprise me, since she launched me into orbit with such accuracy, but it does make it strange that she can't do the same to get me back to the safe-house.

KHUA SEND TRAVELERS USING TWO ENERGY SIGNATURES—THE ORIGIN AND THE TARGET. THEY HAVE TO BE DIFFERENT, USUALLY DIFFERENT PLANETS. GETTING TO QUAIN MEANT LEAVING THE CORE OF FERINNE AND TARGETING THE STRANGE ENERGY OF THE IZIM. THAT MADE IT WORK.

I get the feeling I could spend the rest of my life studying Khua mechanics and barely understand a tenth of what they do.

The Aelo have generations of knowledge. I wonder how much Tiav understands that he wasn't able to tell me.

Thinking about him is less than smart. I thought I'd left the aching guilt behind at the empty spires, but now it returns, doubled as I imagine what he'll think when he discovers what I just did. I want to explain to him—I should have explained everything sooner—but Quain is right. The planetary officials would take too much time discussing instead of acting, and the Agnac in particular will never believe I've knocked a Khua loose for everyone's good. At this point, I doubt anyone will. Asking them to believe that would be like asking me a year ago to believe portals are alive.

I can't worry about Tiav. What energy I have has to go to moving fast and not getting caught. That's more than enough to worry about.

Approaching Cim gives me a good distraction. Some Haleians are out walking the streets, and I don't know whether they've seen the news-vids with "Please help us find poor lost Liddi." Spin-Still gives me an instinct-level sense of where the safe-house is, but I can't take the most direct route. I stick to smaller roads, darker alleys, and finally reach my destination.

Yilt doesn't exactly look happy to see me, but I don't think I've seen what a happy Haleian looks like yet.

"Quain contacted me two hours ago to say you'd returned."

Before I can think of a way to explain the detour, he activates a news-vid. It shows two empty anchors, but I recognize the hills around them. They're not the ones I just left; they're Spin-Still's.

"We've received new and disturbing information about the missing Lost Points visitor named Liddi," the voice-over begins. *"She's*

reportedly interfered with at least two Khua, both of which are now missing from their shrines."

I don't know what shrines are other than another name for the anchors, but it feels like a word the Agnac would use.

"Speaking on behalf of the Aelo Prelacy, Shiin'alo indicates she is unable to tell us Liddi's aims or what effect this will have on the Khua as a whole. The Agnac Hierarchy considers this a capital offense and has asked for an inquiry into Shiin'alo's fitness as Primary Aelo."

The image switches to Oxurg from the council. *"Shiin'alo has had our respect, but we now wonder if our patience with her unortho-dox ways has been in error. Her involvement must be questioned, and our people will provide volunteers to guard as many shrines as possible. In light of these new developments, I have ordered the release of Agnac cititzens involved in the recent riot in Podra."*

Kalkig and the other Agnac are free again, Shiin's under heavy scrutiny, and I'm a fugitive. My head feels skewered by all this news.

Yilt deactivates the wallscreen and turns to me. "Two Khua. Are you carrying the second as well?"

I shake my head and sketch a quick explanation. Two spires with a spark of energy in the middle, then two spires with a spark of energy off to the right.

"You set it free? Quain said you were unbinding the Khua from their anchors. He meant the shrines?"

Yes, the shrines, the anchors, the crystal monoliths of doom ... whatever he wants to call them. I point to the first drawing, with the Khua still anchored, and hold up three fingers.

"You've freed three of them?"

No. I try to be patient as he guesses again.

"You need to free a third?"

Right. I hold up four fingers, five, six, and on until I run out.

Yilt stretches his broad shoulders, but I have no idea what the gesture means. "This is important? You heard them—this is a capital offense. I need to know it's important."

I don't know what "capital offense" means, and it takes a moment for Yilt to see that's the part I'm stuck on.

"If we're caught, our punishment could be death."

Right, that. Tiav and Jahmari said laws allowing execution were still around. I've finally crossed a line that could justify enforcing those laws by anyone's standards, not just the Agnac's.

Is it that important? If it were just my brothers, I would say no, and the admission startles me. I couldn't ask this person I hardly know to risk his whole life for men he's never met. Important to me doesn't make it important to everyone. But Minali's harming the Khua, and that endangers entire planets.

Definitely important.

"Right, we can work out a strategy and get going in the morning."

NO, SPIN-STILL DOESN'T LIKE THAT IDEA. NIGHT IS BETTER. NIGHT IS WHEN THE BONDS TO THE ANCHORS ARE JUST A LITTLE LOOSER.

Interesting. Maybe that's why I can only see my brothers at night. Regardless, if the bonds are looser, I'm all for it. I don't know that my hand can take it if it's any harder.

Yilt grabs my wrist. I didn't realize I was flexing my fingers, but he noticed. The pinpricks stopped bleeding during my run back, but my whole palm stings and aches.

"What happened?"

I shrug. As far as I know, it's just part of the process. It hurts, but it's not going to kill me. I take my hand back and add to my drawing. Three moons and stars in the sky.

"It has to be at night?"

Apparently so.

He tilts his head back. It feels like a sigh. Then he taps several commands on the wallscreen, pulling up something that fills the whole space. A map. Land masses, large bodies of water ... based on the scale, it might be the entire planet. Tiny white lights dot the expanse.

"These are all of the Khua shrines on Ferinne," Yilt says. "Where would you like to start?"

A quick look lets me estimate the number. Thousands. There are thousands of them. There's no way I can get them all.

I DON'T NEED TO. I JUST NEED TO GET ENOUGH. THE RIGHT ONES. MINIMIZE THE DAMAGE BECAUSE I CAN'T STOP IT COMPLETELY. IT'LL HAVE TO DO.

I don't know what's enough.

NEITHER DOES SPIN-STILL, NOT FOR SURE. IT'S BETTER THAN NOTHING.

Here comes another headache. But Yilt asked a question. Where to start.

I point at a random light. Except nothing's random anymore. It's where Spin-Still wants us to go.

So that's where we'll go.

✳ – – – ✳

I've lost count of the Khua. I've lost count of the days since I left Sampati. I haven't lost count of the hours of sleep I've had lately, because I can manage those on one hand. Preferably not the hand I hold the sempu in when I free the Khua, because that hand is mad at me. The pinpricks show up in nearly the same spots every time, again and again. Yilt's healing treatments don't stand a chance before we're moving on to the next location.

Because the thing with a spherical planet is, it's always nighttime somewhere. We're chasing moonlight and there's no time for sleep.

I get in the streamer and study the map briefly before tapping a location. We reached several Khua in the first wave, before many guards were in place. It's trickier now, but we haven't run into anyone yet. Yilt says they can't guard them all. The keeper ranks are just sufficient for their normal duties, there are only a few dozen Aelo, and there aren't actually that many Agnac on this planet.

I'm too tired to hate the streamer anymore. Some rides are short, others long. This one's on the short side, so I don't get a chance to fall asleep.

The routine is the same every time. Approach the Khua carefully in case it's guarded. Yilt keeps a lookout, I set the Khua free, we go to the next one.

This time, Yilt stops me with a mammoth hand on my shoulder. "Are you certain you don't want me to do it?"

I glare at him. We already had this conversation once—as

much as I can converse with him, at least. I know it bothers him to see my hand bleed over and over, but he's a better look-out than I could be. He's faster, stronger, and sees better in the dark.

Besides, I didn't tell Yilt this, but it feels like my responsibility. Even though I don't believe what Fabin said about this being specifically his fault, my brothers and I are tangled up in the situation, so it's our job to untangle it. Because we can. *I* can.

The glare is enough for Yilt to give in and nudge me along. This particular Khua is on the edge of some farmland. The field is full of plants taller than I am, and the air is thick with an earthy, green smell. I never paid much attention to the agricultural areas of Erkir—they're mostly sentimental, with the way we produce food now—but it seems like I saw images of these plants before. Maybe in one of the boys' research projects. I think this is how squash grows. Unless it's beets.

While attempting to complete a vital task to help a newly discovered race, Liddi Jantzen got distracted by questions of vegetable identity.

I almost laugh at my own mental media-cast. I need to get some sleep soon.

For perhaps the hundredth time—maybe less, maybe more—I secure the sempu in my hand, say a mental hello to the Khua before me, and brace myself for the imminent pain.

And it hurts. It *really* does. A little worse each time, either because my hand never gets a chance to fully heal, or because I'm so tired it takes a little longer to push the Khua free.

This time hurts so bad, I'm certain I'll see pinpricks on the back of my hand, too. So bad, my muscles override my brain and pull back. A second attempt ends the same.

"I know it hurts, Liddi. Try to hurry and get it over with."

It's the most sympathy I've ever heard in Yilt's voice. The warmth it brings is short-lived.

"Who's there?" That's not Yilt. The voice comes from farther away, but not by much.

"Wait, it's her. Stop!"

I glance over my shoulder. Maybe it's farmers. Yilt can handle a couple of farmers.

But not when the farmers are just as big as he is. Haleian farmers seem pretty unlikely, and I catch a glimpse of a uniform as they approach. Keepers.

Yilt punches one and kicks the other. Not enough to stop them, just to keep them busy. "Liddi, go!"

Not without finishing the job. Panic gives me the adrenaline I need to shove the Khua free, even with the energy slicing into my hand.

"Now, run!"

I hesitate. I could try to help Yilt. Not sure how, exactly. The two keepers handle themselves just as well as he does. Mostly I could get myself knocked out, but it doesn't feel right to leave him.

"I said run! Finish it!"

The Haleian's expression has never been so clear to me. Steely eyes, set jaw. This is more important than him, than me, than even my brothers.

Yilt is right, and I run, but I hate it.

The keepers came from the direction of the streamer, so I can't go that way. The only option is into the field.

Cornfield. Corn grows on plants like this.

Amazing how my brain comes through when it's the most irrelevant.

I run while I can still hear the fighting, but the whip and rustle of the cornstalks soon drowns that out. The pack of supplies on my back makes moving between the plants awkward, but this situation is exactly why Yilt made me carry it every single time.

They're going to arrest him. The government may be slow, but what if capital offense trials are fast? They can't kill him for helping me. I can't stand even thinking it.

I don't know what to do.

CHANGE DIRECTION.

Sounds as good as anything. I turn directly to the right and keep moving, slower now, trying not to disturb the stalks and give away my location.

Maybe I should keep going.

I SHOULD GET ON THE GROUND AND HIDE.

The heat-blocking material is in my pack. I lie down and cover myself with it.

Maybe Spin-Still should launch me back to Quain's ship.

HE'S ON THE FAR SIDE OF THE PLANET AND SHE NEEDS A DIRECT LINE OF SIGHT TO TARGET SOMETHING SO MUCH SMALLER THAN THE POINTS' PLANETARY CORES.

All I can do is lie here, breathing the soil, not moving. My arms sting with cuts from the cornstalks, but it's nothing compared to the pain in my hand. At least I'm well-acquainted with

silence already. The footsteps of two approaching Halcians are hard to miss. Voices accompany them, just close enough to make out.

"Anything?"

"No. You?"

"Nothing. If it's true she captured and enslaved a Khua, she could've used it to get to the other side of the planet."

Shows what they know.

"All right, one of the flyers is going to do a sweep of the area, just in case. We should get the traitor to Chalu."

The voices fade with the ground-jarring footsteps and scraping of the cornstalks. I stay covered, keeping my ears tuned for the telltale whirr of flyers overhead.

A traitor. That's what they think Yilt is. Someone who just thought this world could use a little jostling, and I was the laserball that came barreling in for a bigger collision than he expected.

I say a silent apology to the Halcian for getting him into this. And a silent promise that if I can get him out of it, I will.

As usual, the workshop was noisy and chaotic, but Mr. Jantzen and the boys liked it that way. And the boys liked it best when their father had the time to spend with them.

Liddi added to the chaos by running into the room and crashing into her father's legs.

"Whoa, slow down there," he said, swinging her up into his arms.

"I'm sorry, Nevi," Mrs. Jantzen said from the doorway. "She keeps slipping away."

"Oh, let her stay, Sav. The boys don't mind, do you?"

A chorus of "No" responded, and Emil added, "Liddi can sit with me."

Mr. Jantzen set her down and reminded them to make sure she didn't hurt herself before moving on to help Durant with a tricky timing mechanism.

The boys kept working, and Liddi entertained herself with various bits left out on the workbench. Some she examined and set aside; others she added to her collection, piecing them together. She even sneaked into Emil's kit to snag a power supply. An hour later, Fabin noticed what she had in her hands.

"Um, Dad? I think Liddi made something."

He came over to look, but before he got there, Liddi's little fingers flipped the switch. The lights she'd cobbled together burst into life as the device flew up from her hands on its tiny hover-motor. It floated there, shining and sparkling as everyone stared at it.

"Boys, did she get that from one of you?" Mr. Jantzen asked.

Another chorus of negatives, and again Emil followed it. "I watched her make it, Daddy."

Vic and Luko responded in one voice. "But she's two."

No one could make sense of it, but Liddi was too little to care. All she cared about was watching her bright little machine, the way its light played off the walls.

"Pretty spark!"

21

TWO NIGHTS LATER, I've freed several dozen more Khua, all of them around Podra. Enough that seeing an untethered Khua floating around isn't all that rare anymore. After falling asleep for a few hours in the cornfield, I woke before sunrise and cleared out. I worried that Podra would be in the most danger, with so many anchored Khua around it, so I had to brave the more monitored areas.

Getting here involved "borrowing" an unsecured streamer, to add to my list of offenses. I don't dare use it anymore, though. Too easy to track. So I rest during the day and spend the night running across the countryside.

The Khua are more likely to be guarded here, but the guards still go on patrol, still change shifts, still wander off to relieve themselves. Half the Khua I've freed since Yilt's capture were guarded when I got there, but I waited, watched, and let Spin-Still be the wind pushing me at the right moment.

It's hide-and-seek all over again.

This one could be tricky. I lie flat on my belly at the top of a ridge overlooking a pair of Khua maybe two hundred yards apart, the closest of any I've seen. Around Podra, there are usually a few miles between them, and away from Podra, it's more likely a hundred miles at least.

These two Khua are close enough to watch at the same time, but they're each guarded by three Agnac. One in particular sticks close to the anchors, hardly moving. Maybe these Khua are extra-special in the Agnac's weird religion.

Spin-Still appreciates their respect, but wishes they'd listen a little more. I think Agnac yell too much, and a bout of induced silence could do them a world of good.

Once in a while, one of the Agnac wanders off, but that leaves two at one Khua and three at the other, plus I have to worry about whether the wanderer will circle around and find me. They each carry small lights—their night vision must be awful, because the light of the three moons is plenty—so at least that makes it harder for them to sneak up on me.

I glance at my watch, resisting the twinge as it reminds me of Tiav. I should leave, find another Khua to free. An easier target. But every time I think about getting up, I get the urge to stay, to wait, to watch. It has to be Spin-Still, and she has to have a reason for it.

All six of the Agnac are in position when the Khua on my left draws everyone's attention. It whirls and flashes into a larger ball of light, just for a heartbeat. When it goes back to normal, an extra person stands in front of it.

Even with just the moons and the light of the Khua, I know that build. It's Tiav.

The Agnac recognize him, too, an instant before Tiav

collapses. They're shouting in their language before he hits the ground.

"Stop, listen to me! You don't understand!"

His voice comes through amid the angry gargles of the Agnac language, but I don't understand, either. He just came out of a Khua without using a sempu. Without "authorization." He broke the Agnac's biggest law, and he must've been in there since before I arrived.

Sparks.

The three Agnac on my right run to see what's happened. Their Khua is left unattended.

Double-sparks. That can't be what Spin-Still expects me to do.

For the first time in days, there's no clear answer. This time, I choose.

Calculations tick away the seconds. How long it would take me to reach the Khua. The odds none of the Agnac would see me, or notice when I freed it. Those odds are okay, with the diversion Tiav's causing.

Then the approach I'd have to take to get to Tiav. The chances of getting out alive. Slim.

Tiav hasn't gotten up. I remember how an "unfiltered" Khua feels.

Someone has a stick. Raises it. Swings it down.

Tiav cries out.

I'm already halfway down the hill, cursing the numbers that say I won't be able to loose another Khua, that those I've managed won't be enough. It doesn't matter—if Ferinne gets torn to pieces now, maybe it's as much their own fault as Minali's.

I don't know what I'm going to do to the Agnac when I get there. All I know is I have to stop what they're doing to Tiav.

Before I reach them, the smallest Agnac grabs the stick, tries to wrestle it away. The larger one throws him off. With the way Tiav's defender twists, the light of the Khua illuminates his face.

Kalkig.

Something's changed. No anger in his face. Just fear.

The other five Agnac don't listen to him, I have no chance of stopping them, but I run anyway.

"Hey!"

"Stop!"

Those aren't Agnac voices. They have Sampati accents.

Vic appears in front of Tiav, sending a very startled Agnac back a step. The one with the stick swings it at Vic, hitting nothing, and the momentum spins him to face Anton.

It's not just those two. All eight of my brothers appear, disappear, reappear as the Agnac whirl and shout and fight. My brothers aren't random, either. They appear everywhere but in my path. They're trying to clear the way, give me a chance.

They're in pain, they're weak, but they're making this effort for me. I can't screw it up. I slip through the commotion, reach Tiav crumpled on the ground.

"That's her!"

Tiav looks up at those words, just as I grab hold to haul him to his feet. The spark is back in his eyes, the spark that sees who I am. Light floods through me, but only sharpens my fear.

"Ignore them. Get her!" one of the Agnac shouts.

Kalkig picks up a stick of his own and swings it, but not at us—at his own people. "Liddi, get him out of here."

The shock of hearing Kalkig use my name rather than *heathen* freezes me for the smallest moment. Long enough for him to look over his shoulder at me. Alien gestures vary, but our eyes all speak the same language. Kalkig isn't sure he trusts *me* yet, but something changed in the days I've been gone. He trusts his friend again, and he's sorry for what he's done.

I'm sorry about all of it.

Tiav can barely stand. There's only one way out. I hate to do it to him when he's already hurting, but the alternative would be a lot worse.

With silent thanks to my brothers, I wrap one arm tight around Tiav's waist, reach for the anchored Khua with my free hand, and hope Spin-Still will tell her friend to drop us off somewhere decent.

— — — ✳

The Khua are by far my least favorite way to travel, but this time is worse than usual. Mind-ripping chaos, more pain than a person should be able to take, that's all normal. The nauseating twist and stretch like someone's trying to make me taller, the choking dimness surrounding us ... those are new. Just when I'm certain we've reached the end, it starts over.

Days. Years. Microseconds.

Then we're out. Tiav's full weight collapses against me, and my own body is convinced its cells have imploded. I struggle to lower him to the ground without dropping him.

The pain isn't real. It's in my head.

Surprisingly, focusing on that thought diminishes the pain, enough that I can take stock of our surroundings.

A canyon between two wooded mountains. The rush of water reveals a river nearby. Two crystal spires anchor a Khua behind us. And it's daylight.

So, still on Ferinne, but the other side of it. I thought we couldn't do that.

WE TRAVELED BY TWO KHUA. THAT MOMENT I FELT LIKE IT SHOULD'VE BEEN OVER, I WAS RIGHT. WE'D REACHED ONE OF THE OTHER POINTS, BUT ANOTHER KHUA WAS WAITING RIGHT THERE TO PICK US UP AGAIN.

Tiav groans and tries to push himself up, but I push him back. Energy charges through me at being close to him again, touching him again, but I can't think about that. I don't know how badly the Agnac injured him. The bruises on his arms will hurt for a few days, and I tenderly check his ribs. He winces, but I don't think anything's broken.

"I'm fine," he insists, even if his voice doesn't sound fine at all. Slowly, he sits up, just partway, and scoots to lean back against a rock. Even that much effort winds him. "Liddi, I'm so sorry. I should've let you explain, but I didn't understand. I felt something wrong in the Khua, like a sickness, and I saw your brothers and thought they did it. Then you had the sempu and the Khua with it. Everything, my whole life has been about the Khua, learning from them, but this . . . I didn't understand, and I was scared."

My brothers *are* the cause, but not on purpose. That's the only thing Tiav misinterpreted, and I can't blame him for that. I lay my hand on his chest, hoping to calm him, but all I can feel is how hard his heart pounds. The tension of his shallow breaths. I wonder how he understands now, what happened to change his mind.

He still knows how to read my eyes. "No matter how we deployed people to guard the Khua, you seemed to go straight for the ones left open. Everyone's saying you imprisoned that one." His eyes move to Spin-Still briefly. "That you're using it against its will. But I thought about what Quain said, about the Khua allowing you to come here from Sampati. Quain wouldn't talk to me, and I started to wonder if the Khua was helping you. I knew I was missing something."

I'm *still* missing something. I rap my knuckles on a nearby rock and point to my head.

"Because I'm hard-headed?"

No, not that—pretty sure I'm harder-headed than he is. I jut out my chin and lean forward on my arms like an Agnac might.

"Kal? I'm not sure if the logic sank in or if it was just seeing how miserable I was, but he agreed something was off. Especially once I explained how the Khua have been getting more and more confusing since *before* you arrived. He told his people he had those shrines covered and I disabled the alarms. Then I went in to ask the Khua if I was right."

I trace a circle on his chest, where a crystal disk should lie but doesn't.

"Without a sempu," he confirms. "It was . . . I'd been told how awful communing was before we had the disks, but I had no idea what it's really like. Hours felt like a lifetime. Too long, it gave that patrol time to show up. Some of those men, your brothers, they found me and tried to explain, but it was hard for me to focus. They're trapped, right? Because of what someone on Sampati is doing, the one who put that thing in your throat so if

you speak, they'll die. And that's why you wouldn't tell me. You were afraid *we* might hurt them if we knew, and they're your brothers, so you had to keep them safe."

He knows. He understands. Not everything yet, but enough. And he's not angry anymore.

Tiav sees my relief and takes my hand. The wrong hand. The sharp sting jerks it back.

"What's the matter? Let me see."

I turn my hand, and he gently holds it by my wrist. His eyes break my heart. He thinks it's his fault.

"The design," he murmurs. "It's the same."

I noticed that, too. The angry red marks on my palm are a perfect match of the engraved pattern on the sempu. That's how the energy cuts through.

Then he traces his thumbs lightly up either side of my hand, outside the edges of the scars, and I don't want to think about Khua or conduits or Minali or my brothers anymore.

I have to kiss Tiav, so I do.

My hair is a tangled mess, and I've been days without anything other than the minimal hygiene kit in my pack. I don't care. Based on the way his arms wind around me, drawing me closer, he doesn't either.

When he pulls me *too* close and winces, I care about that. He only lets me back away a little.

"I said I'm fine."

I trace my fingers over his ear, through his hair, and mouth the word, *Liar.* That makes him smile, but it doesn't last.

"Liddi, what are we going to do? The Agnac are putting out an imminent threat order. They could kill you on sight, no trial. The Crimna are fighting it, the Ferinnes and Haleians can't decide, and the Izim won't talk to anyone. My mother doesn't know what to think, and she *always* knows. The rest of the Aelo know something's wrong with the Khua, but think it's *because of* what you've been doing. I can try, but I don't—I'm afraid no one will listen to me now. As soon as those Agnac report back to Podra, I'll be stripped of my title."

A chasm opens up in my chest, overflowing with guilt. It's all fallen apart. Tiav will lose his status as Aelo—what he's worked at all his life—and his whole world is in chaos. The death sentence hanging over me could extend to him as well.

And Yilt. *Imminent threat order.* Yilt may not have as much time as I thought he did.

I use my finger to draw swiftly in the dirt. A small figure to represent myself, and a hulking figure for Yilt. I point to it and look to Tiav, letting all the panic I feel paint itself into my expression.

"That Haleian who helped you? No, they won't execute him. It would mean war with his people. But he'll be kept in a detention facility, maybe for the rest of his life."

That news is only a small relief. Yilt won't die for helping me, but wasting his life away in confinement won't be much better. I don't have the answer to Tiav's first question—I don't know what we'll do next—but I know somehow in the end we have to make everyone understand. They have to see Yilt doesn't deserve that punishment.

"Okay, one step at a time," Tiav says when I don't offer anything else. "We're safe for now. How are we still on Ferinne? You can't travel by Khua within the same planet."

I don't know how to explain it to him, or everything else he needs to know. Maybe Spin-Still can tell him.

YES, SHE CAN.

It's about time I give back what I inadvertently stole. I lift the cord from around my neck and lower it over Tiav's head. He closes his eyes and his breathing slows as he concentrates on communicating with her.

Meanwhile, I contemplate how strange it feels not to be holding Spin-Still anymore. Not lonely, because I'm with Tiav. But like silence has closed in again, wrapping itself tighter around me. It brings an ache of isolation I'd almost forgotten.

Tiav opens his eyes, and everything in them is more complex. Sad, overwhelmed, anxious, happy, and hopeful. I don't know how he can feel all those things at once and not explode. Then he takes off the sempu and tries to put it back on me, and I definitely only feel one thing.

No. Absolutely not.

"Liddi, yes. She belongs with you. I didn't even know they have names—we never thought to ask. Didn't know they don't need the shrines—the anchors—anymore, haven't for a long time. Didn't know their connection to us, to biological beings, was helping them evolve and grow, rather than already being at the apex of their own existence."

See, he already knows more than I do. He's an Aelo. I'm not.

"I'll only hold on to it if we're going to release the Khua over there, because I'm not letting you do that again."

I'm not letting him do it, either, but neither of us is doing it right now. I point at the sun nearly straight overhead.

"You've never released one during the day. That's on purpose?"

A nod, and I push the sempu toward him. He pushes back.

"Please."

It's too hard to argue when he says please, when he looks at me like that...when he smoothes his hands over my hair and neck as he settles Spin-Still in place. I let it go, but I don't like it. Even if having her back dulls the ache of silence again.

We need time to decide what to do next, to make a plan, but I can't just sit here. My pack has a small medical kit in it, but I don't know what anything does. I pull it out and hand it to Tiav, hoping he'll find something to help him with the pain. While he looks, I go down to the river and refill the water flask. Yilt assured me it had a built-in purifier, so I don't need to worry about anything nasty in the water. If we're going to stay here, we can't sit in the sun all day. The mountains present several possibilities for shelter. We'll work on that when Tiav feels up to moving.

He's fished a pill of some kind out of the kit when I get back and gratefully accepts the offered water. I point to the sun again, but before I can point to the mountains, I freeze.

Vid-cams. I'm being watched.

No, that's not it. Not the same buzz. More of a hum with a grating edge, making my bones itch.

"What is that?" Tiav asks.

The anchored Khua draws my eye, several feet away. Even with the anchors locking them in, the Khua usually float and hover loosely, like a buoy on a wave. Not now. This one is perfectly still, as frozen as I feel.

I hurry over and put my hand to one of the spires. It vibrates. A lot.

This might mean it's too late. That the Khua have been fully locked down and they're fighting a losing battle not to tear everything apart.

NO, NOT ALL OF THEM. JUST A FEW, LIKE THIS ONE, BUT THE OTHERS ARE RUNNING OUT OF TIME. THIS IS WHAT QUAIN PREDICTED, BAD THINGS HAPPENING BEFORE THE END OF THE MOON-CYCLE.

Spin-Still's assurances mean there's only one thing to do. I take her from my neck, wrap the cord tight, and start pushing.

It hurts, it hurts, it hurts. Worse than before, worse than any of them, and it won't move, I can't. Tears flow down my cheeks, the only release when I can't cry out.

"Liddi, stop!"

I can't do that either. The vibrations run through me, ready to shatter my bones, but I have to keep pushing. I can't stop Tiav from getting to his feet. He's unsteady but makes it to me without falling.

No matter how I push, how I throw all my weight into it, the Khua won't budge. I'm not strong enough to break the bond in daylight. My feet skid on the rocky ground, not giving me enough purchase.

Tiav reaches around and puts his hands on mine, leaning against me. We both push.

It works. The Khua breaks free. Tiav and I stumble forward before he grabs my waist to pull me upright.

WE HAVE TO LEAVE. WE HAVE TO GO NOW, USING THE KHUA WE JUST FREED, WE HAVE TO LEAVE FERINNE.

Spin-Still's urgency shakes me. I don't know what's happening, why she's telling me to leave. What about the other anchored Khua?

NO TIME FOR A PLAN, NO TIME FOR THINKING. THE PRIORITY HAS SHIFTED. THE POISONING EFFECT OF THE CONDUITS HAS INTENSIFIED, AND IF WE DON'T GO NOW, THE KHUA MIGHT NOT BE ABLE TO TAKE US SAFELY AT ALL. WE NEED TO FIX THINGS, AND WE CAN'T DO THAT HERE.

But the Khua still anchored on Ferinne—

WHAT I'VE DONE WILL HAVE TO BE ENOUGH.

"Your hand," Tiav says.

Yes, it's bleeding again, nothing new, and we don't have time. I leave his arms, grab my pack, and point to the Khua, still hovering nearby.

"Leaving? Where are we going?"

His hesitance is unmistakable, and I understand. He's been taught all his life that using the Khua to travel is the wrongest of the wrong. And it's not going to be a pleasant trip.

There's also no time to explain. I pull Tiav close and reach for the Khua.

It's time for me to go home.

The Sentinel and the Wraith were once friends, equals who together created the realm of Ferri as a home for the spirits of the Seven Points after they died. As they worked, the pair found they had very different ideas of what Ferri should be. The Sentinel thought it should be soft and smooth, a place for the spirits to forget the trials of their lives. The Wraith thought it should be sharp and powerful, a place of labor to remind the spirits they were unworthy of the protection they were given. Without Ferri, the spirits would be lost.

The two friends discussed, and then they argued, and then they fought. One began to shape Ferri to his liking, and the other tore it down, insisting it must not be so. Destruction and ruin were the only results.

Finally they decided they could work together no more. They drew a line through the foundations of Ferri, the Divide that could never be crossed. The Sentinel created Idyll, full of tranquility and beauty. The Wraith created the Abyss, where the toil and torment would never end. When men and women of the Seven Points died, they would be claimed by the one they most deserved.

Even knowing it wasn't real, young Liddi didn't like the story. If the Sentinel and the Wraith were so powerful, they should've been smart enough to find a better way.

22

THIS TRIP THROUGH THE KHUA is one too many in too short
a space for Tiav. I have to catch him again when we arrive, my
own legs barely holding, and he's breathing too fast.

"Please—can we—not do that—again, Liddi?"

I look to the sky. The angle of the sun has changed, and
beyond that, so has the sun itself. A little smaller, a little whiter
than Ferinne's sun. More important, I know these woods. We're
on Sampati, not far from the house. Keeping one arm around
him without aggravating my injured hand, I pat Tiav's chest to
ask if he's okay.

He nods, forcing himself to take slower, deeper breaths. It
doesn't stop his shaking—or mine—but he keeps to his feet.
When I urge him to take a step forward, he starts walking. Neither of us is very steady, half from the aftereffects of the Khua
and half the protest from our equilibriums about the subtle
change in gravity.

"We've left Ferinne, haven't we? I've never been on another planet before. Plenty of people visit Crimna or Agnac or Halei, but my mother was always too busy. What is this? Erkir?"

His nerves show in his rambling, and I can't blame him. I remember how I felt when I unexpectedly landed on Ferinne. Looking up at him, I shake my head and mouth one word. *Home.*

Tiav's eyes go wide. "Sampati? It's not how I pictured it."

Of course not. It's one of the few parts of Sampati that's not like Sampati at all. He'll probably see that soon, but first we need to get to the house. It's close enough that I still haven't walked off all the Khua-aches by the time we get there. I stop at the edge of the woods, and Tiav waits with me, silent.

Everything looks the same. The garden needs a little weeding, that's all. I can imagine the Triad bursting out the back door any minute. My gut twists with the knowledge that they're not going to.

I've been gone a long time. Long enough for Minali to notice. And possibly long enough for her to set a guard here. Or long enough for her not to expect me to come back somewhere so obvious.

We wait, and we watch, and Tiav doesn't ask any questions. He just takes the medical kit from my pack and treats my hand without a word. Finally, I decide we'll have to go in and see what—if anything—awaits us.

"Welcome home, Liddi."

I almost cry at the sound of Dom's voice.

"That was a rather lengthy absence," he continues, "and not reflected on your schedule. Ms. Blake seemed quite upset not to find you here when she stopped by. I take it you are still not speaking?"

That's obvious, particularly when I pull up the drawing screen and do a rough sketch.

"A vid-cam? No, Liddi, as you're aware, vid-cams cannot function on the property, aside from those installed in the house. Those remain secure."

"Smart computer," Tiav murmurs.

"I'm not a computer, sir, I'm a subroutine running *on* a computer. I am the Domestic Engineer and Itinerary Keeper. You may call me Domenik, or Dom if you prefer."

Despite clear bewilderment at having a computer program introduce itself, Tiav responds. "Nice to meet you. Tiav'elo, call me Tiav. Um, Liddi, that woman who trapped your brothers . . . could she have tampered with Dom while you were away?"

"Absolutely not!" Dom answers for himself. "The Jantzen family knows better than to use simple passcodes like birth dates, sir. My system has quadruple-layered encryption and triple-redundant backups."

It's true, my brothers are beyond diligent about keeping their tech secure, so I move on. For Dom *and* Tiav to be able to help me, I'll need them to speak the same language. I draw again, this time the Eight Points, arranged in their ring. A few simple lines in red connect the Seven, then a few more in blue for connections including Ferinne. I point at it and wait for Dom to make his guess.

"Are those the portals and conduits again? You appear to have included an extra Point."

I look to Tiav and shake my head. He gets it. "No, the blue ones are called the Khua. The extra Point is Ferinne—that's where I'm from."

"Intriguing. I shall update my database."

Okay, we're getting there. I point to the red lines again and nudge Tiav.

"Domenik, what did you call the red lines?"

"The conduits. More reliable than the ancient portals for interplanetary travel."

"Your brothers told me something about false Khua. That's what you call them?" Tiav checks. "Conduits?"

Exactly. I pull up one of the larger news-vid feeds on the wallscreen and point to it and my sketch of the conduits at the same time.

"You want to know if there's been any news here about them, about the conduits."

"There has indeed," Dom says. "Would you like a summary or to watch them yourself?"

One finger for the first choice. Tiav seems startled as he realizes Dom is watching us through the in-house cams.

"Over the past nine days, each of the Seven Points has reported dozens of minor tectonic tremors. Damage has been minimal thus far, except to conduit terminals, which use highly sensitive equipment. Conduit travel is thus restricted to emergencies, but technologists at JTI are currently working on a fix. The coinciding timing of the tremors on all seven planets is also being investigated."

They're saying the earthquakes damaged the conduits when really the conduits caused the earthquakes. Minali has to know that, but it's possible everyone else is buying the story. She'll complete the process of locking my brothers in, and if it works to stabilize the conduits, she'll be praised as the hero who kept the Seven Points connected.

If it doesn't, we'll be buried under too much rubble to point fingers.

I don't care what her simulations said. That eighteen percent chance of failure sounds more like a certainty to me. Her simulations didn't account for the Khua, for *life*. She's working off of incomplete data.

"So, what do we do?" Tiav asks. "Do we tell these JTI people what's happening, how to stop that woman who attacked you and your brothers?"

My expression in response is withering.

"She's *with* JTI? Like, someone they all know?"

I hold my hand high above my head.

"The boss?"

Technically, that would be me, but close enough.

"Would she stop if she knew what she's doing to the Khua and Ferinne?"

The question lodges in my head directly between yes and no. I'm not sure. She didn't hesitate to put my brothers' lives on the line and handcuff me, all in her obsessive certainty that she's saving civilization. But I've known her for years. She's always been a little too driven by calculations and the bottom line, but I never thought she'd take a cutthroat instinct so far. Maybe she can still be reasoned with.

Then I remember one important fact. I'm contemplating reasoning with a murderer. She killed Garrin. Why would she care about a planet we've forgotten, or a race our people never believed was alive at all?

I shake my head. It's like Quain said. Talking to her would only tip her off to any plans we might have. Not that we have any plans yet.

280

"What, then? Do we destroy the conduits?"

I drop onto a couch, my head in my hands. Getting rid of the conduits makes sense—they're what's causing all this trouble—but my brothers are stuck in there. And even if we find a way to get them out first, the Seven Points would become completely isolated from each other. Minali is right that losing the conduits would be catastrophic. Our society for hundreds of years has depended on movement between the worlds. Without the others, each Point is unbalanced in what it can provide. How can I destroy the lives of billions of people?

Spin-Still pulses against my chest. No matter what the Agnac think, the Khua don't mind carrying people between worlds as long as they're asked, not forced. Like Tiav said, interacting with biological beings allows them to grow. They restrained themselves from fully manifesting in the Seven Points at the request of the Aelo, but if I ask, they'll return. We can extend use of the sempu and work together.

If Tiav and I can find a way to save them first. I look up at him and give an uncertain nod.

He sits next to me, runs a hand across my back. "Okay. We'll find a way to do that. If there's one thing you've shown Ferinne lately, it's that you know how to sneak around and sabotage things if you want to."

I clamp a hand over my mouth to keep a humorless laugh from escaping. Maybe it's a sob. He has no idea, but he might as well find out now. I pull up several old media-casts in rapid succession.

"Liddi Jantzen, seen here at Syncopy last night—"

"Top fashion designer Igara confirmed that his new shoe line will be worn by Liddi Jantzen at—"

"No word yet on whether the Jantzen girl will debut anything at this year's Tech Reveal."

"With the deaths of Nevi and Savina Jantzen, control of Jantzen Technology Innovations passes not to one of their sons, but to six-year-old Liddi—or it will when she's old enough to—"

Tiav watches the screen, expressionless, so I scan the feeds for something current.

"There's still been no sign of Liddi Jantzen on any of the Seven Points. We all remember that strange morning she wandered barefoot into the borders of Pinnacle, but she hasn't been seen since a few days after that incident. JTI officials have refused to comment, and the Jantzen boys likewise cannot be reached, leaving one question. Where are the Jantzens?"

I turn it off, and Tiav takes a deep breath, processing it.

"Okay, I guess sneaking around won't be that easy after all. But we'll figure out something."

We will. I need to think. But it's hard to think when I feel dirty and smelly. I hold up a tangled lock of hair and roll my eyes at Tiav, which makes him laugh. After steering him to the guest room, I go upstairs to get cleaned up.

Liddi Jantzen died of happiness upon returning to her own bathroom after a long time away.

Once the dust and grime is gone and I'm wearing my own clothes, I'm ready to go back down and get to work. Except something catches my eye. I keep images of the family on screens throughout the room. An image of Durant and me on Yishu is next to my bed. We went to a concert on that trip.

The stringed instruments captured my attention at the time. Each string vibrating, held down on the ends. Then the musicians would press their fingers somewhere, pinning the string so it held still in that spot and vibrated to one side. The music harmonized when the vibrations were at related frequencies.

Related frequencies...

I run down the stairs two at a time. I know what to do. At least, where to start.

The space between the back of the sofa and the wall was tiny enough that only Liddi could fit there. Only if she turned herself sideways and squeezed in at just the right angle. It was the one hiding spot of hers the boys didn't know about, so when all the strange people arrived to offer their condolences, she was nowhere to be found. Each of her brothers assumed one of the others knew where she was, and there were too many people, too much going on to realize she was missing. Too much noise to hear her crying.

That was true at first, anyway. Then the crowd thinned out, and Durant spoke from somewhere nearby.

"Fabin, I still haven't seen Liddi. Where is she?"

"I don't know. With the Triad, maybe?"

"She's not with us." That was Marek.

"We haven't seen her, either," Luko said.

Durant's voice took a hard edge, and Liddi could picture the face that went with it. "Find her."

He sounded like their father. That made her cry harder.

"What? Where's that coming from? Liddi?"

Moments later, hands reached into the small space and pulled her out. Part of her wanted to scream and squirm, but she didn't, and once Durant had her out, he held her tight. He didn't say anything until they were in Liddi's room, with no more strangers looking at them. Then he sat on her bed with his sister on his lap.

"Why did you hide, Liddi-Loo?" he asked. "You scared us."

"I—I don't know." She hiccuped. "Because I'm sad."

"We're all sad. You don't have to hide it."

"But when I'm sad, Mommy makes me happy again. Mommy's gone, and so is Daddy, and I'm alone."

Liddi's oldest brother hugged her tighter than before. "There are eight of us, Liddi. You'll never ever have to be alone."

23

WORKING WITH MY OWN COMPUTER, even without my voice, is such a release. All the familiar icons and subroutines, and Dom is still set to fill in the blanks where he can. Time to draw. I point to the existing picture for Tiav.

"Right, blue are the Khua, the red are those false Khua—conduits."

He's got it, so I minimize that drawing. For this to make sense, I'll have to simplify. Just two planets, connected by both a Khua and a conduit. After some fiddling, I get the computer to animate the red and blue lines vibrating at the same rate, exactly aligned like a single plucked string on Yishu's instruments. Each planet holds the ends of the "strings" like children holding skip ropes.

"You want to get both on the same frequency. Why? They're already getting too close. That's the whole problem, right?"

I move that drawing aside temporarily and try another, eight people standing on a red line, arrows drawn from there to a blue line, and finally arrows drawn out from the blue to a house with a tree.

"If we get the two synced, you think your brothers can cross over fully to the Khua and come out like we do?"

Yes, that's exactly what I think.

"But there's no way to do that. Khua are filtered to one 'frequency' using sempu, but only in one place, or on one 'end.' The filtered part makes sort of a bubble around us when we go in. The rest of that Khua's being stays unfiltered on all the other Points, plus at their secondary connections to other planets like Agnac. Your conduits don't seem to work that way. And besides, the only sempu we have right now is holding Spin-Still."

He thinks it won't work, but at least he understands. I go back to the animated drawing and slide the anchor points off each planet, moving them along the "strings" toward the center until they're practically on top of each other. The tiny lengths in between still vibrate as one.

The four loose ends swing randomly, chaotically.

"Bringing everything together into one 'bubble' somehow?"

I nod. Something like that.

Tiav just stares at the picture for a long time. "Liddi," he finally says. "Is this something Spin-Still is telling you to do?"

Good question. Sometimes it's hard to tell what's mine and what's the speaking-through-instinct from her. As I wonder, though, the answer comes through clearly enough. No, this is my idea, because I see the Khua from the outside, as they can't see themselves. I shake my head.

He gestures to the diagram. "Even if I knew how to focus a Khua that way, and even if I knew how to force your people's conduits to align with it, I don't know what would happen. I

don't know what these 'loose ends' would do. The Khua embody powerful forces. The destruction could be severe, and I don't mean the minor tremors they've been talking about. The stress could tear into the planetary cores."

Part of me doesn't want to care. Part of me says I'd destroy half of every planet I've ever set foot on if it would save my brothers. More of me knows I can't be that irresponsible. More of me *does* care. But freeing my brothers dovetails with undoing the damage Minali has already done to the Khua. There has to be a way.

As usual, Tiav sees all that I'm feeling. "Can I see what Spin-Still thinks?"

I hate that. The sempu around my neck is his. He shouldn't have to ask for permission, and the answer is always yes.

He slips his fingers beneath the crystal, brushing against me. I'm not sure if it's my pulse or his that I feel, but I count the beats. It's eight before he lets go, and his hand doesn't move far, just enough to rest on my cheek.

"She says the Khua won't be well again until your brothers are released, and if they aren't well again, worse things will happen. She thinks if we tell your brothers your idea, one of them will know how to do it."

That means finding my brothers. It's hours until sunset, and we can't wait that long. Hovercars aren't anywhere near as fast as streamers, so getting to a place on Sampati where night's fallen isn't an option, either.

We can talk to them inside the Khua. Not the "narrowed" Khua that Tiav is used to. I couldn't hear my brothers in there. It'll have to be the unfettered, full-blown, on-*all*-the-frequencies kind.

The kind Tiav didn't want to go into again.

I take his arm and lead him out to the yard. Looking for a Khua on Sampati is nothing like finding one on Ferinne. I wonder how we're going to do this.

THE KHUA ARE ALL CONNECTED. THEY TALK TO EACH OTHER IN THEIR OWN WAY. SPIN-STILL CAN CALL ONE TO US. THOSE I UNANCHORED ON FERINNE WILL BE THE STRONGEST AGAINST THE GROWING CONDUIT INTERFERENCE, SO SHE'LL CALL ONE OF THEM.

Just like making a wish, a Khua winks into existence, ready and waiting.

Tiav sighs. "We're going in there, aren't we?"

I squeeze his arm. He likes it about as much as I like streamers. I'd go without him, but I need him to do the talking.

"This is definitely not what I expected in all the years my mother trained me to be an Aelo. But I guess important things are often unexpected, aren't they?"

We enter the Khua, and I focus everything on not *going* anywhere—none of the other Points—just letting my brothers find me. Through the chaos and the freezing heat of dark fire and the screeching silence and the pain-pain-pain, I have to keep my focus.

Fabin is first, then the others one by one, gathering around us as they did when they took me to Ferinne. As then, their presence blocks most of the pain, but they're weak. They won't last long, not in a Khua twisting and pulling like this, poisoned and sick.

But we're together. All of us.

"Liddi had an idea," Tiav says. He's better at focusing through the chaos than I am, and he dives into explaining.

My brothers listen, not interrupting, not questioning until he's done.

"That works on the figurative," Luko says. "But we have to work out how to make it happen on the literal end."

"I might have a piece of it," Fabin says. "We came in through the conduits, but our biological energy pulls us toward the Khua, because they're drawn to life. The eight of us are what's getting the two tangled in each other. We're the glue."

"If that's true," Durant says, "getting us out will let them untangle and separate, fixing everything."

"After all this, the conduits will probably collapse," Ciro adds. "They're too damaged."

Emil gives an uncharacteristically dark look. "Good."

Tiav is watching me and sees what I want to say. "We still need to know *how* to get you out so all this can happen."

"I have an idea," Fabin says. "But we'll need help from the Khua, if they're willing."

He talks about convergence and nesting energies and things I only half understand, but I get enough. Tuning several conduits and Khua to match, creating the "bubble," pulling my brothers free . . . and Spin-Still. We'll definitely need her.

Ten minutes and five eternities later, we have a plan.

It'll take a lot more wishes to pull this off.

※ — — — ※

I'm pacing. I know it won't accomplish anything, but there's nothing else to do. We've slept—my brothers insisted on it

as we left them in the Khua—but all it's done is make me restless.

Through a lot of drawing and gesturing, I got Tiav and Dom working together on fabricating a blank sempu. Between the two of them, they got the right crystal composition, and Tiav's engraving it now in the workshop. When he's done, Dom will make exact duplicates, some for the Khua and some modified to interface with the conduit control systems, ready to filter the Khua and bring those conduits into harmony with them. Temporarily.

My job is to figure out how we're going to get to the conduit terminals to set things up. Eight conduits, one for each of my brothers. Not just any conduits—the ones they were working on when they were trapped, which they made Tiav and me memorize. We have to get to them even though the second I go into any city, the vid-cams will be all over us. Minali will know I'm back, and she'll stop us.

I can't let that happen, but I also can't find a way around it. If Tiav goes alone, the vid-cams will ignore him, but he has no voiceprint, no one knows him, so no access to anything. I need to be there, because Liddi Jantzen would be let into a restricted conduit terminal, but I can't go, because Liddi Jantzen can't go anywhere without getting noticed.

I'm an idiot.

Tiav is sitting at Fabin's usual spot in the workshop when I come in. I don't want to mess up his engraving, so I wait until he notices me. It's difficult when I'm ready to explode.

"You have an idea?"

Yes, but I really don't know how to explain it. Then I remember one of the news-vids Dom summarized. I pull it up and scan to the right moment.

"JTI technologists are working on repairing the damage to the conduits."

I freeze the image accompanying the words—people in JTI uniforms entering a conduit terminal. I point to one of them and point at myself.

"We'll disguise ourselves as repair workers from JTI?"

No, not that. Vid-cams use sophisticated face-recognizing algorithms, so disguises are useless. Before I can think of a way to be more specific, Dom jumps in.

"Liddi hardly needs to disguise herself as a JTI employee when she stands to inherit the company."

Perfect. With a nod, I put on a stern face and act out marching around giving people orders.

Tiav slowly smiles. "You'll go as yourself. With something as big as all the conduits being down, of course the head of the company should oversee repairs personally. Will it work? Will people believe it and let us in?"

I scan through the news-vid again until I find an image of Minali. Freeze. Point. Shake my head.

"That's her, the woman who did this? So everyone but her? Okay. Then we definitely watch out for her."

We'll need a few things from Dom. I didn't want to resort to this, but I can't think of any other way to explain it, so I fish into Tiav's pocket for his com-tablet. Not connected to the Ferinne network anymore, but it still has the read-aloud program. He keeps engraving while I work out a message.

"Dom mayk mee tock nooz-vid."

"I don't believe I understand," Dom says.

Of course not. He wasn't programmed to interpret something so broken, but Tiav's become an expert at it.

"She wants you to make one of those news-vids with her talking, but she can't talk, so you'll have to fabricate it. Can he do that?"

"Certainly," Dom answers for himself. "It depends on what she wants to say, naturally, but with the number and variety of recordings on file, it's quite likely I could find the right words."

"You want to announce that you're going to check progress on the conduits?" Tiav asks. "Is that smart?"

It'll be a little bit tougher for Minali to quietly get rid of me if everyone knows what I'm doing. I nod. I need something else, too, but I think I can draw this one. A sketch of myself standing at a door, little sound waves traveling from my mouth to the receiver.

"Voiceprint," Dom says. "Yes, if a conduit is unattended, you'll need to use it, and that will be difficult if you can't speak. Shall I prepare a high-quality recording of that as well?"

Another nod, and I get to work writing the exact words I need for the news-vid. No shortcuts, no skipping anything. Word-for-word.

By the time Tiav finishes engraving the sempu and fabricating the duplicates, I'm finished, too. Dom pieces together the script, remodulating it so it sounds natural, and I practice mouthing along a few times so it looks convincing before we record. Tiav has a strange expression, so I give him what-face.

"First time hearing your voice, sort of," he says with half a smile. "But I'm still holding out for the real thing."

With the plan as we worked it out with my brothers, he'll hear it soon enough. We link Dom to one of my own com-tablets in case we need him and head out to the hovercar.

Time for me to show Tiav around Sampati.

Being the oldest also made Durant the busiest, so when he offered to take Liddi to visit Yishu, just the two of them, she was thrilled. She wasn't sure what they'd do there, but time with her brother was good enough.

They got there, and she was confused.

First stop was an art institute where they saw students working on paintings and sculptures, and walked through the galleries. Sometimes Liddi could identify what the piece depicted. A painted landscape. A sketch of a child's face. A sculpture of a dog. Others made no sense. Splotches of color and random shapes.

Next they took in a series of concerts. Stringed instruments. Metallic instruments. Big drums and little drums. Some of the music had rhythms that spoke to Liddi's sense of patterns. Others felt discordant, unnatural.

Finally, a dance performance. More music, and then the movements of the dancers. Some fluid, some sharp. The lines and angles of their bodies forming patterns of their own, moving again before Liddi could fully take them in.

During an intermission, she couldn't take the confusion anymore. She tugged on Durant's sleeve. He turned to her, but she waved him down to her level so no one else would hear.

"What's the point?" she asked quietly.

"What do you mean?"

"On Pramadam, I get it. They cliff-dive for adrenaline, and they play sports because they want to win. But what's dance or any of this for?"

Durant's response confused her more. He looked concerned. "When they were dancing just now, what did you feel?"

"I don't know. That I didn't get it."

"You're thinking too much, Liddi."

At eleven years old, Liddi had never been accused of doing that. Thinking too little, maybe. "You're all always telling me we're Jantzens and we use our heads."

His expression softened as he smoothed her hair back. "I know, maybe we say that too much. When we go back in, try not to think about what they're doing. See what you feel, okay?"

It wasn't easy. Liddi just wanted the answer, and hated that Durant wouldn't tell her. Not thinking wasn't natural.

Then a new dance started. Just a man and woman dancing with a younger boy.

Parents and their son, she thought.

And the music was sad. So were their movements, their dancing. Aching and yearning.

They lost him. Or he lost them.

Like we lost Mom and Dad.

Tears fell, and Liddi was glad vid-cams weren't allowed in the performance hall. As the audience applauded, Durant put an arm around his baby sister and whispered in her ear.

"That's the point of art, Liddi. It reminds us that thinking is well and good, but feeling is what makes us alive."

24

DURING THE DRIVE TO EDGEWICK, I get the jittery feeling of luck running out. The first conduit was easy. No one was there working on it, the voiceprint recording got us in perfectly, and the redesigned sempu fit into the modulating unit just as Fabin promised. It took us five minutes at most.

The next two weren't quite as simple. A few JTI techs were at each, falling all over themselves when they saw me. Tiav filled his role perfectly with things like "Miss Jantzen is here to check the unit's configuration" and "Please don't disturb Miss Jantzen while she's working." The techs were scarcely more than entry-level employees and didn't have any expectation that I would speak directly to them, so they didn't comment on my silence. They didn't even dare question Tiav's out-of-place accent.

It makes me a little sad.

Regardless, three conduits are set, five remain. Vid-cams have caught sight of us, so far just media-grubs marveling over the Jantzen girl finally showing up and getting some work done. We're doing well, but I don't like this feeling.

"Liddi," Dom says over my com-tablet, "you have a new message in your queue from Minali Blake. Would you like to hear it?"

I guess I'd better, so I tap the icon for Yes.

"I don't know where you've been or what you think you're doing," says Minali's disembodied voice. "But stop it. Your checked genes may not be able to grasp it, but this is what will save the Seven Points. It has to be done, and don't forget that implant. That news-vid was almost clever, but I know the implant's still active."

The message ends, and I rub the bridge of my nose. She didn't say anything I didn't already know, but the reminder isn't helping.

"What did she mean, 'checked genes'?" Tiav asks.

Dom handles the answer. "Parents have the option of holding certain genes in check during the early stages of pre-natal development. Mostly it's used by particularly vain individuals who want to ensure their offspring's ears don't grow disproportionately."

"So what did your parents hold in check?"

I tap a finger to my forehead, and Tiav's eyebrows go up.

"Your mind? That's ridiculous."

Sweet of him, but he doesn't know the full Jantzen history I've failed to live up to. When he sees my doubt, he presses his claim.

"First of all, why would parents do that to their child? Second, you're brilliant. All those gadgets you made on Ferinne when *nothing* here works the same way? How would someone with 'checked' intelligence pick those things up so quickly?"

I don't know. Somehow the technology on Ferinne made sense in a way nothing on Sampati ever did. It's not the same.

"Dom, do you have access to Liddi's medical records, her genetic code? And her parents'?"

"I do."

"Could you tell if they'd done anything to modify her genes?"

"I could. And they did."

I'm stopped from giving Tiav an I-told-you-so look by a sucking emptiness exploding inside me with the confirmation that my parents really did that to me. Despite the evidence of my whole life, part of me wanted a different answer.

Only Dom's not done yet.

"However, it had nothing to do with limiting her intelligence. Rather, it was a minor modification to intuition and flexibility, enhancing them slightly."

I'm so stupid, I didn't even think to ask. Of course, getting the information out of Dom on my own, without my voice, would've been impossible.

Tiav takes my hand, squeezes it tight. "That woman lied to you, Liddi. Or maybe she wants to think it's true. I don't know why you believed her."

Because it made sense. I'm the failure of the Jantzen family. I pull up my news-vid queue and find the packet I've played dozens of times—my brothers at the Tech Reveal, everyone wondering when I'm finally going to show up, and I never have.

After Tiav watches it all, he's silent for a long moment. When he speaks, his voice is low. "Liddi, how old were you when your parents died?"

I hold up six fingers.

"And you inherit the company, not your older brothers. Everyone on seven planets knows that, right?"

Knows it and won't let me forget it.

"Don't you think that kind of pressure would make anyone lock up? Most Aelo take up their full duties by the time they're twelve. Instead, I almost quit the whole thing because I was sure I'd never be as good as my mother. Maybe your brilliance showed through on Ferinne because no one had those expectations, there was no pressure. Maybe you just need to relax and let yourself be brilliant in your own way, which might be a little different from your brothers'."

I like his maybes better than mine. But I'm not sure it's true, not when I've always struggled, always lagged behind.

Not always.

A memory flashes: the workshop, Dad and the boys so young. A sparkling contraption full of light hovers in the air. Something I made. It looks a little like a Khua.

Pretty spark.

How in the Wraith's name did I do that?

Spin-Still tells me something I don't remember. I saw a Khua when I was a toddler. I escaped into the yard at night and chased the pretty spark. Fabin found me with the Khua hovering near my face like a curious firefly. He never told anyone.

Did the Khua pass something on to me, so all my ideas are theirs?

No, that Khua was just intrigued by a child who wasn't afraid. That's all. Tiav's right—I've been letting the pressure get in the way, because I'm the one who chooses.

I choose to prove Minali wrong.

＊– – –＊

Liddi Jantzen broke two nails today . . . climbing a disposal chute.

I'm too anxious for a laugh to tempt me. My hands and feet are barely keeping me wedged in the chute as it is. We still have at least ten feet to go, inch by inch. A slight slope keeps it shy of vertical, but close enough.

All necessary because I was right that the ease of the first three conduits couldn't last. Minali's stationed police officers at some of the conduits, including this one.

No problem. Dom got us the building schematics and we found a back door—or rather, I disconnected the recycler at the end of the chute and we climbed in. Not the most elegant solution, but the best I could come up with.

"This would be a really bad time for another tremor, wouldn't it?" Tiav whispers from below me.

I miss my hand placement and slip a few inches before catching myself, wishing endlessly for the tethers and harnesses we used during the Daglin. I do *not* want to think about tremors right now, as often as they're happening.

"Sorry!"

Once I'm sure I won't slip, I resume climbing, and Tiav follows. The small panel at the top is meant to open easily enough from the outside, whenever a lab tech has material to dispose of. It's unlikely anyone ever considered opening it from *inside* the chute, but that's what I need to do.

I reorient my body to wedge myself with just one hand and both feet, and claw at the panel with my free hand. If I can just

get under the edge and apply a little upward force, the assistive motor should kick in.

There goes another nail, but the panel's open. A little more maneuvering, and I tumble out onto the lab floor. Before I can get back to help Tiav, he's made his own way through. My arms and legs are screaming from the exertion, so I try to shake them out.

"And now back down again, right?" Tiav says.

True enough, though it makes me want to groan. The conduit's on the first floor, while this lab is on the third. With the police standing guard at the building entrance, there was just no other way in.

Getting around inside the building isn't too bad, though. Out of the lab, down an emergency stairwell, and onto the first floor. No police stationed inside. The voiceprint recording gets us into the conduit facility, and I get right to work.

It's simple enough. The conduit terminal consists of a raised target area for travelers to stand on with some emitters and receivers embedded in the ceiling, and a console next to it for the operator. I just have to remove a coverplate under the console to get at the modulating unit. Old components out, sempu in, another conduit tuned to a Khua frequency.

Just as I get the cover back in place, the floor bucks beneath me, smacking my head into the console.

My vision swims. The room swims. I'm not under the console anymore, but I can't get my bearings.

"Liddi!"

Tiav's voice sounds far away as the shaking continues. My arm stings, and I don't know why until my eyes focus a bit. It's bleeding. I cut it on a jagged crack that formed in the floor. That fact quickly moves down the priority list.

Another crack is in the ceiling. A larger crack going right to the conduit terminal.

Three of the embedded emitters have been knocked loose.

A chasm opens up to swallow my heart, to suck the air from my lungs.

The tremor trails off, and I push myself to my feet. Try to. I'm too dizzy and my balance skews. My knees don't hit the floor like I expect, though. Something's holding me up. Hands on my waist. Tiav's saying something, but I'm not listening. I'm moving my feet forward toward a maintenance locker, dragging him with me.

"Hold still and let me stop this bleeding!"

No, that can wait. I wrestle out of his grip, still scarcely able to breathe. The conduit assembly only uses full power when someone's actively traveling, but it's always running, always maintaining the conduit's connection to the network. If the quake damaged it too much, I don't know what it might do to people trapped inside.

It might hurt them. It might do worse.

This one is Emil's conduit.

Tiav doesn't understand, not until I start pulling tools out of the locker, thrust my com-tablet into his hands, and point emphatically between it and the damaged emitters. Then he stops arguing about the cut on my arm.

"Dom, I think Liddi needs you to tell her how to repair some damage here at the conduit terminal."

It takes some back-and-forth between them before Dom has a lock on the situation and locates repair procedures. Moments later, I'm sitting on Tiav's shoulders—not great for my recovering equilibrium—so I can reach the ceiling and follow Dom's instructions.

My hands are sure and steady because they have to be. Any harm to Emil might be temporary, might just be while the few emitters are offline. There's no time for mistakes.

One emitter repaired. Then two, a little trickier. Finally, three is secure, its indicator lights glowing again. Back on the ground, Dom coaches us through a diagnostic to ensure the conduit is fully online. Green, green...

"Worst one yet, I—hey, what are you—Miss Jantzen!"

The disjointed declarations come from the doorway. I whip around, certain I'll face a dark green police uniform, but I don't. Just a pair of women wearing the coveralls of JTI techs.

"The officer didn't mention you were here," one of them says.

"He said he just came on shift, though, didn't he?" her partner adds.

I busy myself gathering up the tools I used, keeping my injured arm out of view, while Tiav jumps in to answer.

"Just trying out a possible fix for these conduit problems. That tremor slowed us down a little. You'll want to seal these cracks. We should be going, shouldn't we, Miss Jantzen?"

After glancing at the diagnostic display to verify the last icon turned green, I nod and leave the room with Tiav. Back to the stairwell, back to the lab, back to the disposal chute.

Sliding down is a lot faster than climbing up was.

We're in the hovercar and on our way with no sign of the police out front being aware of us. The technicians will probably mention my presence when they leave, but I can't worry about that.

I'm too busy shaking.

It's nothing to do with Tiav finally tending to my arm, nothing to do with the bump on my head that makes me wince when he runs his fingers through my hair. When he wraps his arms around me, the shaking only gets worse.

"I'm sure your brothers are fine."

The warmth of his whisper on my cheek tempts me with its reassurance. But we both know he isn't really sure. We know we can't spare the time to summon a Khua and check. We know we have to finish the job, and only then will I see if Emil's all right.

Tiav's words aren't meant as truth, though. They're meant as hope. I snake my arms around his neck and hold him back even tighter.

Hope is better than nothing. I'll take it.

✳ – – – ✳

The seventh conduit still has no police presence and no workers, proving Minali hasn't figured out exactly what we're doing, which conduits we're visiting. Almost all of my brothers were captured while investigating on other Points. Tiav and I traced out the Sampati ends of those conduits through the planetary rerouter, so our targets would look random to Minali if she hasn't done the same backtracing. Which it seems she hasn't, at least not yet.

The last one's going to be impossible for Minali not to pick up on, though, because it's not a public conduit terminal at all. It's at JTI headquarters. Anton had the bad luck to get caught in a conduit that traces back to one of the labs. We saved it for last, knowing it's where we're most likely to get caught.

An assistant spots us in the lobby and flags me down. "Miss

Jantzen! I didn't realize you'd be coming in today. Has there been any progress on the conduit outage? Is there anything I can help you with?"

"Miss Jantzen is very busy, but I think we can manage," Tiav says. The woman is persistent, but another word or two succeeds in brushing her off as we get into an elevator.

"Which floor?" Tiav asks.

I hold up nine fingers and bounce anxiously on my toes. Minali will have been alerted as soon as I entered the building. We'll have to move quickly.

The voiceprint on my com-tablet gets us through two sets of doors. A Banak police officer waits inside. Even though I told myself to expect it, I'm startled and freeze.

Tiav doesn't. Two punches, a knee to the groin, and a blow to the back of the head add up to an unconscious police officer who didn't even have a chance to pull his gun. The man had focused on me and didn't expect Tiav's reaction any more than I did.

"Spending half my life fighting Kal has its advantages," Tiav says, answering the question in my eyes. "Just don't tell my mother I did that."

Right, behavior not befitting an Aelo, I'm sure.

He drags the officer to a storage locker while I work on the doors. We don't have any time to spare, but if I can slow Minali down, I might buy enough. I enter the first level of locks easily enough, using the standard icons and my voiceprint. Then I have Dom enter some code we came up with on the drive here.

It won't last forever, but it'll have to do.

This part of the dance I can do in my sleep by now. Open up a panel, slide out two components, slip the sempu in, and tap the icon to reconfigure.

We're done, and they're going to find us any second.

"Okay, Liddi, time to finish this," Tiav says, closing the access panel. He steps toward me but stumbles as the floor shifts beneath us. "Sparks, not now!"

He's right—not a great time for another tremor, though at least it waited until my head was clear of the console. It's not a bad one, but I'm pretty sure we're about to make it worse.

"We have to hurry. Tell Spin-Still to call the others."

She's already glowing so bright, I'm afraid the heat might burn me. They're on their way.

They're here.

Ten Khua burst into life in the middle of the room. Not like on Ferinne, so calm and controlled. They writhe with the pollution of the conduits' energy, sparking and twisting, dancing around each other as they instinctively try to escape something tied to their very foundation.

It's gotten bad. But they're strong, holding themselves together and staying in this room despite the nearness of a conduit—the source of their pain. One for each of my brothers, to pair with his conduit. One for Tiav and one for me, to complete the chain and pull them out.

Hopefully.

"Unidentified energy signatures in Conduit Lab, Level Nine."

Leave it to the computer to state the obvious. If Minali had any doubts about where we are, she doesn't now. All I can do is hope my locks will hold as Tiav and I get to work. We take the remaining sempu disks from our pockets, one to bring each Khua to the same "frequency" we've tuned the conduits to, and set them on the floor in a circle. Or as close as we can get to a

circle while the room's shaking. Spin-Still burns even hotter, warning the others not to join with the disks until we're ready.

We're as ready as we'll get once we stand back from the circle. I take Spin-Still off my neck so I can hold her in my hand. The heat is just about as much as I can take.

The other Khua fly to their sempu like drops of water joining together, and the room explodes. Not literally, but the blast of light and color sends Tiav and me both back a step. The shaking stops, but I'm not sure whether it's because the tremor's done or the force of the Khua overpowers it.

Just like on Ferinne, each Khua forms a length of energetic fabric centered on its sempu. Only now, with no spires to confine them, the fabric extends to the edges of the room, floor and ceiling. And with ten of them, they intersect each other, forming seams of searing-white energy. But not all at the same point, and that's what we need. One intersection, all together.

Something jerks inside my chest as Spin-Still's will ties to my own. I have to direct the Khua, line them up, she can't without me. I see them from outside, and she doesn't. Tiav and I stand in a wedge formed by two walls of energy. All I can see of the others are the bright lines where they cross each other, so I focus on those. The line in front of us, where those two walls meet— that's where I want the others to go. I set my attention on one, imagine it moving.

The weight of ten thousand worlds presses into me. I can't breathe. But the line moves, so I keep pushing. It inches closer to the center seam, finally making contact. The energy in the room spikes, echoed by my heart as it threatens to go into arrest.

That was just one, there are more, too many. I can't do this.

Something heavy pounds on the door. We don't have time.

Tiav clasps my hand in his, pressing the sempu between our palms so we can both maneuver the Khua into position. He's not even looking. His eyes are closed, his breathing steady.

"You don't have to push, Liddi," he says. "Imagine them *wanting* to fall into position, like it's where gravity would naturally make them settle."

No one has ever conceived of anything like this before, but clearly his years of attuning himself to the Khua make him the expert, not me. I close my eyes and shift my focus. The Khua are like grains of sand falling into a cone, hitting the sides, sliding down, but always coming to rest at the point.

A single point. The center.

I feel it working, but only because the weight is still there. It's not the weight of pushing. It's the weight of holding myself together, of not letting every neuron in my body explode with the energy pouring into the room.

I'm not the only one struggling. Tiav grunts with the effort, Spin-Still burns hotter, and the floor vibrates beneath us. Then more than vibrates—it trembles. Not like before. This time is more like every molecule in the room is going to fly apart. The light of the seam flows red through my closed eyelids. It'll be too bright to look at directly, so I turn toward Tiav before opening my eyes.

He's already looking at me. Determined. A little scared, a little overwhelmed, but determined is what wins. Because he knows how much I need this. Not because of the Khua or his duty as an Aelo, even though those are good reasons. Not to save eight worlds. He's standing here, ready to do something that could get us both killed, because he knows I need to save my brothers.

That's the moment I know I love him.

"It's ready," he says.

I nod. I feel it, too. The sand has settled.

Careful to keep our eyes averted, we step together toward the seam, the center where all ten Khua-fields meet. Even without looking, it's not difficult to find. The energy's pulling us there.

"Close your eyes." We turn to face the joining of ten Khua, so bright it nearly blinds me even with my eyes closed. "Ready... now!"

We thrust our clasped hands into the seam, the sempu between them.

Placing Spin-Still inside what she is already inside. Creating the bubble, the space where the attuned Khua and conduits can all gather.

Taking us with her.

It's like communing with the Khua on Ferinne... only terrible.

It's like my first chaotic, agonizing trip through a portal... only cleaner.

We exist in a white emptiness of everythingness with too-sharp focus cutting to the point of pain. But the pain is like joy that's just too much, that's more than one person can bear so it hurts. It hurts and I want out, I don't want more pain, because this joy is twisted and wrong and not happy at all. It's death wearing the face of joy and it lies.

"Do you feel it?" Tiav whispers, only it slices through the roar of silence. "It's killing them."

My brothers? No, that's not what he means. I _do_ feel it. The false joy, the lying death, it's the tainted energy of the conduits poisoning the Khua. My brothers are part of that, they're the

bridge between Khua and conduit, but they aren't meant to be. That's what we have to break, what we have to undo.

"Liddi?"

That's not Tiav's voice.

Emil fades into view, the effort clear on his face. He's here and he's okay! But it's not like on Ferinne, there's no barrier keeping us apart. I know because I can hear him, and nothing stops me from throwing my arms around him.

It worked. We matched the frequencies.

I look around. In the whiteness of this non-place, I can still see the extra spark of the sempu holding Khua within, ten of them floating around us. Spin-Still isn't in my hand anymore—she's around us in the everywhere, holding this place separate from the loose strands.

I take one of the sempu and press it between my hand and Tiav's like before, then do the same with another, holding Emil's hand. Luko and Anton are here, too. The others are arriving.

The poison-pain cuts into me again, sharpest in my hands where I hold the sempu, where the Khua have felt the pain for eternities already. And weight on my shoulders, on my chest, it hasn't left. It gets heavier every moment.

"Everyone take a disk," Tiav says. The strain shows in his voice. He feels it, too. "Hold it between your hands, like this, and form a ring."

We'll complete the chain, then one final push to free my brothers. They take their places, a Khua between each... only there's one left over, still hovering free.

Fabin isn't here.

DESTRUCTION. BAD THINGS. EVERYWHERE.

It's Spin-Still, telling me what's happening outside in the "real" world. I feel it around us, behind us, beyond us. The chaos of the unbound energy. Like a ship in a storm, tossed on the waves, riding the peaks and valleys.

A ship ready to capsize.

But Fabin isn't here.

My brothers have closed the circle, with Ciro joining Tiav on the other side from me. Without Fabin.

Tiav doesn't know my brothers, but he can count.

"Someone's missing, right, Liddi?"

I nod, but the waves beat closer to us now, hammering the weight into me. I almost lose my grip on Emil.

"It's time, Liddi, we have to go," Vic says.

That's ridiculous. It's not time until we're all here.

Something hits my brothers on the other side of the circle. They wince and double over.

"Now, Liddi," Marek says. "That Khua can't hold this together much longer."

I shake my head so hard it hurts. Everything hurts.

"Where's the other one, the one missing?" Tiav demands.

"He's not coming," Durant says. Agony radiates from him, more from his words than what's happening to us. "Liddi, do it."

It's collapsing. The bow of the ship is breaking. My body shudders under the waves of chaos, tears squeezing from the corners of my eyes. Tears that match my brothers'.

I won't go. Not yet. My brothers' voices blur together. One voice, a hundred voices.

"We have to."

"There's no choice."

"Liddi, go."

"No time."

"Go now!"

"Not coming."

"Liddi, now!"

The pressure, their pressure, my heart bursting through my chest—it all breaks.

I shout.

"Not without Fabin!"

And because I speak—because I trigger the implant, using Minali's pulse as the final push—without Fabin is exactly what happens.

An explosion, an implosion, or an infinite expansion of nothingness—something shoves me away, delivering the real world in the form of the floor slamming into my back.

I suppose it was my back slamming into the floor, but when I can't breathe through five thousand points of pain, I don't care about the distinction.

Something else stops me from breathing—clouds of dust choking the air. I'm in the same lab, but nothing's the same. A section of the ceiling has collapsed. I push myself up to look around.

Most of the lab equipment is intact, the conduit platform is crushed, and some items are just knocked over. The others sprawl on the floor around me. A quick headcount confirms it. Seven Jantzen brothers, all unconscious, and one Ferinne Aelo.

Fabin isn't here.

I set off the trigger, and he wasn't in the safe zone of Spin-Still's energy.

The weight I felt from the Khua was nothing compared to what hits me now. Weight to crush my soul, to hold me down on

the bottom of the ocean. I deserve more. I deserve worse. I want to sob and dissolve and lose myself to the emptiness of failing.

Metal screeches across the room as the door is levered open in a damaged frame. Minali and three guards spill into the lab.

They have guns drawn. Including Minali.

"Nobody move," she says. "Don't. You. Move."

I may have failed Fabin, but this woman is the reason. She sacrificed my brothers instead of finding a real solution. She had Garrin killed to hold on to her secret. She nearly destroyed the Khua and turned me into little more than a piece of equipment.

The guards' guns point at the ground. Minali's points at me, but it shakes.

And I don't have to keep silent anymore.

"Computer, voiceprint override. Identify Liddi Jantzen."

Minali fires. I flinch as the shot hits the ground two feet to my right.

"Liddi Jantzen, identified," the computer replies. "How may I help you, Miss Jantzen?"

Tiav is dragging me toward a console to shield us, but I have to talk fast, before Minali steadies her aim, or worse, goes for my brothers.

"Disable JTI weapons in Conduit Lab, Level Nine."

The power indicators on the guns go dark, but I'm not done.

"Minali Blake is to be terminated immediately. Relay such to all news-vid sources as well as authorities on both Banak and Neta. And get the police to JTI headquarters to have her arrested. If you three don't want to get arrested with her, go help my brothers."

The guards start climbing over the debris. Minali doesn't seem to inspire much loyalty. Despite what I said, she's not

looking at me anymore. She's looking at a monitor and has gone pale. "You stupid, stupid girl! I nearly had everything fixed, and now you've destroyed them, the conduits . . . they're gone. Do you think anyone in the Seven Points will listen to you when you've cut us all off from each other?"

"They will when I tell them about the Eighth Point and explain a new way to get from world to world. Or an old way. And especially when I tell them everything *you've* done. It's all about how you spin it, right?"

She grits her teeth with half a growl, coming at me past the rubble of the collapsed ceiling. Maybe she'll try to tear my limbs from my body with her bare hands. I'm not convinced that pain would be any worse than what I've already experienced. Tiav is worried enough to get between me and her, but it's not necessary. As long as one particular thing in this mess is still working.

"Computer, is the neural incapacitator online?" I ask.

"Confirmed, Miss Jantzen."

I glance at my brothers, who are just starting to come around with the three guards tending to them. I think about everything they've been through. I swallow the despair when I see Fabin still isn't here.

This is letting her off easy. I'll have to see if the authorities can come up with something more fitting. But for now, this will do.

"Calibrate for Minali Blake and engage."

The sky turned so dark, Liddi thought maybe it was already dinnertime, but no one came to bring her in yet. So with the stubbornness of a seven-year-old, she kept climbing the tree. She looked up at the dark, bloated clouds just in time for a fat drop of water to land in her eye. Thunder rumbled in the distance. Then a crack of lightning, not so distant, with a bone-shaking boom half a second later.

Retrieved or not, it was time to get inside.

Raindrops pummeled the girl, like they were trying to push her down the tree faster. She was soaked instantly, and her hand slipped as her foot reached for the next branch.

She missed.

Liddi tumbled down, grabbing at branches and getting nothing for her trouble but bark-scrapes all along her arms and legs. At the last second, she caught hold, but only for a moment. The force of stopping so suddenly broke her grip again, and she fell to the ground. She had no way to right herself, no way to keep herself from landing awkwardly with a thud . . . and a snap. Her scream used up any air that hadn't been knocked from her lungs.

Fabin rushed over, finding his sister just a few seconds too late. "Liddi, what happened?"

"I slipped. My leg."

He took one look at it and got to work, finding a couple of branches that he broke to a particular length, and then cutting strips of cloth from his shirt. "I've been looking everywhere for you," he said, fashioning a splint. "Why did you wander so far from the house?"

"The trees here are taller."

"Why does that matter?"

"I wanted to be closer to the stars when the sun went down. I wanted to try to find Ferri to see where Mom and Dad are."

Fabin's hands slipped as he tried to bind the sticks with the strips. His voice was as heavy as Liddi's rain-soaked clothes. "Ferri isn't a planet. It's not real. You know it isn't."

"But I want it to be!"

"I know you do. But even if it were real, it wouldn't be the kind of place you can see."

That couldn't be true. Liddi's parents had to be in the sky, watching over her and the boys. They wouldn't have left the children alone. "So I can't see them?"

He carefully lifted her up, kissing her forehead when the pain made her cry out again. "Of course you can. Every time we close our eyes, we all see them. And sometimes that's enough."

25

THE COUNTRY HOUSE HASN'T been so full since right after Mom and Dad died. To my mind, though, it's just shy of full enough.

My brothers are weak after so long in the physically non-physical state of the conduits. I smuggled Jahmari in from Ferinne to look after them. He says it's nothing they won't recover from—they just need to get their strength back, and that takes time.

They can have all the time they need, but I could use a few more hours in the day.

Our stunt with the Khua had an impact everywhere. The collapsed ceiling in the lab was nothing compared to some places. Structural damage to buildings, terrible rockslides in the mountains of both Erkir and Pramadam, an amphitheater on Yishu was a total loss. And people were hurt. Concussions and broken bones, mostly. But some deaths.

Deaths I'm responsible for. At least in part.

I almost shut down when I found out about all the people. Spin-Still gave me impressions of how much worse it would've been if we hadn't done it. Cities full of people dead and some of the Points no longer habitable for the survivors.

That's definitely worse, but I can't tell whether it should make me feel better. So instead of thinking about my choices, I've kept busy. I talked to engineers about finding the best, fastest ways to rebuild and repair. That was just the beginning of the talking.

Talking to top technologists about the collapse of the conduits and reinstitution of the Khua, talking to government officials on Neta about interplanetary implications, talking to law enforcement chiefs on Banak about crimes committed, talking to historians on Tarix so they can get the record right . . . I never thought I'd miss silence.

Others want to talk to me—media-grub demands are at an all-time high—but I'm too busy, with the fallout, with the company, with my family.

Today, I'm busy doing nothing.

"They're beautiful."

Emil's voice startles me. He's supposed to be back at the house, not crossing the river to the small clearing, and the walking stick he holds isn't doing that much to help.

"You shouldn't be out here," I say, supporting his other side.

"I'm fine." The words are strong enough, but the way he leans on me says otherwise. His color's still not right, his eyes worn and weary. He really ought to be resting, but I'm not going to argue. "*You* shouldn't be out here alone."

"I'm not alone." Three Khua float lazily around the clearing, and that doesn't count Spin-Still. "When did you know the Khua were alive?"

"I'm not sure. Not right away. But when we held one here so you could use it, I think we knew. It felt wrong, like holding someone prisoner. We shouldn't have done it, but we had to get you safe, away from Blake."

Understanding pulses through me from Spin-Still. "And you didn't know how to ask. They forgive you."

"Good. But I still say you shouldn't be out here alone—I don't mean with or without the Khua. We left you on your own too long. We all hated it."

He's saying they've worried about me, and maybe that they still do. Maybe they're right to. Maybe they don't need to. It's hard to tell anymore, so I choose not to say anything about it. We stand and watch the Khua dance.

Silence has been with me too long. Even with all the talking I've done, one piece of silence has followed me, and I can't let it stay anymore. Not now. My question might barely be loud enough to hear, but it won't remain silent.

"Emil, why didn't Fabin come?"

His arm across my shoulders pulls me closer, and I feel his sigh more than hear it. "He didn't tell us. We didn't know until we found you and he wasn't there. Liddi, it was very strange in there, the way we could sometimes know and understand things and then not."

"What did you understand?"

"The pulse triggered by your vocal implant wouldn't have disrupted enough. It might have set *us* free, but the conduits' energy would still have been entangled with the Khua. They'd still be suffering. Fabin knew. He knew if one of us was outside

the safe zone, taking the hit from the pulse, it'd be like an explosion, enough to knock the conduits loose. No more parasites for the Khua."

A rock lodges in my throat, or might as well. "But what happened to Fabin?"

"I don't know. I really don't. These things, these energies, they're still so new to us. He could be lost in a different strand, separate from the conduits *or* the Khua. I don't know. One thing I *do* know. You found us and freed us. Our little Liddi unlocked cosmic energies and got it done. So maybe we can still find Fabin."

It's hard to be hopeful when my heart only feels the emptiness of Fabin's absence, but Emil's right. Maybe we can. The checked genes were a lie. I can trust my instincts, and maybe they'll come up with something unexpected.

"Now, why are you out here on your own, watching Khua, when every other day you've been so busy we hardly saw you?" Emil asks.

"I'm waiting. Tiav said he'd come back today . . . if they let him come back."

"Is it possible they won't?"

Why does he have to ask me that when it's the last thing I want to think about? "Sure, it's possible. It depends on what happened after we left, everything I did when I was there, if they still think Tiav acted against his duties . . . I don't know. I don't know anything about Ferinne right now and that's what kills me. They could arrest him, or they could let him come back."

"Tell me about this boy. Clearly not another Reb Vester."

Just when I thought I'd have no reason to laugh today. "As

different from Reb as it gets. He trusted me without knowing anything, Emil. I mean, none of the things that everyone in the Seven Points knows. I could be anything or nothing, but what he saw was me. Then he finds out what being 'Liddi Jantzen' means, and he *still* sees me. At least, I think he does."

"Good. That's important. Now we just need to make sure he can stare down your overbearing big brothers."

My smile grows. Tiav stared down his own government and the leaders of three alien races. He can handle Durant and the others.

Just as quickly, the smile drops. Tiav's been back on Ferinne for days. Facing his mother, trying to convince her that I was acting on behalf of the Khua, not against them. Trying to convince the Agnac that the Khua have more to say about the situation than they have in a long time. Keeping Quain and Yilt out of trouble for helping me.

Because they could be in a lot of trouble. So could Tiav.

"I should've gone with him to help explain," I murmur.

"You heard what Tiav said. You already had seven worlds to explain yourself to. He can handle the eighth."

More arguments wriggle through me. How the Seven Points didn't have to put up with a strange girl who couldn't and wouldn't explain herself the way Ferinne did. How I gained trust and broke laws and turned allied races against each other.

Those arguments stop because one of the Khua does. It holds steady at eye level several feet in front of us.

It's not like the insane maelstrom I used to leave Sampati, and it's not quite like the Khua in their crystal spires on Ferinne. The knot of energy blossoms, then contracts with a snap. When I blink, Tiav stands there and the Khua floats away.

I don't have to ask how it went. He smiles. Emil isn't leaning on me anymore, so I close the distance to Tiav. He sweeps me into his arms, and I pull myself even closer.

"I missed you." His breath tickles my ear.

"How long will they let you stay? How bad were things there? The damage? Yilt? And your mother and Kalkig? Why are you laughing at me?"

"Because I like hearing your voice."

Probably as much as I like using it. After so much struggling and silence, I can tell Tiav anything and everything I want. The relief blankets itself around me, even when everything else has made me so anxious.

"I can answer everything," he continues, "but first let's help your brother back to the house."

I twist in Tiav's arms to look back at Emil, but he's not where I expect. He's already started walking back toward the bridge and waves us off.

"I made it out here on my own, I can make it back on my own. I'll yell if I have a problem. Besides, if I stay here, I'll give in to the irrational urge to beat Tiav with this stick."

Emil keeps going, and he does look strong enough, so I let him and turn back to Tiav.

"Answers. Now."

"Things were pretty bad," he admits. "After we left, the Agnac were calling in people from their home planet, possibly getting ready for war. The Haleians were divided, some of them siding with your friend Yilt—who's been released, by the way— and no one knew what the Izim might try. And that was *before* we destroyed the conduits and everything fell apart. By the next Daglin, they'll still be repairing the damage, especially from the Khua you didn't knock loose—tidal waves flooded coastal cities, tremors leveled buildings, even some volcanic eruptions. In some ways, that was good, because it helped me convince everyone you were helping, not sabotaging. It would've been so much worse without you freeing a couple hundred of them in just the right places. But I can't take credit for much of the convincing—Bright-Fade here did most of it."

He's still wearing the sempu holding a Khua—the one he and I were holding when we freed my brothers, the only Khua who chose not to separate from the sempu when we were done.

"She has a name, huh?"

"Yes, *he* does." He runs his thumb along my palm, tracing the scar matching the sempu patterns. "It...it's going to get interesting, Liddi."

"How?"

"The Izim and Crimna want to make contact with the Seven Points. We used those plans for the interlocks on the linguistic monitoring system, so my mother and Voand are going to start talking with your leaders on Neta to work it out. The Haleians are still discussing, and the Agnac are still being the Agnac. But Kalkig says he'll be the first Agnac on Sampati to see what you 'heathens' are really like, because obviously he'll have to visit."

I think I know what he's saying, but I need him to say the words. "Why is that obvious?"

"Because with the Khua resettling all the Points, everyone agrees you need an Aelo here."

"So you're staying?"

"I'm staying."

Those are the only words I need. I work my fingers into his dark hair, guiding his face to mine so I can kiss him. He kisses me back, tightening his arms around my waist to hold me closer. He's not afraid of breaking me anymore.

I'm not so afraid of being broken.

When Tiav pulls back, he stays close, touching his forehead to mine. "What your brother said . . . Do I really need to worry about getting beaten?"

"Not while they're recovering, but once they do, yeah, you'll have to get used to the threats. Especially from Emil, since he's closest to me. And Durant, since he's the oldest. Really, pretty much all of them. Except . . ."

"Except Fabin," he whispers.

A sob wells up instantly, threatening to break free, but I refuse. I already spent a day and several nights crying. "Yes. Fabin. But I might have some ideas. I'm not giving up on him yet."

※ – – – ※

When I ask if it's possible, Spin-Still doesn't answer. She just shows me how to make a very particular sempu. The engravings are precise, intricate, complicated. Not like anything the Aelo have ever done—Tiav confirms that.

It's done, but Sampati isn't the place for it. Tiav comes with me to Erkir. The Khua have become plentiful here already, but that also means more people lingering, watching, gawking once they get their own sempu, a token for travel. Khua tourism. I hope the effect fades once everyone gets used to them.

We go to the plains, where I once flew a glider with the twins. The place I have in mind is a long hike out. It's not as picturesque as the forests, mountains, or beaches, so no one's here.

No one biological. A single Khua hovers a few feet above the grass, waiting for us.

"Are you sure you can accept the answer?" Tiav asks.

"I need to know. The truth isn't something to be afraid of."

A squeeze of my shoulder, a kiss, and he lets me take the final few steps alone.

The new disk is in my pocket. From around my neck, Spin-Still pulses her encouragement. I take the disk in my hand and hold it out to the Khua. It hovers, questioning, investigating, before joining it in a flash of light and color.

When I can see again, I'm not sure *what* I'm seeing. Not a Khua. Not an Izim. Both of those glow like white starlight. This small whorl of energy is a nebula spinning, colors shifting and weaving with hints of brighter lights within.

It floats toward me as though curious, with none of the intimidating power of the Khua. I don't need to run or back away.

Still, I'm startled when it grazes my arm. A breeze of lightning. There are no words—not even the vague impression of my own thoughts like I get from Spin-Still. Only feelings.

Worry. Confidence. Watchfulness.

Guilt. Sadness.

Something in it . . . it's so familiar.

"Fabin?" I whisper.

No confirmation. I don't know if this is what Fabin's become, or an echo of what he was, or just my desperately wishful thinking.

It doesn't matter. Silence still traps me, because I can't talk with him. Can't tell him I'm sorry and he should've let us find another way and the Khua could've done it without him.

The whorl brushes against me again, and my protests melt away, leaving the truth I haven't wanted to face.

Fabin is dead. I killed him when I spoke, and there's no hope of freeing him.

My legs threaten to give out, toppling me backward, but they can't. My back stops against Tiav's chest, and his hands on my waist keep me to my feet. He knew I needed him and came to me.

Again the bundle of energy comes closer, touching my cheek, sparking against a tear. Sparking words. So few. So faint.

Clever girl.

Those words fill me with warmth just as they always have. Always when Fabin said them to me. Knowing he always meant them.

The energy floats back away. It—Fabin?—whirls and snaps, rustling the grass at my feet before breaking. Disappears in an explosion that threatens to take my heart with it.

I squeeze Tiav's hands reassuringly so he'll let go, then kneel to find the disk in a tangle of wildflowers. It's shattered within its frame.

SOME JOURNEYS CAN ONLY BE MADE ONCE. SOME PART-INGS AREN'T WHAT THEY SEEM. SOME ENDINGS MUST BE SO SOMETHING ELSE CAN BEGIN.

Spin-Still's saying she won't show me how to recreate the disk. And I understand, but it hurts.

SHE WISHES THERE WERE NO PAIN, BUT THAT COULD ONLY HAPPEN IF I DIDN'T LOVE FABIN.

 326

I understand that, too, so I let the pain be. "I'm making a choice, Tiav," I say softly. "To believe my parents have been watching me. And now Fabin is, too."

"I know they are. They love you too much not to." He pulls me to my feet, tucks a stray lock of hair behind my ear. "What now?"

"It's time to make them proud."

ACKNOWLEDGMENTS

THIS BOOK HAD SOME amazing help leaving the station. Huge thanks to Lisa Yoskowitz for getting me on the right track, Julie Moody for keeping me there, and both Kate Egan and Kieran Viola for pointing out that if I didn't throw a switch or two, I might end up derailed.

That's enough train metaphor, I think.

Thanks to Jamie Baker and everyone on the Hyperion team who work so hard to cheerlead for our books, both publicly and privately. Thanks also to the design team for making a book that's oh-so-striking on the shelf and just as lovely to look at inside.

Thanks to my agent Jennifer Laughran for not bailing on me when I get all mathy-sciencey on her and for keeping it real.

I'm lucky to be friends with some fantastic writers who happily gave this a once-over. (Maybe twice, in some cases.) Mindy McGinnis, MarcyKate Connolly, Riley Redgate, and Charlee Vale all helped immeasurably in bringing this story together.

Particular thanks go to Charlee, as well as Tess Sharpe, for showing such enthusiasm in my choice of fairy tale when I wasn't sure. Their thoughts on the root of the tale were invaluable. Also, to everyone whose face lit up when I said "The Wild Swans" and didn't need a summary—thank you for the motivation.

To my family for putting up with deadline testiness.

To my fellow teachers for supporting my non-mathematical activities.

To my students for making sure I keep my head in the game.

Thank you, all.